"Is this acceptable?" Margery asked, furt... exploring the areas he'd allowed, behind his ear and along the rim of it.

"What?"

"My hand here?" She gently pinched his earlobe before going over his temple, then his brow.

Evrart closed his eyes briefly as her palm skimmed to explore the other side. "It's...different."

It was as if his bones were mountains, his skin the earth. She wanted to explore him. "How?" she asked.

"You touch me all the time. On my shoulder, on my arm, on my hand..." he said.

He held so still she wasn't certain that he breathed or that his heart beat.

She shifted closer.

This man... She wanted him.

Reason told her that she should keep boundaries as large as the fortress. That she should play the game of false smiles and false words and then hide. Not be alone with him...not want to kiss him. But hadn't she already realized he was different? That despite their differences in size and gender, they shared similarities? They were alike. He needed to defend himself, too.

Keeping her eyes on his, she continued what she'd started, what she seemed unable to stop.

Author Note

Here is a story that wasn't meant to be written. Not so much because the rest of the Lovers and Legends series didn't have "Oh, look who's arrived! I must tell their story now!" moments, but because I had plans! Dreams! I was meant to write the last book in the series. I was supposed to write *Malcolm's* book, but...

I had a crush on Evrart, and when Margery defended him against her sister, Biedeluue, I knew I had to write their story.

Yet how to tell their story when they meet at the exact time and place Louve and Biedeluue meet in *The Maiden and the Mercenary*? Only one way for it: there's one event and many, many differing opinions on what happened.

No worries if you haven't read the previous book. This story begins before and ends after *The Maiden*, so there will still be surprises. But if there are some scenes from *The Maiden* you need to know more about, Evrart and Margery are there to tell you all about them.

They certainly told me over and over, but I'm so very glad I got the opportunity to listen and write one extra book. I hope you enjoy their tale, too.

NICOLE LOCKE

—

Her Honorable Mercenary

HARLEQUIN
HISTORICAL

HARLEQUIN®
HISTORICAL™

Recycling programs for this product may not exist in your area.

ISBN-13: 978-1-335-40735-1

Her Honorable Mercenary

Copyright © 2021 by Nicole Locke

This edition published by arrangement with Harlequin Books S.A.

For questions and comments about the quality of this book, please contact us at CustomerService@Harlequin.com.

Harlequin Enterprises ULC
22 Adelaide St. West, 40th Floor
Toronto, Ontario M5H 4E3, Canada
www.Harlequin.com

Printed in U.S.A.

Nicole Locke discovered her first romance novels in her grandmother's closet, where they were secretly hidden. Convinced that books that were hidden must be better than those that weren't, Nicole greedily read them. It was only natural for her to start writing them—but now not so secretly.

Books by Nicole Locke

Harlequin Historical

The Lochmore Legacy
Secrets of a Highland Warrior

Lovers and Legends
The Knight's Broken Promise
Her Enemy Highlander
The Highland Laird's Bride
In Debt to the Enemy Lord
The Knight's Scarred Maiden
Her Christmas Knight
Reclaimed by the Knight
Her Dark Knight's Redemption
Captured by Her Enemy Knight
The Maiden and the Mercenary
The Knight's Runaway Maiden
Her Honorable Mercenary

Visit the Author Profile page at Harlequin.com for more titles.

To new friends brought about because of 2020: Taylor DeLong, Mary E. Montgomery, Isabelle Peterson, Arell Rivers, DeLisa Smith and Libby Waterford. You all are the reason I and this book (but mostly me) made it through.

Chapter One

France, 1297

'What do you think, my dear?'

Ian of Warstone waved before him. His posture, voice and sweeping gestures all indicating that there was a correct answer, and Margery of Lyon knew for her very life, she'd better know what it was.

Aware there was an audience waiting for her reply, she craned her neck to take in the tilled fields and orchards leading downwards and then up to a sprawling village winding around a dark monstrosity of a structure which blotted out the soft blue sky.

Warstone Fortress was…menacing.

Giving the guards who circled her a smile, Margery adjusted her reins from one hand to the other in the vain hope the horse she rode would somehow understand what she needed.

It didn't—just as it hadn't understood all the other hints she'd given it on this journey for the past sennight. For instance, her begging it to gallop away, to dash off in a different direction, to help her escape. No such good fortune for her, however.

The horse wasn't to blame; it simply followed its master—who wasn't her. The expansive lands and the forbidding fortress before her weren't hers either. Nor was the man, Lord Warstone. She wasn't even Ian's mistress, but it was a role he meant her to play for however long he wanted.

In truth, if she were to give her true opinion on his home and lands it would be Warstone Fortress was beyond frightening. That she feared the moment she rode under the portcullis she might never see her family again.

That opinion, she knew, wouldn't be the correct response.

'It's impressive,' she lied.

'You can't even see it from there,' he clucked.

That was because the horse wouldn't swerve around the guard in front of her, and most likely wouldn't move until Warstone's horse did. They were both following Warstone. The horse she rode, however, was blessed with the ignorance of not knowing its fate. She knew hers all too clearly.

'It's difficult to miss,' she added. 'What with its… vastness.'

Ian's pale grey eyes swept over her. She could have sworn his lips curved before the wind brushed his black hair across his cheek, hiding any sign of amusement.

Had she amused him? She wasn't sure she wanted to. But at least now he'd turned to a guard and they were conversing. So his attention was—

A burst of laughter from the two men and she jumped. Judging from the sneer of the guard nearest her, her fright had been noticed. And frightened she most definitely was.

Ian of Warstone was dangerous.

She hadn't needed him to abduct her to know that.

All it had taken was his reputation, rumours and the fact over a week ago she'd caught him in a darkened corridor with a dagger at a whore's throat.

She'd run before she'd known what had happened to that poor woman, but she hadn't run fast enough not to be caught.

Pretending to stretch, Margery tried to slow her breath. This was only nerves. She must just think of this situation like all the others she'd found herself in in her life. There was no doubting Lord Warstone was a bit more challenging than her past adversaries, but it was nothing she couldn't resolve. She was still alive—which meant she'd lasted longer than she'd expected at least.

'Is everything well?' Ian said. 'That palfrey isn't any trouble, is she?'

Not for the reasons he suggested.

Margery patted its neck. 'She's lovely. I'm looking forward to seeing your home, that's all.'

He gave her an indulgent smile. 'Of course you are.'

What did he truly want with her? She hadn't wanted to hear him talking to that woman about a missive to be delivered any more than he had wanted her to overhear it. She certainly hadn't wanted to see terror in the woman's eyes. In truth, she'd never wanted to live the life she was living, but there was no one to blame for that except herself and poverty.

Her brothers tilled the fields, her eldest sister had left their village to find coin in other employment, and she…?

She had agreed to Josse of Tavel's offer to become his mistress. Then Josse's gambling losses had resulted in her being sold to Roul. And living in Roul's debauched residence had led to her stumbling across Ian of Warstone in a corridor late at night.

For months she'd avoided everyone in Roul's residence by never entertaining, by only eating in the privacy of her chambers or, when that wasn't feasible, by sneaking into the kitchens late at night. She'd gone to find food when Ian had caught her. No one should have been up. She should have been safe.

Yet if he was as evil as was reported, why hadn't Ian slit her throat? Instead, after he had corralled her in a corner with a lone sconce, an arrested gleam flickered across his sharp features and settled in his unnatural gaze. A gleam she feared indicated something worse than a quick death. That gaze had contained something she'd been plagued with all her life: interest.

Even as a child she had noticed people's stares. Her sister Biedeluue had recounted when she was an infant, she had often been taken by the villagers just so they could hold and gaze at her.

She knew it had had nothing to do with her soul or her demeanour, which at that tender age had consisted of eating, sleeping and relieving herself in linens, but everything to do with the lavender colour of her eyes, the flaxen colour of her hair, and perhaps the berry colour of her lips—or whatever fanciful colours she'd been described as having upon her birth.

It had nothing to do with what she had done, only what had been given to her, and it was something within the very marrow of her bones she didn't want. It had caused her nothing but grievances for her and her family.

'Shall we continue?' Ian urged his horse forward.

The guards and her palfrey lunged forward as well.

The sudden movement lurched her sideways. The horse didn't acknowledge her imbalance, or her tight grip, but merely lumbered on, step after step, because the others did. She'd seen horses that were docile before, but this one practically slept whilst it was awake. She wished she could ease her thoughts so easily.

On they went, past the orchards and into narrow streets which seemed to be closing in on her the farther they rode.

What did Ian want?

She feared she'd keep asking herself that question and would never come to an answer. When she'd asked him, he'd just smiled and ordered her away. Along the journey, whenever it had been time for bed, she'd undressed for him, but he had frowned and ignored her. She'd wandered around the camp, looking for opportunities to run, but always she'd been blocked by Ian's mercenaries. He didn't seem to want her like Josse and Roul, didn't hold a dagger to her throat either, but still wouldn't let her go. He threatened, but never harmed.

To think she'd been frightened of indulgent Josse and cruel Roul. At least they'd wanted her in the way men always did. Ian never looked at her as a man would a woman. He played his own game and she didn't know the rules!

'Such a frown upon your face,' Ian said. 'Is there something wrong with the streets of this village?'

This man observed too well. Living with Roul, a passively spiteful man, it had been essential not to give her emotions away, and it had worked. Roul hadn't noticed anything of her moods. Of course he'd drunk and bedded much. Still, she knew she had some skill to distract men.

She widened her eyes and gave him a beaming smile. 'This village is charming.'

Ian's eyes narrowed. 'Different from Pérouges?'

Pérouges. The answer she gave as to where she was from. Of course it wasn't where she'd grown up. But it was close enough to her home that if asked for details she could give them, and far enough from her family to keep them safe. She needed to keep them safe.

Did Ian have a family? Were they in the courtyard even now? Maybe he didn't have a family that cared...

Hers did—very much—and she missed them terribly. The irony was her family had tried to protect her from just this kind of situation. Abduction. Men. And here she was. Although, in truth, she didn't know how long they have could protected her.

Her family were poor, and against their wishes she had accepted coin from men like Josse, like Roul. She had never regretted her decision to go with Josse, but she had been hurt by his recklessly throwing her away to Roul. Yet none of that compared to this journey with Ian of Warstone.

'Your village is very much different from mine,' she said. 'Pérouges has all those stifling walls. This is very... winding.'

His eyes scraped across her—searching, no doubt, for truth—before dismissing her for the landscape instead.

Releasing her held breath, she tore her gaze from her abductor to three scampering dogs and the boys running amongst them. Trailing far behind them, a much smaller child attempted to catch up. Ian, and even the sneering guard next to her, slowed to give the child room.

It was one of the best-kept villages she'd ever seen. Not many houses—she expected that most people lived inside the castle—but there were well-tended land and fields.

The Warstones were wealthy, but in her experience wealth did not equate with well-tended *anything*. Josse's estate provided him with a heavy purse, but his tenants wore threadbare clothes. Roul hadn't seemed inclined to survey his property, but his servants kept to the corners and did their duties so as not to be seen.

Here, there was no fear in the people's eyes, and the children had shoes. Finding sympathy from any of them to hide or protect herself from a despicable lord seemed unlikely, since the villagers who came out were reserved, but respectful.

Which begged the question: what maliciousness was Ian of Warstone hiding? Was his evil reserved for darkened corridors and mysterious missives? Did these people only know him in daylight?

'I am pleased you are pleased with my...' Ian trailed off, his eyes going distant, almost melancholy, before he shook his head. 'I wouldn't want my mistress to believe I don't care for my tenants.'

He did this. Spoke in half-sentences, on inconsistent topics, and then looked off into the distance. When he'd first forced her upon this journey, she'd tried to hide from his notice. When harm hadn't immediately come to her, she'd realised she might live. Then she had wondered if there would be a chance for escape on those occasions when he muttered to himself and strode away, as if he meant to do something but had forgotten what it was. He always came to himself before she found the courage to flee. But flee she must.

She didn't know whom she feared more. This man who seemed to hold no reason, or the cold, malevolent predator who had held a dagger to a woman's throat.

They'd somehow reached the open gates, but her horse had stopped. Was it only now listening to her hints?

It was too late for that—and it was too late for her to take back what she had done before they'd left Roul's residence.

Trapped and guarded by Ian, that morning he had left

her side only once. She had assumed he'd done so to bargain with the man who'd won her in a game. At the time she hadn't known of either Ian's cunning or his distraction. She had been acquainted only with his arrogance and the knowledge he could kill her.

So she'd stolen a piece of torn parchment, ripped it again, and hastily written two messages. One to her brothers, to tell them she was in danger, the other to her sister, to tell her that she was well and having a grand time with a charming man.

Would her sister receive the letter that should keep her away? Would her brothers receive theirs, telling them to rescue her?

She moved in her seat to urge the palfrey forward. It still didn't budge. Sweat prickled under her arms. It was too late for the horse to back away now!

Too late not to have sent those messages.

The guards were going through, hails were being shouted, and she watched as Ian realised she wasn't directly behind him. She saw the deep frown, the cold eyes before he turned his horse around to stand beside hers.

'What is the matter? Am I not benevolent?' Ian said. 'I could have simply killed you.'

She felt again the terror of being cloaked in his benevolence. 'It's my horse…' she choked out through a throat that was closing.

'I should have killed you,' he went on, as if he didn't hear her. 'I even let you out of my sight whilst I took care of…' He trailed off. 'Unfortunate circumstances… foolish ones.'

Had it been foolish to beg her brothers to come to her aid? She was beginning to believe so. Maybe her brothers wouldn't receive her message. Maybe Biedeluue wouldn't be protective and check up on her at Roul's.

She knew these were maybes. The most she could hope for was that the messages would never be received. Her siblings always came to her rescue, and Biedeluue was the worst—or the best.

Always, if Margery so much as snagged the end of her gown on a twig, Biedeluue was there to sweep her up and carry her away from any harm. She loved her sister for it, and understood why she did it. As a child, one moment Margery had been safe in her basket, the next Biedeluue hadn't known where she'd gone. But her sister was stifling.

For once Margery wanted to carry her family away from harm. That was why she'd gone with Josse. And it was why she was trying to find a way to escape Ian without their help.

His eyes narrowed on her, as if he'd guessed her thoughts. 'I shouldn't have let you out of my sight. Fortunate for you that my men reported you spoke only to servants who had already been there and remained there.'

That was because she'd asked the young man not to deliver her messages until they'd left. The coin she'd given him had been enough for twenty messages, which had helped, but there was no certainty he'd done it.

She wouldn't have sent them had she known how little reason but how much fierce cunning Ian seemed to have. For all she knew, he'd left someone behind at Roul's to watch for messengers, and she'd risked that poor man's life.

'Now you refuse to ride into my home whilst my people are watching?' Ian hissed. 'Perhaps I might have given you some leave, but since you abuse the freedom I've given you, no more! You'll stay in my private chambers. Never to see anyone else. Never to go outside again.

Yes, I like that very much. For your slight that is fitting, isn't it?'

Margery felt the mercenaries' anticipatory stares. They expected violence. As if she was in some trap or waiting for a flogging.

'It's my horse,' she repeated, almost begging. She spoke louder, hating the almost strident tone, but Ian's eyes were wide, wild... 'She's stopped moving. It's not me!'

Ian stared at the palfrey, then at her, and then at his men. He looked back at her...then, slapping his thigh, he chuckled.

There were dots before her eyes, and her heart beat so weakly she thought she'd faint. She wasn't used to this constant fear...wasn't used to threats. His laughter was terrifying.

'Why didn't you say so?' Ian laughed again, as if they'd drunk the heartiest of ales and told the bawdiest of tales. The men around them laughed as well.

No, Ian wasn't distracted...he was mad.

Grabbing the palfrey's reins from Margery's frozen fingers, Ian tugged.

Margery felt that tug as if she truly was being led towards a public flogging, and as she went under the portcullis she was certain she'd entered the place of her punishment, perhaps her death.

She couldn't help but wish she hadn't been hungry that night, or that she'd run faster so as not to be caught. She regretted sending those letters, which might harm her brothers if they came, and yet she hoped they'd get here as soon as they could to rescue her.

Chapter Two

Evrart knew before the announcement was made that Ian of Warstone was returning to Warstone Fortress.

It wasn't the shouts from the different sentries along the path, or the franticness of the steward as he organised the household. Nor was it the old porter who hobbled across the courtyard to open the doors. It wasn't even the village boys, who usually raced down the slight hill, trying to be first to notify him because if they did they'd get a treat, or food, or a trinket they could gloat upon for weeks or months to come.

It was the damn hairs on the back of the neck that warned him. Some shift in the air.

It was always a turbulent time when the Lord returned from his missions, having left Evrart to defend the fortress, but never more so than now—because he wasn't anywhere near the fortress courtyard but in the lake behind, scrubbing off mud, blood and sweat.

Bathing in the middle of the day would be a perceived shirking of his duties that wouldn't escape Ian's observant eye. It didn't matter that he'd spent hours in the lists that morning and had worn out Ian's men. It wouldn't matter that he was just getting clean. It would matter that

Evrart wasn't there when the Lord arrived. Appearances were everything to Ian of Warstone.

Sluicing water over the remaining soap on his body, Evrart shook his head to release the excess. The lake was outside the fortress walls, near the back gate, but not close. It would take him some time to return and be in position.

Swiping the too-small linen from the rock, he rubbed the cloth over as much of his body as he could.

One factor worked in his favour. Ian always liked to arrive at his residence slowly, for the greatest attention. Evrart could only hope this would be the case today. After all, the Warstones were one of the most formidable families in France and England, but they hadn't gained their fame by fair deeds or their coin by good fortune.

Tossing the soaked linen to the ground, Evrart wrapped his braies and tugged on his breeches. No, the Warstones and their four sons—Ian of Warstone being the eldest—weren't revered because of any goodness. In the ten years Evrart had worked as Ian's personal guard, he hadn't got used to it—not once, not ever. Just when he thought he'd seen enough intrigue or horror, they'd surprise him.

Which begged the question: why didn't he leave his position as Ian's guard and find employment elsewhere?

He pulled his tunic over his head, tied his belt, and sat on the largest rock to lace his boots. Evrart wasn't of noble blood or good connection. He was nothing more than the third youngest of a poor family, and who had been tilling a field on the outskirts of the Abbey of St Martial when Ian spotted him.

His entire family were often noticed, because there were trees smaller than his father and houses smaller than his mother. His sister, oddly enough, was finely boned, as if whatever had made up the rest of their family was trying to correct itself. Unfortunately for his ears, or any continued peace, when last he'd seen her, Peronelle had been taller than any of her friends—a fact she bemoaned to no end.

Evrart strode across the land towards the castle. The watchguards on the ramparts were already conversing and positioning themselves along the walls.

He ran.

Such was his life now. Castles and swords. Ramparts and great halls. All he wanted was a fine plough and some oxen. A thick roof and a well-stoked fire.

Ian had been gone longer than he'd reported. Anything out of the ordinary with Ian was concerning. Ten years of being his personal guard, and Evrart had seen many changes. But not like the ones over the last year.

Ever since his brother's Guy's death, Ian's behaviour had turned from merely cold-hearted to terrorising. Frequently, he'd left Evrart behind. Going off on missions, leaving Evrart to hear rumours of legends, of treasures, of betrayal. Recently, he'd become certain Ian had tried to have his own brother, Balthus, murdered, and lately he'd looked at his steward in a way that didn't bode well for the old man. He talked more frequently of his wife and children, how they had been lost and saved.

And something about a dagger had been lost and found but lost again. That appeared to agitate him the most and Evrart had had to step in once or twice to save a wayward strike towards a servant.

Ian's reason was slipping day by day, which made his time away all the more concerning. Who would Ian be upon his arrival, and why had his schedule been disrupted? It either meant celebrations or punishments. The latter was more probable. Thus, if he wasn't in position where he was expected, Ian would take his wrath on him.

It wouldn't be the first time. Such would be his life until his death. And it wasn't for the coin, or the position, or the power.

Oh, he'd amassed some fortune for himself in the ten years he'd been with Lord Warstone, after Ian had trained him to be his personal guard. More coin than he'd ever wanted or desired. However, unlike his two older brothers, Yter and Guiot, Evrart had been content to stay at the village and help his surviving mother and youngest sister. He hadn't wanted to go anywhere.

It wasn't loyalty that kept him. It was Ian of Warstone's threat of a brutal death to his mother and sister if he was ever betrayed. Evrart didn't question the threat. If a Warstone made such a statement it was fact—like the sun rising and setting.

So, though he loathed every moment in his employ, he did it. He did it and would do it until he rotted in some unmarked grave.

Rushing through the back gate, he bolted around the south tower into the courtyard.

The front gates were already open.

He was late.

Ian had already dismounted, and men surrounded him. Horses were being led away by stable boys. Some of the men wore Warstone colours; some did not. A few Evrart did not recognise. But it wasn't the men who held his attention. It wasn't Ian either, though the Lord acknowledged the distance between them with a raised brow.

No, what held his attention was the child on a palfrey. The cloak looked like one of Ian's and it swallowed the poor creature.

Ian had a wife and two boys, all of whom he had taken away six years ago. They had never returned. Rumour was that his wife had taken the children and run somewhere that Ian wouldn't find them.

This creature was too small to be Ian's wife, and yet she didn't peer around the hood with the curiosity of a child.

Whoever she was should be inconsequential to him within the thick stone walls and heavy gates of the fortress surrounding them. Insignificant to the duty of his sword and him sword arm. Whoever was on top of that horse shouldn't hold any meaning in Evrart's world—but she did. Merely because she had been brought here by Ian of Warstone, and Ian didn't bring anyone here who wasn't a guard or a mercenary…who wasn't meant for battle, death, or to serve him his wine.

With a sweep of his arm towards the diminutive shape, Ian grinned. The mad Lord was showing off.

Something vigilant and dark struck deep through Evrart's bones, and he strode through the parting crowd to enter Ian's circle.

The fact many had to scurry around him was not his concern. He was Ian's guard. He was expected to be close to the Lord. He knew whoever rode the palfrey was either dangerous…or in danger.

Ian grasped the creature around the waist, parting the cloak to reveal a gown underneath. When her feet touched the packed dirt, her hood fell to her shoulders.

Reeling, Evrart widened his legs. Ian had brought back a woman, but she was not his own. Her hair was light, her eyes were clear, innocent… She didn't belong to Ian—to whom *did* she belong?

Ian's arm went out and she placed her hand on it, separating the enormous cloak from her body, revealing gently curved breasts, a sharply indented waist above ample hips. A woman finely wrought. But innocent? She couldn't be—not if she was here.

Something wasn't right. They were...awkward with each other. Something that went beyond the formalness of Ian's mannerisms, and her stiff-backed response. She smiled, and so did Ian, but both smiles were forced, both were playing a role. With certainty this was another game then. Perhaps she was innocent, perhaps she was here by force—but that wasn't what alerted him.

In truth, something had eased within him when he saw she was a woman, not a child. Though he couldn't quite shake that feeling of vigilant protectiveness. But that would go soon once the newness of her arrival had disappeared.

Ian was speaking now, introducing her as his mistress. Margery.

In ten years Ian had had no woman, no mistress, and never had he lain with his own servants.

Another intrigue, then...and brought to his home. She must be a powerful ally, but Evrart didn't recognise her name. Her clothing was fine, so it was possible she was from a noble family, but he'd never seen her before at any residence or castle.

However, it appeared everyone around him knew something of her that he didn't.

Then he knew what was wrong. It was the crowd... they seemed rapt with attention. As if they were witness to some display of great entertainment. The woman again? But why? Her features were fine, with almost a perfect symmetry between her nose, her mouth and her eyes. She had two arms and legs and hands...

But someone gasped and pointed. One child clapped, and a few of the guards at the gates, who hadn't travelled, were elbowing each other and looking at her meaningfully.

Was his own poor background to blame for why he didn't recognise her? Or was it something older, and established before the decade he'd been here?

It was a possibility.

However, the two little girls giggling at her, and being shushed by their mother, made no sense. They wouldn't know who she was, and yet they appeared to be beside themselves with delight at her appearance here.

Was it that Ian had brought back the woman because she caused such a reaction? Another possibility, since Ian had stayed faithful to his wife, Séverine. But these possibilities were all guessing. There was nothing that should cause him concern, and yet he felt it. Those raised hairs on the back of his neck weren't going away.

Evrart swept his gaze farther afield, to the ramparts and the various buildings that butted against the great wall, to any movement around the chapel's garden. All was as it should be.

Most of the crowd had disappeared now. The horses were gone, and Ian was talking with the woman. Her gaze was going from one man to another, to him, to the cordwainer at his side, to the child next to the pantler.

He waited until her gaze swung to him again. Everyone looked at him. Then her eyes gentled as she looked at the kitten clenched in the child's hands.

He waited some more, and matters changed again. It was quieter, and there was an air of expectation. Evrart stopped looking at this woman, this... Margery...and looked instead at Warstone, who was looking directly at him. He realised that Ian had asked him a question, and he needed to answer.

When he didn't, Ian's smile became sharper. 'See,

my dear? Evrart's as silent as the walls of my castle; you won't notice him being your guard whilst I'm gone.'

Her guard while Ian was gone.

There—right there—was the danger.

Chapter Three

Margery kept the smile on her face, her hand gently resting on Ian's arm. All the while her heart thumped and her body shook.

Staring at the kitten had felt like a reprieve—until Ian's words had registered. She was to have a guard.

She was days away from anything and anyone she knew. She could barely ride a horse. Roul certainly hadn't fought for her to stay—she knew he wouldn't be coming after her. Now she was in a castle courtyard, with enormous stone walls and mercenaries surrounding her. And she had…a guard. Right next to her. This man—this Evrart.

Ian had been correct. He was silent like the fortress' massive walls. And just as cold and unfeeling.

Except… There was a flash of something in eyes that were blue but wanted to be brown. Or were they brown and almost blue?

Margery had seen many hazel eyes before; they were often a blending or mixture of colours. But Evrart's were different. Distinctive in that parts of them were blue, others were brown. She could almost trace the swirling…

The longer she looked, the more she noted other

things about him: the broadness of his nose, the heavy weight of his brow. Everything about him was brutally carved except for his lips, which looked soft, and his ears which peeked out from his oddly cut dark brown hair.

His expression had turned wary at her scrutiny and he looked away. No, it was not wariness, most likely displeasure. She needed to stay strong.

For all she knew Evrart was indeed like the walls, and that meant he was only good enough to secure her and no good for anything else. That would bode well if he was to be her guard. She'd need some freedom if she was to escape—and she *would* escape.

She might be terrified now, but that couldn't last. She'd been frightened, but resolute when she had accepted Josse. Then betrayed and angry when she'd been forced to accept Roul's bed, but she had survived that.

Although neither of them was like Ian of Warstone. Neither had threatened her life, her family, nor held a dagger to a woman's throat. When they'd left that afternoon, she hadn't seen Roul or that woman. Ian killing them both—killing *her*—wasn't outside the possibilities.

She needed to get around this guard and escape.

With an enigmatic look towards her, Ian swung away. Evrart was immediately at his side. They were steps away before she realised she was meant to follow them across the open outer courtyard and through another wall opening into a smaller courtyard.

She faced an imposing castle, numerous buildings, unusual sounds and then the abrupt lack of them. Margery looked to the people hastily jostling for a better view. None of them came up, as they had in the village, except one man, the steward, whose reedy voice gave her goosepimples.

Ian treated him horribly, and from Evrart's expression he didn't like him either. Still, the man scraped and bowed before he was dismissed.

Other eyes were not so oily…most were curious. One large man, with his arms crossed over a bloody cook's apron, looked almost friendly. None looked prepared to rescue her, though, and Margery dutifully climbed the steps into a great hall. Here, she slowed her steps to gaze at the tapestries, the ornate carvings, but Ian only hurried his pace, and then suddenly stopped.

'I need to gather my men,' he said to her, before turning to Evrart. 'Take her to my chambers. Secure her in the room with the bed. You'll need to set a guard until we get a blacksmith to fashion something of a lock for the outside. But do it now.'

She was to be locked in a room? 'Do I not get fare to eat, or somewhere to clean my hands?' she asked.

Ian gave one of those smiles he gave when they were being watched. 'I'll have something sent, my dear. Now, if you'll excuse me?'

Margery stood at the bottom of the stairs along with Evrart as Ian went swiftly out through another archway.

She felt the weight of his stare, heavy against the back of her neck. What now? She'd asked for food, to get clean. How else to delay?

'I'm thirsty,' she said.

Nothing.

Did she dare ask again?

'Can you ask if I can have some watered ale?'

Evrart pointed at the stairs.

She glanced up the staircase, which was neither dark nor light. There wasn't any indication as to whether it would be safe or dangerous, and this man…somehow embodied both.

Which made little sense.

It was the fear of the journey, the exhaustion of the ride. She was seeing things that couldn't be. This man? Safe? He was large, strong. If he was safe, it was for someone other than her.

With a frown, he pointed up again, and something in her snapped.

'Oh, is that some sign that I'm to go up the stairs?'

A muscle ticked in his jaw; she tensed for the strike. Nothing again. There was no one else in the corridor. Not even voices to indicate that someone would hear her scream.

She could see no way out of this.

Gathering what courage she had, she ascended the staircase. At the top, the corridor was wide and slightly curved. On one side were arches open out towards the inner courtyard down below, and on the other side were several doors.

Before one of the closed doors, her new guard opened it to wave her in. She glanced around his body and saw furniture, some windows. But mostly she saw the latch on the door that had a lock.

'I thought he needed a blacksmith?'

Her guard pointed to her left where another door didn't have a lock.

'So I'm to stay here now, and there later?' She wasn't ready. He might have to resort to physical violence to get her in there.

'I need to relieve myself,' she said.

He frowned. It wasn't a nice frown.

'He'll fetch me some food,' she said. 'He might not fetch me an empty bucket.'

He kept his eyes on hers too long. Would he hit her now?

She braced herself, but his eyes flickered over her head and down the empty corridor.

She looked, too. 'Is there…do you have an inside garderobe?'

He waved ahead, which she assumed was a signal for her to proceed down the corridor.

When Ian had said Evrart was like a wall, had he meant it literally? This man didn't talk. But it didn't matter how much waving he did, she didn't want to walk any further down the long corridor either.

Mostly because she didn't truly need to relieve herself. She'd hoped her request would lead them outside, or on some errand to fetch a bucket. Anything not to be corralled and cornered again. That had happened to her with Ian…that was how she'd been caught.

Ian wasn't around now, but her terror wasn't easing. Could she run faster than him?

Not from where she was standing, and not with his size. He'd merely have to reach out and grab her hair. Even if she did dash past, how far would she get within the walls and gates?

She needed to keep walking forward.

The man kept his steps even with hers. They barely made a sound, and he made no other movement. Not a swing of an arm, not a brush of his tunic against the stone walls.

The mercenaries she'd travelled with had jeered, made every bodily sound possible, and when Ian hadn't been looking they'd grabbed their cocks. They'd constantly talked, constantly gestured, and when they'd had a woman, they'd constantly passed her around.

She had been frightened every moment in their company—especially when she'd slept, or tried to sleep. This man…didn't move. But that wasn't comforting either. His restraint was disconcerting. He hadn't stared like everyone else in the courtyard. He'd barely acknowledged her at all.

She was still overwhelmed by the fear she'd felt at the sight of Ian, haunted by the woman in the corridor who was now most likely dead. And she couldn't stop her mind from replaying the memory like the iron crank of a portcullis.

But this man, keeping his silence, scraped across her already frayed heart and made it worse.

Slowly she proceeded down the corridor, which was solid on one side but resplendent with views on the other.

Another step. Was her guard still there? Of course he was.

Why was her heart pounding? Why were her feet stumbling? The trembles…

She couldn't take another step. She stopped.

He stopped as well. He didn't speak. He didn't point.

She swallowed hard. 'You're very quiet.'

He said nothing.

She looked up…then up again. His arms were at his sides, his eyes steady, and all that stillness caused something to seethe within her. He was large, but then everyone was larger than her. It was how it had always been.

But being in this fortress, trapped and threatened by Ian of Warstone, wasn't how it had always been. If only she could wave a sword or conduct her own threats.

The seething turned to roiling. If only she had some way to protect herself! Not just standing here staring out of a window, feeling waves of helplessness, as this man—this warrior, her guard—watched her tremble, heard her teeth chatter whilst he was constant stillness, relentless silence.

'How will you guard me if you don't speak?' she asked.

His brow rose, and she swore she saw the corner of his lip twitch.

Maybe it was the terror, maybe it was because her reason had finally fled, but Margery laughed. It was a choked laugh. More strident than joyful. More sobbing than anything humorous.

And when his brows rose more and his eyes widened…when wariness that couldn't just be wariness entered his eyes again…the noises she emitted came out harder, until tears sprang from her eyes and she had to brush them away.

She noticed the poor man hadn't moved, but he seemed to be leaning back. Not with displeasure or cruelty. Not to smirk or laugh—though he should be because of her ridiculous question. But simply to stand there, a bit away from her. And whereas before she'd equated his silence with displeasure, his restraint with formidable trapping walls, now she saw it wasn't. It truly wasn't.

It was the way he blinked, and his careful movements as he straightened himself. He was disconcerting because for days she'd been plagued with violence and threats. For months…years…before that, she'd had Josse, Roul, the mercenaries who'd leered and calculated.

When her hood had fallen, he hadn't elbowed the man next to him. He'd simply looked at her as he looked at her now. Like…a person. And maybe it wasn't wise, maybe she was wrong, maybe she truly had lost her reason, but she didn't care that he was quiet. It didn't mean *she* had to be.

Resting her hand on his forearm, she said, 'Don't mind me—truly. I am harmless. Well, maybe not completely, but I'm not likely to cause any permanent wounding.'

Patting his arm before releasing her touch, she brushed

her hands down her skirts, gathered herself, and gave him as reassuring a smile as she could. He wasn't like Ian or those other guards. Maybe he was like that man with the bloodied apron—the butcher who'd had a happy smile. Maybe they could start again.

Maybe they couldn't.

His eyes were the size of the moon and his hand gripped his forearm where... She was right. His hand was gripping his arm, right where she'd touched him. His knuckles were white.

With anger?

Was he injured and she'd inadvertently harmed him?

'Oh!' she said. 'Did I hurt you?'

He said nothing, but his eyes grew intent. She felt terrible.

She grabbed his fingers to pull his hand away. 'Here, let me see it.'

She didn't know what she'd do, but there she'd been, laughing because she couldn't harm him, and then she had. She was worried, terrified, but this man hadn't done anything to her and here she was—

'No,' he said, and pulled his hand away from her.

All the while he kept his gaze on her. His hands were rough, his fingers felt thick, but his touch was inordinately gentle.

It was his voice, though, that made her shiver. Deep, gruff. Exactly the voice she'd expected from a man with shoulders that could protect her from a storm.

She held still. 'Say something else.'

He stared at her so hard she thought he would see to the other side of her before that corner of his mouth quirked again. Was he trying to smile but couldn't?

'No,' he repeated.

Something came over her. Something that wanted him

to smile. What was wrong with her? She didn't need to laugh with this man or ask if he was hurt. His hair might be wet as if was like everyone else who bathed, and he might look vaguely annoyed rather than cruel, but she needed to escape!

As if he'd guessed her thoughts, he abruptly let her hand free and pointed again.

Resolved to do what she must, she continued down the corridor. Before she closed the garderobe door, though, she said, 'And you'll stand out here? Then take me to that room and lock me in?'

When he crossed his arms, she answered herself.

'Of course you will.'

Chapter Four

Evrart closed the door to the chamber he'd left Margery in and opened the adjacent one.

He wasn't surprised that Ian was already at his desk. He'd heard noises down the corridor when Margery had been in the garderobe, and Ian spent most of his time behind that table, scribbling on parchment or standing at the few windows surrounding it.

'What is it, Evrart?'

Evrart knew better than to answer. Ian was too manipulative with conversations. Evrart might say he liked the colour blue, but Ian would construe that to mean he liked the colours of another family. Back home, he'd taken after his mother and been the quietest of his siblings, but now he knew silence was how he stayed alive and kept his family safe.

Ian wrote his message and handed it to the man standing patiently by his side. Evrart waited until that nameless man had left the room before he looked again at Ian, who had leaned back in his chair.

Evrart stayed still.

'This is about my mistress,' said Ian.

Evrart nodded.

'You secured all the doors?'

As much as he could. All the rooms here, save for his, were Ian's private chambers, most of those were connected by inner doors. Some hallway doors had locks, one did not. She was in the locked room next to this one, which was also attached to his. Something that shouldn't have mattered but did. He felt her there.

He nodded again.

'You have questions on my wants and needs?'

No, but he did have questions of his own. She'd touched him—freely, and without an agenda. And she'd looked at him as if he was no different from the cordwainer, who was half his size. That kitten had received more of her attention than he.

It had been…startling. But that didn't compare with when she'd laughed, her eyes filled with fear, and he had felt that need to protect. He'd leaned away, to put some distance between them, but the brush of her fingers against his had riveted him next to her. Made his body burn and made him question if he had any reason.

She was danger—or she brought danger. She wouldn't be in a Warstone fortress, as a prisoner of Ian's, if she wasn't, and yet… He knew if she touched him again, he'd let her. He'd never been so irrational before. He was questioning himself on his response to Ian's mistress, but he wouldn't ever question Ian. He wasn't a fool.

'Never.'

'This is about your role.'

'Yes, my lord.'

He shouldn't be anyone's guard except Ian's. Until this last year he'd hardly left Ian's side. Now his men questioned his position and his role in this fortress. If Evrart was Ian's personal guard, how could he be left behind? Almost worse was the rumour that he'd fallen out of favour with the Lord of Warstone. Not that Evrart cared for idle gossip, but his job of training the Warstone soldiers was made easier if they believed he had Lord Warstone's ear.

If the guards questioned him, he quickly met them in the lists, but still… He might not like his role in this household, but it was his role, and he would do it well until he could find an end to it.

Ian steepled his hands. 'You didn't question me in front of my men when I told you to bring her to my rooms.'

'No,' he replied. Again, he knew when to keep his silence, and was rewarded when Ian's mouth curved into a smile.

'After all these years…still saying so few words to me,' Ian said. 'Did it ever occur to you that if you said more, I might let you go. I do like to understand my guards, and at this pace I'll never understand you.'

A rhetorical remark Evrart would never answer.

Ian did flash a grin, but then his brows drew in and he looked to the side.

Evrart stood his ground. Ian hadn't been stable for many years, and his condition had rapidly deteriorated since he'd packed up his wife and two children and deposited them in an undisclosed location. He'd always liked Séverine and Clovis, and the infant Pepin was adored by all. But it had been years since anyone had seen them. Ian's thoughts weren't good, and since last year, they had grown darker yet. Right now, Ian could order his death or ask him to play chess.

When his gaze slid back to Evrart, he looked no more or less like a cunning wolf.

'She interrupted me when I was persuading a messenger to gather information whilst a certain man was suitably occupied. The task of delivering a message she had no issues with—the method of getting the information she refused. Naturally, she had to be persuaded... Margery happened upon me during our negotiations.'

Did that mean Margery wasn't his mistress but was inadvertently involved in a Warstone scheme? No wonder she'd fought being locked in a room. No wonder she'd given such a fearful laugh. That didn't excuse his response to her, though...

'You look surprised,' Ian said.

He looked no such thing. He knew better than that. But then this could be simply another rhetorical question.

'I, too, am surprised not to have killed her. I actually had to negotiate with Roul for her services.'

That grabbed Evrart's attention. Roul was the youngest son of a noble family and he amused Ian. Evrart couldn't recall what he looked like because his face was always buried in some woman's breasts.

And this Margery had been under his care? Was Roul the reason she frequently looked over her shoulder?

'Said he won her in a game of chance, but that man can never be trusted. Still, it was a fool who lost one such as she, since she is utterly beautiful—don't you agree?'

When people talked of beauty, Evrart never saw it. He looked at form, or deeds, and since he'd become older, he'd realised he had another skill most did not have. He could determine someone's character. He had known immediately not to work for Ian of Warstone, but being able to determine character did not mean he had any power.

He wondered if this Margery had any power. Had the scheme being played started with Ian or Roul? Because Ian, one of the worst men Evrart had ever known, thought Roul couldn't be trusted.

The woman appeared innocent, but she couldn't be if she was Roul's mistress. This would bear some thought.

'Her beauty, whether it exists or does not, isn't my concern,' he said. 'My concern is my duties. For ten years I have trained the men you have brought into your home. Even now you have brought new recruits. Now you have asked me to oversee a mere woman. I simply want to understand my role.'

Ian shook his head. 'I truly don't understand your preference in women, nor why you cannot see beauty. I am happily married, but to call Margery "a mere woman" is astounding. As to the rest—your role is to ensure she doesn't talk. To anyone. She can use Jeanne for a servant, but that is the only person she's to have contact with.'

'Is she to remain in your chambers?'

They were large and consisted of several rooms. When Ian was in residence he often stayed in the rooms and didn't venture to the Great Hall for meals. Busy with schemes, and untrusting, he rarely interacted with anyone in residence.

Ian nodded. 'Tomorrow I will be journeying. I'd like to see my children soon.'

Evrart looked out through the window behind Ian as quickly as he could. There was no hiding his surprise this time. As far as he knew Ian had tried a few times, unsuccessfully, to find his wife, but now he seemed certain. He could be wrong, but—

'Oh, you are very surprised!' Ian chuckled. 'You should be. There will be changes soon, though I'd wish for it differently. My brother is forcing my hand.'

Evrart swung his gaze back. Talking with Ian was like fighting a bog. 'Is she to begin these…changes?'

'No, but that is an interesting proposition. Do you think her beauty would be enough?'

Evrart said nothing. A bog would be less murky than Ian's thoughts, and he'd be foolish to step into either one.

'Quiet again… You are fascinating. I do wish you'd give me some suggestion whether you think her suitable or not.'

Suitable for…*him*? If she was beautiful, as Ian purported her to be, she wouldn't be suitable for—

Ian shoved back his chair and stood, then looked down at his desk and swept everything off to crash on the floor. The ink arced for a moment, but the pot stayed intact.

Brows drown, Ian tsked and picked it up to set it back on the desk. 'I hate wasting words.'

Evrart stayed still.

'They're all wasted now—did you know? That fool of an Englishman my parents hired lost the dagger again. Not his fault, he told them. How could he know it had been switched? That red-haired clan figured it out, but they don't have it either. No one does. And that's supposed to comfort me because Reynold doesn't have it. But he's after it—so where's the comfort in that?'

Evrart felt the blood drain from his body, and nothing but instinct kept his legs holding him up. Ten years with this family. Ten years during which he had heard of their schemes and their pursuit of the Jewell of Kings—a gem that was hidden inside a hollow-handled dagger. It was a legend like Excalibur…like the Holy Grail. Whoever held the Jewell of Kings held the power of Scotland.

It was a story. The Warstones, even the King of England, believed it. Evrart liked the story, and didn't like to think of Ian's mutterings about a treasure and a parchment safely hidden being part of it, though he knew it was.

A treasure? He didn't want to think of the Warstones gaining more wealth for more power.

And truly he wasn't supposed to know that the Warstones were after any of it. Ian had never, not once, spoken of it directly to him before. What would the Warstones do to his mother and sister when they realised that he had?

Ian tsked again. Shook his head. 'Lost! And now it may be too late for me. At least there are a few things I can do to catch my parents unawares, but I have planning to do for that… I do.' Striding towards the door, he added, 'Get someone to clean that up. Keep her in my chambers. She's not to go anywhere. *Anywhere*.'

Evrart needed to find his voice. 'The garderobe?' She'd asked for it once; she'd ask for it again.

'This is why I like you. Specific. She can go there, but you're to accompany her.'

Evrart swallowed hard. 'At my own convenience?'

Ian's expression turned dark, but Evrart held firm. The men already questioned his position, if he had to stop for a woman's needs, he couldn't keep order.

'You have new men and they need to be trained, my lord,' he added.

'Ah, yes,' Ian said. 'Again you prove to me why I keep you. And I like it that she is to be restricted. It might prove to be amusing.' Ian eyed Evrart. 'And if you don't see her beauty now, I'm certain you will soon. There may be many interesting things whilst I am gone…'

The hint of speculation in Warstone's eyes didn't bode well for him, but at least he strode out the door without another incident.

Evrart looked at the wrecked room. There were other signs that Ian's temper wasn't controllable. There were slashed cushions on the bench under the window. He wondered whether the messenger had been privy to that display—if it had been a warning to him to ensure the scroll was delivered.

What would Margery think of this room?

Evrart looked at the thick wooden door that led to her bedroom. Silently, he stepped towards it, fisted his hand and thumped it.

A gasp and a scurry of feet.

Just as he'd thought. His instinct told him she was innocent. She'd seemed distraught, and she'd kept looking behind her as if an enemy was at her back. Maybe she had been forced to come here...but maybe not. Her innocence didn't accord with the Warstones and their schemes.

And Ian... He was acting as if he didn't quite know what to do with her, but he had brought her here to his home. To be here, she must be tied into Ian's need for power and information. It couldn't be simply that she'd come across Ian threatening a messenger. He would have killed her otherwise.

Unless she truly was that beautiful...

Was that why the courtyard had been full of such surprise and chatter? For beauty? Evrart couldn't imagine such a trivial thing holding so much sway. No. This was about Ian, whose intentions were layered and far too vast for him to make mere conjectures.

And her? What innocent would press her ears to doors to hear private conversations? Had she heard anything?

He didn't know!

Evrart was tempted to storm into her room and demand answers, but his duties awaited. And, in truth, it would be safer to wait.

He'd been careful all these years to keep himself and his family safe; he would continue to be so. Despite her size, and the fear in her eyes, despite what he thought she might be, he'd wait.

He hadn't been around Ian for so long without picking up skills besides his ability to judge character. This woman changed matters around here. He didn't know how, or why, but she was outside the realm of what had been occurring for ten years. Ten years during which he'd been away from his family and from the life he wanted.

If Ian was keeping her, it was for something. And now that Ian was leaving again, it was up to Evrart to find out why she was here, and if she was useful to him.

Because if there was any means to get home, he'd take it. If only for the fact he could bathe in peace again.

Chapter Five

Margery faced the bed, the window, the door. Then faced them again. It had been five days since Evrart had waved her in here, and she had willingly walked across the threshold. The room was more than comfortable, and no luxury had been spared; however, five days with nothing but her thoughts to keep her company wasn't good.

She worried over those letters she'd sent. Now she was here, she saw the futility of her brothers trying to help her at all. And how long would the words she'd sent her sister Biedeluue hold her back?

Her siblings were all she had. Her father had walked away when she was just an infant and her mother, already frail from births and grief, had never recovered. She had been broken in both body and soul. As a consequence, Biedeluue had become like a vigilant mother, Mabile a gentle nurturer, and her brothers had doted on her and indulged her.

As a child, she had once watched a game her older brothers had played of throwing hammers. All had been fine until a hammer had gone astray. Her brothers had tried to protect her, but not before she'd been hit. She had bruised far too easily, and although she'd covered as much as she could, Biedeluue had found every injury. Her scolding of Isnard and Servet had been talked about for weeks afterwards.

Oh, she missed her family—but she didn't miss the village she came from, and it had been a long time since she'd been there.

Leaving with Josse had been the right decision, but difficult. If her family had had any way of surviving without his help, she wouldn't have done it. But given her mother's frailness, and her siblings toiling as hard as they could, what else could she have done? She'd needed to help them because they'd lost so much simply because she had been born.

The reason she'd left with Josse had been to help her family. And the coin she'd earned had helped. But she hadn't received what she should have from Roul before she'd been ripped from his home, and Ian wasn't paying her.

It was all the worse because Mabile had written to her about her latest pregnancy. She'd need help with taxes and food and such, and now she was stuck here with silk cushions and generous helpings of fine food while her family went without.

'Stuck!'

She shook herself. Muttering, pacing. It was only a matter of time before she didn't finish her thoughts or her sentences, like Ian.

Ian—who had left the day after they'd arrived. His goodbye had held more distraction than actual words. In a moment of clarity, she had seen a man who was fighting against himself and losing. Yet she couldn't pity him. Not when he had trapped her here, not when he had most likely killed that woman, and not when he got that look in his eye as if he was prepared to do the same to her.

She'd asked again what he intended to do with her, and he'd answered that he'd know when he returned. As if that was an answer!

She moved to the window again although she tried to avoid it as much as possible. Ian's courtyard was extensive, and at least provided much to watch, but her interest often went to the far corner, and if she sat just so… strained her neck a bit…she could see the lists, where day after day the men trained.

Some days they trained with swords, others they just wrestled. Then there were days when their weaponry was laid out on wool blankets or stretches of leather, when one man would lift it and display its worth and purpose.

One man…one warrior…who held the attention of many as he gave instructions, as he ordered dangerous men as if they were mere boys.

Evrart held *her* attention, too.

It wasn't just that he was easier to see because he was wider and taller than the rest. It was because…he was different. He didn't look as if he belonged. Maybe it was because he held himself a bit apart, or maybe because after the training the men avoided him. She didn't know.

But it was the interaction between them that intrigued her, despite her knowing better. Despite him not speaking to her again since that first day.

Day after day he'd—

A tapping on the door.

Not a knock, not even a fist.

Margery, feeling a bit lighter, called out for Jeanne to enter.

Jeanne stood with a tray. A guard was behind her, with his hand on the latch before he closed the door. The servant was younger than Margery and no wider than a broomstick, with light brown hair and eyes. At first she had stuttered when Margery talked to her. So Margery had kept trying.

It hadn't taken much to draw the poor girl out, and she was decent company. No, better than that—she could almost see them being friends if it wasn't for the cruel man who kept her trapped.

'Is this where you want the tray?' Jeanne indicated the table with her chin.

Margery tried not to smile. 'Perhaps.'

It was a game she had played since the first day: ordering different food or asking Jeanne to arrange the placement of a spoon or a bowl in a certain way, to delay her from leaving the room too soon.

That first day Margery had been certain Jeanne thought her mad. Though even then Jeanne had answered some of her questions. The second morning, however, Jeanne had caught on to what Margery was doing when she'd asked for a small tapestry to clean her hands, and if there wasn't one to supply thread so they might do one together.

Jeanne had laughed and continued the game, as well as answering questions and letting Margery know a bit about the people here. They had delayed so much since that first day that the guard who was there had stopped banging on the door for them to hurry. Jeanne might have changed her mind in thinking her mad, but the guard had clearly had his opinion confirmed.

'Is this satisfactory?' Jeanne looked up through her lashes, moved the spoon a little to the left, and then more.

'So how is Thomas today?' Margery asked.

Thomas was a little red-haired boy who had been trying to help Cook in the kitchen. But the man drank, and apparently there had been an accident. She only knew any of this because on that first day Jeanne had kept fumbling until Margery had been certain she'd collapse. It hadn't taken much encouragement for Jeanne to share her worries.

'The swelling around his nose is easing. Still can't see through his one eye, though.'

'And Cook?'

'He's...' Jeanne mouth tightened. 'He will be well.'

Why the man hadn't been banished, Margery didn't know.

She must have frowned, or made some sound, because Jeanne said quickly, 'It isn't his fault—it just isn't. Thomas set him off, that's all—surprised him. And Cook thought Thomas was—' Jeanne shook her head. 'He picked him up, but then the light hit him, and when he realised it wasn't... He tossed him away,' she said. 'It's only been a few days. He needs time, that's all. Time... He prepared this for you.'

On the tray was some overly buttered *raston*, well-aged cheese, and finely cut meat. It was a meal that in childhood would have delighted her. Now such a meal came at a price she didn't want to pay. She truly just wanted some firm bread she could chew on. It would last longer and it would remind her of better days with her family.

As for Cook... It wasn't her place, Margery knew it, but she couldn't let children be harmed. She knew what it was like to be suddenly lifted at the whim of an adult. And she'd never been harmed. Thomas had.

'Why doesn't the steward do something?'

Jeanne looked horrified. 'Steward avoids Cook—Michael—and long may that last.'

Margery didn't understand this household. Something tragic had happened with Cook, but Jeanne was loyal and wouldn't tell her. Still, if there was anything she could do...

'Will you tell me why? I promise not to say a word. Or maybe I could say something to help, and—'

There was a bang on the door. Margery dropped the hard cheese onto her lap, and Jeanne turned around.

'I've got to go.'

The guard hadn't given them any time today. 'Why are you following his orders?'

'They're not his orders.'

Evrart's.

Whatever thoughts she'd had that he might be different had been just wishes or false hope for escape.

'No asking me to help you escape today?' Jeanne said.

Margery laughed, shocked that this woman she'd met only a few days before could somehow discern her thoughts so well. She would like her as a friend.

'I'll give you rest for today—but maybe you should warn Evrart that matters won't be so easy for him.'

Jeanne's eyes widened. 'I don't believe that would be good.'

Why did everyone fear him?

'Why? Perhaps it would provide some entertainment.'

'Oh, you truly shouldn't provoke him! No. That wouldn't...' Jeanne pressed her lips together, seemed to come to some decision. 'Are you truly planning to escape?'

Margery blinked. Jeanne hadn't asked a direct question before—especially not about who she was or why she was there. Her first response was to answer in the same teasing vein they'd established, but seeing the earnest concern in Jeanne's expression, she answered with the truth.

'I do want to. I shouldn't be here, and I fear I've made

a mistake that may harm people I care about. But I don't see how I can. Not with the guards, the walls, those vast fields. And the fact I can barely ride a horse.'

Jeanne's expression eased and her eyes softened. 'Doesn't mean you don't wish for better things, does it?'

Margery poked the soft bread on her tray. 'Better things like some true bread.'

Though she smiled, Jeanne narrowed her eyes. 'You won't make me go down there again...'

'Ian did say you were to serve me anything I desired,' she said, though she wouldn't force Jeanne to run around today simply to give her more company. The guard was already impatient. But it was an idea that could be used another day...

'How about something else?' Jeanne asked suddenly.

Margery almost blurted out that Jeanne shouldn't be concerned. The servant had other duties and might get into trouble with the steward. But Jeanne looked almost eager, so she said, 'Such as?'

Jeanne snatched the tray and stared at the door behind her. 'Let me see.' Jeanne gave a quick nod, and then carefully went out the door.

Margery caught a glimpse of the guard who'd followed Jeanne up here before Jeanne shoved the almost full tray into his hands and talked to him, her words continuous and never letting him say a word in reply. Then Jeanne's hand was on the latch as the door closed.

Margery waited for the distinct scrape of wood and iron as the door was barred. When that didn't happen, Margery waited some more. Then she realised what Jeanne had given her instead of bread.

A way out.

Chapter Six

Evrart blinked, then blinked again. He wasn't mistaken. Margery was in the corridor, heading towards the stairs. He stopped his long strides up the staircase. There were no others behind her, and he heard no other sounds other than his footsteps. This tower was empty save for its captive—who shouldn't be freely roaming any corridor.

Evrart cursed. If Ian had been in residence she would have lost her life, her toes, her feet. She could have been hurt in any of the numerous ways he'd watched Ian use to torture his enemies. She could have been passed to some of the newer mercenaries who were out to prove themselves to the Warstones.

He didn't trust those new men even when he faced them in the lists. Until he'd gathered all the information on their families, something Ian insisted upon to ensure loyalty to the Warstones, every day he was prepared for some act of betrayal.

What would a faithless man do to a lone woman who was reported to be uncommonly beautiful and Ian's mistress? If there was an enemy amongst them, and they thought she was important to Ian, she'd be used as bait.

Of course if she was captured by Ian's enemies she'd be killed. Ian wouldn't bother to rescue her.

And that dark thought of another man touching her, of any of those new men touching her, let alone slicing a blade across her throat, brought again that sense of dark vigilance inside him. Something far more seething than the desire merely to protect.

How difficult could it be to keep her locked in a room? He'd checked on her three times a day since Ian left. Five days of opening the door and waving her towards the garderobe whilst he waited down the corridor. Five days of guarding her from those new men, and from any acts she might do against the Warstones.

He hadn't talked to her since that first day because it wasn't safe. Not with the way she was with him…not with his reaction to her.

He needed to know more about her. He'd tried to get information from the men Ian had travelled with, but they had not been forthcoming. Any knowledge they had divulged had made his hands curl to fists, though what they'd said wasn't anything more than what any man had said. He just didn't like it. Not when it came to her.

Training was hard for them all that day.

Yet all his precautions had been for nothing, for here she was, taking a few more steps closer to him as if he wasn't about to unleash himself upon her.

He took the final stair. All the responsibility for this woman fell on his shoulders. If he failed in his one task, his family would be at risk. And this woman played *games*?

'Did you just growl?' she said.

He was about to do so much more.

Jeanne had done this. That quiet girl had obviously left the door unlocked so Margery could escape. What was the name of the guard who had accompanied Jeanne today? It was his last day.

He saw her eyes move to the door to Ian's chambers and then past him. Did she think he'd let her pass?

'Are you simply intending to stare at me?' she said.

No, nothing as simple as that. This woman wasn't Jeanne. She was someone who couldn't be reasoned with. She would incur his frustration and his threats.

He rolled his shoulders just once before he said, 'What would it mean if I answered?'

Her eyes went wide and her mouth twitched. Was she going to cry?

The other day she'd had such a reaction of fear and laughter he hadn't known how to respond or even if he should.

Women did this...but more so around *him*. Fright, tears, fainting! Any movement startled them, any words said often made it worse—and not simply because he couldn't choose the right words, but apparently because his voice was gruff...as if he had any control over that.

Her lips were trembling and there were tears at the corners of her eyes. Evrart looked behind him. Maybe he could—

Margery laughed.

Evrart started to take a step back and only just remembered where he stood. Her eyes widened more, and the soft laughter grew bolder. This wasn't like before. These weren't tears choked out by fear.

'What could be humorous?'

She chuckled and shook her head. 'It's your expressions, and that shoulder-rolling thing you do.'

If he rolled his shoulders it was because his shoulders had tightened from frustration, or anger. From all the danger, intrigue and lies. Because lives were at stake. It wasn't a jest.

This didn't bode well. He was four times as big as all of her, and she wasn't intimidated by him at all.

Again, he knew the right course would be to put her back in the room and be done. Again, his reaction wasn't typical.

Wrenching his gaze from hers, he leaned against the arches to stare outside. 'It isn't safe.' *For either of them.*

She wiped her eyes. 'But he's gone, isn't he? When is he to return?'

He didn't know. Not this time. In the past Ian had rarely left him behind, but now he seemed to do it all too often. Something was escalating and there was nothing Evrart could do about it.

As far as he could tell Ian's brothers were turning on him. But Reynold had turned on the family long before Evrart had become a part of the household, so it made no sense other than the rumour that the youngest, Balthus, was also turning away from the parents and Ian.

But Balthus was a favourite of his mother's. His betraying the family must be false.

'You do know you haven't answered me?' Standing near a different arch, she continued, 'I'm assuming you know how long he'll be and you have been advised not to tell me.'

This was disastrous. He should have opened the door and put her in the room. He should have returned to his duties—though none of them had held any appeal from the moment he'd seen her stepping towards him.

'Your silence isn't loud enough for me to hear,' she said. 'How about you nod or make some other affirmative physical gesture if I am saying something true?'

Something light shifted in his chest. Was he going

to laugh? He didn't know this woman. Ian had ordered him to lock her in a room, either to keep her safe or to keep his home safe. Either way, he should be obeying.

Evrart allowed himself to gaze at the woman at his side. The days he'd escorted her out of the room he'd been careful not to stare too much, though he'd wanted to. He felt she wouldn't like it. But it was the way others still talked about her. Her hair...the way she moved her hands...and her lavender eyes.

But lavender's distinct fragrance wasn't what clung to him after he left her presence. Her scent was something more distinct, something... There were times when he opened the door and instead of stepping back he held it, so she'd brush against him to enter the corridor. That scent wasn't lavender. Lavender wasn't addictive. And it didn't make his body tighten or make him wish he could bury his nose in the crook of her neck.

'You should go to the garderobe whilst I wait here.'

'I have already been. That's where I was when you interrupted me.'

How long had she been free?

'It's right down the corridor.' She pointed. 'You expected me to wait for you?'

He expected her to stay safe.

He almost winced. She wasn't safe, was she? He wanted her in that room so he could do his duty to Warstone, so he and his family stayed safe. But her being in that room wasn't beneficial to her at all. Unless she was dangerous—which he couldn't believe. Not when her wide eyes were on him, allowing him to see every emotion.

Still, for all their sakes, she needed to obey.

'You've been waiting for me for five days,' he said.

'It's not always convenient. What if you don't arrive on time? I'd have to clean up my own—'

'Don't say it.'

'Now you want me to be quiet?'

Why had she stayed in her room before? Because of fear or a sense of safety? Or because the door had been locked? Now apparently Jeanne had brought food and hadn't locked it behind her. He might need to install permanent guards.

'Are you thinking of putting guards outside my door?' she said.

He almost growled again. Who *was* this woman?

'Not only thinking…intending to do it.'

'Will *they* take me to the garderobe, then?'

That sense of dark vigilance he hadn't quite been able to shake since that first day he'd seen her roiled in denial. He shook his head.

'You don't trust them?'

She leaned her hip against the sill, a movement which outlined the shape of her body. Everything about her was bright…almost brazen. No, *brave*. Her body reflected it—from her eyes upturned at the corners to the flick of her nose, the determined chin. Her breasts were moulded tightly by her gown binding. The curves were barely discernible, making a man wonder what her nipples would feel like against his tongue. But her hips… Those were fully rounded, and even in his hands they'd be a handful, something he was being made viciously aware of.

Was she as beautiful as Ian purported her to be? She was…*something*. In all the women he'd come across, never had he wished to know what one truly looked like, but he did her.

'The chapel with the gardens is beautiful,' she said.

It was quite a view when Ian left his private rooms

to see such changing beauty through the multiple archways along the corridor. Not that he could see beauty the
way others could—something he'd been made aware of
when he was a child.

'The chaplain won't let you claim sanctuary,' he said.

She huffed—some sound between amusement and
frustration.

'Why do you keep laughing?' he asked.

Her brows drew in, but her mouth still held that soft
smile. 'You keep being humorous.'

He'd never been accused of such a thing in his entire
life. 'You're not afraid of me.'

'Am I supposed to be?'

Everyone was. Maybe not when he was but a boy in
the field, maybe not to his own mother. But since he was
grown, since he'd gained skills, everyone but Ian treated
him as if he was deadly…always.

For ten years it had served its purpose. He was to protect Ian—his reputation assisted that.

But with her… Did he need to protect her from Ian,
or from himself?

His instinct said she was innocent, that Ian had trapped
her in some game of his. But when she walked, she looked
around her as if she was surrounded by enemies. She did
it less now than when she'd arrived, but it was still there,
and it didn't seem as if she knew that she did it. That kind
of habit meant there was something in her past. As if she'd
had enemies all her life. Innocent people didn't do that.

'How do you know Ian?'

'I don't,' she said quickly, turning to gaze out through
the archways again.

The slight breeze brushed her hair about, casting almost a halo glow around her head.

'You're his personal guard?'

'I am.'

'And now mine?'

He wouldn't lie to her. 'My loyalty must lie with him.'

'Must…'

She mulled that word over, but he saw no problem with what he'd said until she continued.

'Then you're in a similar predicament to me,' she said. 'Trapped here?'

For his family's sake, he could not side with this woman. 'I've been with Lord Warstone for almost a decade.'

'That long? Is there no hope for me?'

Evrart let his breath out slowly, trying to gather his thoughts, which were chaotic. It was because of the desperation in her voice, the worry, and the fact he wanted to help her when he couldn't help himself.

'Do you want to leave?'

'You mean I shouldn't? Is it because of the fine food or because Ian might kill me?'

He pulled back from the archway in case anyone looked up. It would do no good if they were spotted conversing.

She did the same. 'You must know his intentions for me.'

Ian's cryptic words about her suitability still made no sense to him. 'I don't.'

Her eyes narrowed. 'If you did, would you tell me?'

He should have said no immediately. His response should have been instant loyalty to Warstone, who held his family in the palm of his hand. But he wasn't certain if that was true.

'Does he know of your family?' he asked.

She tilted her head. 'I told him I lived in Pérouges.'

'But you don't?'

She looked away.

It didn't matter if she told him or not. 'I won't tell him, but that won't deter him for long.'

'So they are in danger?'

He didn't have to answer that.

'Is he a threat to your family, too?'

It had been a mistake to talk to her. It was more of a mistake to believe he could help when he knew he couldn't.

'How many are there?' he asked.

She narrowed her eyes, but that did no good.

'Your expressions are as open as the sky. Ian can't have questioned you else even your silences would have given you away, and if he hasn't questioned you, he doesn't care to know.

'So you do talk,' she said. 'I have two brothers and two sisters, all older than me. My father… My mother isn't well…' She gasped.

'What is it?'

'It's difficult remembering them. There are matters I need to…' She looked away. 'I can't do anything about it now.'

He could tell she was close to her family. That there was pain in her past, and too many family members she cared about to escape Warstone's notice.

'They are all together?'

She glanced at him again, but her gaze didn't stay with him. 'No.'

'What aren't you telling me?'

'If I leave soon, it won't matter.'

She wouldn't be leaving—but he shouldn't be asking her questions. It would only complicate matters since he was always the one who carried out Ian's terrible deeds.

How much innocent blood had he shed? If he knew her, would he be able to spill hers?

'Help me escape,' she whispered. 'I mean no harm.'

'You could be tricking me,' he said.

'Do you believe that?'

There was always an ulterior motive with the Warstones. Margery was Ian's mistress—but he hadn't slept with her. She was to have the honour of his private chambers, to eat the finest food and have whatever she wanted—except she was to be banned from all other rooms and escorted to the garderobe at the convenience of a lowly boy from a poor village.

'There you are being quiet again,' she said.

He hadn't been talkative as a child. As a man, he had trained himself to be quiet.

'Are we to stare outside for the rest of the day? Or will you shove me back in the room?'

'You're not safe running about.'

'So you keep saying—and I wasn't running about,' she said. 'I was using the garderobe.'

'And heading to the stairs.'

Her eyes darted. If this woman had schemes, she wouldn't be able to hide them. 'You can't lie easily.'

'How would you know? And I'd be a fool not to attempt an escape.'

Or ask him to help her. People didn't usually ask him for anything nor did they talk to him for any length of time.

'I'm still not scaring you.'

'Why do you keep asking me that?'

Her eyes never left his. For once, he didn't look away. He needed to know.

She huffed again. 'You don't scare me when you're not quiet. Or when you move.'

He opened his mouth, closed it. 'My quiet scares you?'

She shrugged.

He wanted to stay here longer. Ask her more questions. But he'd do it not to find out her purpose here, but because he wanted to know her.

Forcing himself, he faced the room behind them and opened the door.

Something like disappointment flitted across her eyes. 'I thought we were past that.'

'We're not past the harm that could come to you, and until then...'

She raised a brow. 'There is an "until then"?'

He could make no such promise. Ian had said matters would be 'interesting' whilst he was gone. Evrart couldn't shake the idea that whatever was happening inside him, whatever was changing because of her, was part of it.

He couldn't let it be! He'd been part of Warstone's schemes once, when he had been brought here, but he refused to be part of them anymore. Simply talking with Margery was likely a trap, and one he slowly was falling into.

Thus, it was a relief when, without another glance, Margery entered the room and he locked the door once again.

Chapter Seven

'What are you doing?'

Margery stopped with the spoon halfway up to her lips. It took her a moment more to close her mouth and straighten. Another moment to realise the contents of the spoon were dripping and set it down.

It would take more than a moment for her to find some semblance of calm when the object of her entire morning's thoughts stood on the opposite side of the table where she sat.

Evrart.

It had been a few days since Jeanne had left that door open for her, and she hadn't done it since. Margery had specifically asked her not to, and there had been no mistaking Jeanne's relief.

Margery was simply happy she hadn't been punished. The guard, however, who had escorted Jeanne, had been banished from the fortress. Margery didn't know what that entailed, and thought it prudent for her ability to sleep not to ask Jeanne nor Evrart, whose expression now looked as formidable as ever.

He must have come straight from the lists. Someone

most likely notified him she was dining in the Great Hall, and he didn't look pleased.

From her window, she could admire his training— the sweep of his arm as he extended his sword, the way he crouched and dug his heels in so no man could move him.

Outside, he looked implacable. Fierce. However, something between them had changed since that day in the corridor.

It wasn't so much his allowing her to use the garderobe, though they did exchange a few words now, it was the way he looked at her.

Unlike when she had first arrived, his gaze lingered now. Stares from men she was used to, but Evrart's were different.

He looked at her as if she was something unusually intriguing, and he never stared at her hair or her eyes. No, when she caught him he was usually staring at her wide hips.

She could almost swear his neck would flush, but couldn't be sure. However, just thinking it so set her imagination off in ways she hadn't expected.

Men were men, and she tried desperately to avoid them. Josse, her first lover, was much older than she, and he had been gentle. As far as doing what she'd had to to gain coin, it hadn't been as terrible as she'd thought. Roul, however, was cruel and liked pain.

Though both men had treated her differently, both had had the same territorial gleam in their eye. The same one Ian had had the night he'd caught her: a look of cold interest that had nothing to do with her as a person, and everything to do with her as a possession.

Evrart had never, not once, looked at her that way. If she hadn't been so certain he'd ignore her question, she would have asked him about it. Because not knowing what was in his eyes when he looked at her and failing to contain her own wonderings about it was keeping her up at night. And instead of worrying about escaping, or Ian's return, or her family, she thought and dreamed of Evrart.

He'd caught her escaping in the corridor, but he hadn't punished her, or raised his voice. Instead he'd asked her questions of her family. She could think of no purpose for that except he thought he could help them. He was Ian's personal guard…but she was beginning to believe he was something for her, too.

She no longer avoided the window but stared outside constantly—not just at the lists, but elsewhere, in the hope of catching a glimpse of him. And now here he was, mere feet away.

Up close, she was enticed by the dusting of dirt, the sweat of the man. The way his skin glistened and his chest heaved. She could hear the cracking of his neck as he snapped his head to the side and she scented hot iron, some herb he'd bathed with, and *him*.

Before she knew what she was doing she inhaled again, drawing in that scent a bit more, until there was a tightening inside her. Her body had reacted the same when she snuck into his room the day before and lifted his abandoned tunic to her nose before she caught herself. And all the while he watched her, his eyes moving from her slightly parted lips down to the table.

Was he frustrated not to be able to see her hips? She'd always thought her body an odd shape. Unlike her sister, who was round all over, she was small on top and large on the bottom—something no gown could completely disguise. No man had ever commented on her flaws, but Evrart appeared to like them.

What colour were his eyes? That strange cross be-

tween brown and blue? His hair, damp with sweat, was
a much richer brown, and cut brutally short in places,
but left oddly long in others. As if he cut it for his own
purposes and not for any fashion. It suited him.

It suited her. A section that she could run her fingers
through, and another she could lay her palm along to
feel the prickle and tingle that would begin but wouldn't
end there.

Just imagining how it would feel was causing her
body to react, her breaths to feel a bit short, her nipples
to tighten for want of soothing. That spot on his head…
she'd cradle it when she tugged him closer, when she—

His gaze swung back up to her face, his eyes holding
a question that darkened the colour there. Was her food
of any interest, was she?

The hall was silent. Jeanne had left after setting the
different plates in front of her just so…after Margery had
asked her all the questions she'd been able to think of
to keep Jeanne close for company. Today the topic had
been parts of the fortress she couldn't see. Information
she'd need to escape. None had been forthcoming, but
that didn't mean she wouldn't try.

And she'd keep trying, because she had more of a
chance to leave now with Ian of Warstone not here, than
when he returned. She had more of a chance of escaping
when she wasn't locked in her room.

Something this man—this warrior—seemed to understand as he stood there, his gaze changing from questions
to something more forceful, more demanding.

What was he demanding? Margery looked at the multitude of dishes before her as if they could answer. They
could. Ah, yes, he'd asked a question.

'What am I doing? I'm eating fresh cheese,' she replied. 'It's newer than most and requires the spoon as well as bread to not waste any.'

'And that?' he pointed.

She didn't look down. 'Beans.'

He breathed in deep and exhaled roughly, as if whatever he'd been thinking had tightened something inside him as well. She could tell nothing of his thoughts from his expression, though.

'Cooked with wine?' he said.

This was what he wanted to question her on? No, he wanted something else—she could almost see it. But what?

'Ale, and I requested extra buttered onions to top them.'

'Buttered?'

'I find the taste of oil flavourless.'

As if she could ever get used to such luxury as olive oil! She'd eaten well with Josse and Roul, but the Warstone wealth was unsurpassed. Perhaps the King of France ate such fare, but she couldn't get used to it, and it wasn't what she craved.

It didn't hurt that asking Jeanne for different dishes also kept her close, so more questions could be asked. She truly wished they could be proper friends...

'How many meals has Jeanne provided to you today?' he said.

She tried to keep a straight expression. 'Ten.'

His lips tightened. 'How many did you refuse.'

'Nine.'

'Jeanne has other duties.'

Margery was certain she did—but that didn't suit her purposes.

'How did you get to the hall?' he asked.

'I suggested it would be more prudent for me to eat

my meal here as it's closer to the kitchens, and she could do her other duties.'

Sweeping his gaze around the cavernous room, he pulled out a bench.

There was ample space along the giant table, but when Evrart sat down the space between them wasn't more than the length of her spoon, and when he rested his arm on the thick oak table it shook.

'Do you want some?' she said.

He eyed the heavy, thick bread, vastly different from the fluffy buttered *raston* Jeanne had first offered her and grabbed a roll. She pushed the bean dish over, and he dipped.

He was merely eating, but she felt as if something was in the balance. Something she needed to understand. Because she didn't want to lose this small victory…didn't want him locking her up even more than she was already. Ian had several chambers, and the garderobe was down the corridor. But she was aware she could be locked into only one room with no opportunity to be outside it ever again.

'I'm not outside,' she said. 'The private chambers are just up that staircase.'

He chewed, swallowed, dipped his bread again.

'If I stepped outside, you'd see me because you're always in the lists.'

He stopped chewing, stared at her. When his eyes narrowed and he audibly swallowed, she realised what she'd just confessed.

That she watched him. Not simply looked outside, but at him. That she knew exactly where he was, and what he was doing.

There was nothing, absolutely nothing, she could do about her blush.

Evrart grabbed the cup in front of Margery and downed the liquid. He wasn't surprised it was ale, given the food in front of her. But he was surprised, greatly, that this woman had been watching him.

Him.

Not the lists or the guards. She'd mentioned nothing of the weather, nor the fact the pen around the pigs had been broken by some boys playing, and there had been squealing hogs running loose. They had caused chaos during training, though with one order from him the men had got in line.

Evrart set down the empty cup, but didn't take the final bite of the roll. His ravenous body was suddenly not interested in food. It was wanting something different— something also at this table but not for his consumption. So tiny, but not delicate. He wanted to devour her.

When people first noticed him, they stared. Most didn't blink, and some were bold and walked up to test their height against his before they even introduced themselves.

When Margery had first seen him, her eyes had swept over him the same as everyone else. When Ian had assigned him to her, he'd been treated as no more or less than Jeanne. She talked to him the same way, she touched him the same way. Now she had invited him to sit and dine with her.

Who *was* she? It was not the first time he'd asked himself that question, and it wouldn't be the last. There was still more to know about her. Anything she'd told him could be a lie. Perhaps she did know Ian, and she was here for some other purpose. Maybe she was a spy Ian had planted whilst he was gone.

Yet none of that mattered as it should because…she'd watched him.

The true question was: did she want to know about him? Not as a conquest or to gain position in the household, but him as a man?

As she shifted in her seat and picked up a bread roll, only to set it down, then pick it up again, he thought she might. And just the possibility, just the thought that someone could want him, blasted through every reason he had for staying away.

She wasn't staying in the room as it was. When he'd stand in the corridor, and she'd walked to the garderobe and back, she'd stare out through the archways to the grounds below, and do the same again on her return towards him.

And Jeanne, as quiet and shy as she was, always kept the doors open for Margery to gain access to the corridor. He knew she'd been in his room yesterday when his worn tunic wasn't exactly where he put it. Already the servants were taking risks against Warstone's wishes, and that was significant.

So why shouldn't he? Because he hadn't done it before. There had always been something or someone to jeopardise his family. Was this woman worth it? Reason told him he didn't know, not with any certainty. But the way he felt sitting across from her... He didn't want to let that go. Not yet...not if he didn't have to.

If he was intelligent there wouldn't be much danger—at least not while Ian was away. No one would question him if he acted the way he always did. Who was to say he wasn't guarding her still? It was safer to keep her closer. Today she'd been in the corridor; tomorrow she could be elsewhere.

If he watched her, made certain she didn't talk to others, what harm could there be?

Also, if he was wrong. and she wasn't trustworthy

or innocent, keeping her close would allow him to extract information that he or Ian could use. It would be easier to catch her in some misdeed if he allowed her the opportunity.

It would be completely against Warstone's wishes, though, and a risk. But he'd take it. Because he wasn't starved for food or drink—he was starved for something he hadn't known he was hungry for.

Her.

'What are you thinking?' she said.

Evrart chewed on the bread and beans that would provide him strength, but little else. The woman before him was what he needed, and whatever measly touch she gave, whatever tiny offering of kindness she pushed across the table to him, he'd take.

'How did you get into my room?' he asked.

Her fingers fumbled with the abused bread roll in her hand. 'How did you know I'd got into your room.'

Because he'd felt it before he noticed his tunic hadn't been draped over the chair the way he did. Had almost been able to smell her scent in the fabric, as if she'd didn't just move it, but clutched it as she picked it up.

He no more wanted to threaten Jeanne than he would a small kitten. Whenever he entered a room, Jeanne always found a way to leave it. No, he couldn't reprimand Jeanne. But Margery...

'You only guessed that's what I did, and I just confirmed it!'

She grinned and leaned her elbows on the table. He was all too aware it brought them closer.

'Is this cheese your favourite?' she asked.

Her hands were flat on the thickly textured wood table. How easy it would be to touch her!

'Which cheese?'

Why was she talking of food when her eyes danced as they did? Had they looked this way when she'd entered his room? Now he wondered what else she touched.

'This one.' She laughed and pointed. 'The newer kind—so soft you have to eat it with a spoon or spread it on a dense loaf?'

How did she...? The bowl was empty. Whilst he had sat and thought of her, he must have eaten the lot.

'I'm willing to guess you don't like to talk,' she said. 'So, if I say something wrong you could just blink twice.'

She wasn't going to force him to speak. He could do this. Say a few words, and no one need know why he was here. He was just her guard. That was all. Simply guarding her...

'You're like me,' she said. 'Small village? Perhaps your family tilled the fields? Perhaps they're poor and you've had to make the decisions that led you here?'

This was the flaw in his thoughts! He might not talk. He might be guarding her. But he would be exposed to her and her thoughts, her words and deeds...

Evrart set the roll down and brushed crumbs off his legs. Not this. They couldn't talk of this.

She reached out. Her hand was right there.

'I'm sorry, did I—?'

A mistake. How long had he been here? Enough time to eat a bread roll, and in that time he'd made a mistake. His proximity to her put his mother and his sister at risk, and not just because of the Warstones.

Perhaps if they were caught he could explain to Ian why he'd allowed Margery outside the room. But telling her of his family? Of himself? It was too much.

He shoved the bench away from the table and stood. 'You aren't to leave your room for anything or anyone. I will, however, accompany you every day on any walk that you wish to have. Your games with Jeanne must stop. They put you, and more importantly her, at risk.'

'But if you take me out—'

'I have no risk,' he said. 'Now, finish this meal and I'll walk you upstairs.'

'Evrart, I didn't mean anything. I didn't know...' She slid to the end of the bench and stood. 'I asked, but you didn't answer, and now I know—'

Despite himself, despite knowing better, he said, 'What do you know.'

'That he's threatening your family, too.'

Chapter Eight

Margery glanced at the man walking beside her. True to his word, he no longer trained his men all day, no longer locked her in the room all the time. Instead, for the last few days, he'd roamed the castle with her.

It was a welcome but fragmented reprieve.

That day in the hall, when he'd eaten all her food, he'd seemed to come to some conclusion. But then she'd asked of his family and he became as the fortress—a wall of cold stone.

He'd stopped talking and she hadn't known what to say or how to apologise and return to something approaching amicability between them.

By the time they'd reached her door she had been in a panic. She'd clutched at it, then at his arm. When he'd finally looked at her all she'd been able to do was apologise again. Vow not to talk of his family—or him. She'd felt the tension ease from under her hand, and she'd had the impulse to track that small movement. To feel more of him.

The next day he had been at her door, pointing not at the garderobe but towards the stairs.

And now here they were, though it still startled her

to be out in the air, and that he'd allowed her suggestion for what they did. Of course he stayed close, which precluded her from attempting to run or looking for a way to escape.

Any freedom was impossible with the men at the gates. Every glance she made to the ramparts, or around the courtyard, revealed how well trained they were—and she was hardly a gifted escapist. She'd learnt to watch people to protect herself. Flinging herself into a dangerous situation wasn't a skill she possessed.

At least by walking with Evrart she was able to observe, and maybe an opportunity would present itself. People avoided Evrart, and as a consequence her as well. She wasn't certain Evrart would allow her to interact anyway, but to not be given the opportunity was an odd sensation. Margery was used to people running towards her. Now she received stares, but they were quickly averted, and no one dared approach them.

Unfortunately, however, the first few times she'd attempted to investigate the kitchens or greet Jeanne had been a failure. There had been no visiting Jeanne or being introduced to Thomas. As for Cook—she'd seen him, more often than not slumped in a chair asleep. She couldn't imagine it was he who was preparing her food. Not that she minded the simple fare...

Had something happened to Cook? She didn't know and didn't know how to ask—not with Evrart at her back and people walking as far away from them as possible.

It wasn't all terrible. Being avoided gave her some freedom. She was able to roam the chapel gardens as much as she'd like.

But after a few days of walking the inner courtyard, and a day or two of access to the outer courtyard, Margery wanted more—and not only for herself. She was all too aware of the stares she garnered, but she was aware that Evrart had his fair share, too.

Did it bother him? His expression was as stoic as ever. The man truly was like the walls of the fortress. But something weighed on him. She'd touch his arm to gain his attention and he'd roll his shoulders afterwards. Or she'd stand on tiptoes to whisper closer to his ear so as not to be overheard and he'd flex his neck.

Sometimes it was the things she'd say, and he'd get a pained look on his face. Though she avoided talking of his family, and quickly told him of hers, she still bothered him.

Was it her choice of conversation? Her requests to wander farther and farther? She didn't know. And she wouldn't ask—not while he allowed these odd outings.

Right now, however, Evrart's expression was as impassive as it had been when he'd greeted her this morning and she'd announced she wanted to pick quince in the orchards. He was just as quiet, too.

Despite those two things, he still gave off premonitions of his displeasure—and yet there was some eagerness in him which was at odds with his reluctance. It was odd for her, too, for she recognised her happiness to have his company. If she'd truly hated it, she would have stayed in the room.

If she told someone of Evrart, she'd say he wasn't good company. Except he was exactly the company she wanted. He had been ordered to guard her, but she felt comfortable around him when everything about him should have repelled her. Not because of the sheer size of him, but because he was Ian's personal guard and anything she did would be reported to him.

She'd never been comfortable or trusting with a man. Josse had coddled her; Roul had exposed her. And being ripped from that world and put into Ian's, which was more sinister than anything she'd experienced before, should have terrorised her.

But this time with Evrart wasn't frightening. How could it be when she teased him about his cheese or when he agreed to their picking quince?

'The days would go much faster if we could converse, or you could give an opinion, or...'

'I need to train.'

'Why didn't you tell me you needed to do something else today?'

When he said nothing more, she sighed. Maybe she was comfortable around him because he wasn't comfortable around her. He'd said he had a duty to watch her, but she wondered again if that was the reason he allowed her out of the room.

'We can walk after midday if you wish,' she said.

'No.'

There were days when Evrart was almost congenial—this didn't seem to be one of them. Still, she did like to tease him. His expressions were always good for some amusement.

'Because you don't want to see me?' she said.

'No.'

The tenor of his denial seemed different, deeper... more raspy...and he had hesitated. She'd jested with him, but maybe there was a story here...

'Is it because you're not that good a guard?' She glanced over, trying gauge his response. 'I can understand that. You wouldn't want me reporting your poor skills to Lord Warstone.'

'No...' he said slowly.

'But he did leave you behind,' she prodded.

He clamped his mouth shut. So much for that conversation. They continued up the small hill. It wasn't far to the orchards, but far enough. It was also late in the morning, and there wasn't anyone else on the winding path. This might be another dull day unless her companion—

'You keep looking at me,' he said.

'You are walking next to me.' She switched her bucket to the other hand. 'Of course, that's all you're doing.'

'You're not doing it.'

'Doing what?'

'Looking around.'

What a peculiar topic—but it was conversation from her recalcitrant guard. 'Because it's easier not to walk into walls if I'm looking ahead.'

He shook his head once. 'You look forward rarely. To the sides often, and every twenty steps you look behind you. But right now you're looking at me.'

Margery stopped. That was very specific. Had she stopped doing the most basic thing to protect herself?

'You won't talk of picking fruit in an orchard, but you want to talk about me looking around.' Did he know why she always observed her surroundings? She needed to be more careful. Any sign of weakness and her previous two lovers had taken advantage of her. Did she feel safe around Evrart? Yes, she did. But when Ian of Warstone returned...

'Maybe I'm not used to my surroundings, and I am curious,' she said.

'But you came to the fortress this way.'

'I came this way?'

Her legs wobbled and she grabbed his forearm. He didn't acknowledge her forwardness, but a muscle in his arm flexed and her own fingers gripped tighter before she let go. It was almost as if she didn't want to let go… No, she *knew* she didn't want to let go. She wanted to touch him.

What she didn't want was this conversation.

'Did you change the subject because you didn't want to discuss how terrible a swordsman you are?' She hoped he wouldn't notice her voice breaking.

He stared until his eyes narrowed, until whatever it was he was determining eased. 'Yes.'

He was lying, but he said it anyway. A jest? Or a way to make her more comfortable? She didn't care. What it was, was kindness, and she was grateful. This giant of a man had observed her, seen she was wary, and been considerate enough to let her change the subject.

She patted his arm, gave him a smile, and decided to forget everything else as they continued their walk.

'It isn't far, is it? I thought the quince trees would be near the other gardens.'

He grunted. 'There are servants for what you want to do.'

'There are servants for everything at this fortress,' Margery replied. 'If I let the servants do it all, then there'd be nothing for me.'

He kept his steps small and even with hers, so she didn't miss the side-glance he gave her.

'I know that's what Lord Warstone wanted of me,' she said. 'But we've already been through this, so that argument is finished.'

'Finished?' Evrart said. 'Not when he returns.'

'Are you intending to tell him?'

'Won't have to with you roaming about—someone else will.'

She stopped swinging her basket. 'You told me you weren't at risk.'

He didn't say anything.

She should have known better! 'Let's go back.'

'Too late,' he said. 'You've been roaming for days. This is just one of many.'

'What will he do?' she asked.

If she was to be the cause of his punishment, she needed to know what it was so she could mitigate Ian's response. And if she couldn't, she needed to suffer the same, or at least be brave enough to face it. Ian was a Warstone—they were meant to be bloodhungry.

'He will do what he has always done,' Evrart said.

His deep, pleasing voice was not softening his words at all for her.

'That sounds…dire.'

'It is nothing but truth,' he said.

'That's worse,' she said. 'That has to be worse. You are talking as if he's done this many times in the past.'

'He has to others, and I expect no less for myself,' he said. 'I made a vow to him, and I am breaking it.'

'What argument, then, to defend yourself?' she said.

'I won't.'

She stopped. They couldn't possibly have much farther to walk, and she didn't want others to hear. She wasn't reserved so much because of the words she was about to say, but because of their meaning.

Evrart was right when he said she looked around all the time. She did so because there was danger everywhere for her. If she did not pay attention while walking down a corridor a sudden hand might appear and drag her into a dark room. If she did not look behind her a reckless horseman might run her over before he ever impressed her with his skills.

She looked around her because all her life she had been stolen. Her sister had told her of the times when she was an infant, when she'd disappear from her basket, only to be found at a neighbour's home, being passed around.

She was always trying to protect herself, and now this man told her he would simply take his punishment. Not while she breathed. Did he do it because he was large, because he felt unworthy?

Something changed within her.

Men weren't like this. They took and demanded. She'd never known, hadn't known a man could be like him. Evrart was strong, invulnerable, and yet…

'Evrart, you listen to me,' she said. 'You must defend yourself.'

'I am Lord Warstone's guard,' he said. 'If I have gone against his rules, he is within his rights—'

'No!' She slashed her arm in front of her.

This she had heard all her life. She had lavender eyes, therefore the neighbours were within their rights to take her. They couldn't help themselves. Her hair was like the stars, therefore she had no right to protest when another child pulled on it.

She had made one decision in her life. It hadn't been a good one in hindsight, but it was the one she'd taken. When Josse had come through and wanted her for himself, she'd accepted. He hadn't snatched her or stolen her. She'd gone with him in order not to be burden on her family anymore. And she wasn't. She was a burden on herself—but that was beside the matter.

'No?' Evrart repeated slowly, with heavy measure, as if the word couldn't be the one he'd heard.

'It doesn't matter about anything. You defend yourself. You defend yourself because your worth isn't that he's your lord, or that he pays you, or that you're in his debt, or that you're *this*—' she waved her hand around him, indicating his breadth '—or that you're a terrible swordsman. Your worth is something far beyond any of those or anything else we can think up.'

Was he understanding what she was trying to say? He was simply staring at her. She'd have to take some faith from that.

She pointed at him, then pointed again. Just to get her thoughts across physically. 'You're worth defending—and if no one else does it, it's up to you to do it.'

His mouth tightened, as if he held back some words. Had no one ever told him these things before? Maybe that was why they'd been put together. So she could straighten him up.

She patted him on the arm and tugged him forward. 'We're almost there, aren't we? Let's get going.'

He kept still a bit longer, so she looked behind her. 'Aren't you coming?'

Evrart wanted to say no, simply because there was a feral need inside him that wanted to say yes. He wanted to say yes to everything when it came to Margery. He had been agreeing to everything she wanted, and he wondered if he had any discipline or restraint left in him. Was he to be domesticated like a horse or dog? Was he some great task of hers?

What she intended with him he couldn't fathom.

The fact he even asked himself what a woman intended to do with him was alarming. He was three times as large as her, and one hundred percent more scarred. She might be a mistress, but he was a man who killed, who did tasks that no man should at the request of Lord Warstone.

The fact he did it to keep his family safe was no excuse. If his mother knew it came down to him committing murder or herself killed, she would beg him to protect his own soul. Except, he argued with himself, wouldn't her death also be on his soul if he couldn't prevent it?

So here he was—a man who did deeds because he must.

Everything had been as it should and would be until his death. Then Ian had left him in this woman's clutches and he didn't know himself any more.

She was tiny…insignificant. If he told her to close the door, she should close the door. If he said no to picking fruit, she should cower in her corner and not pick fruit— not carry her baskets as if they were on a pleasure trip.

They finally crested the hill and could observe the orchard below. Tree after tree, all in bountiful lines, with loads of people chatting and picking.

'Oh, look at the colours—this will be great fun!' Margery exclaimed.

The orchard was full of people. It would be a nightmare. It wasn't as if they were trying to escape notice, but this would be openly defying his lord's orders. He would be punished. All he could hope was that she wouldn't be.

What would he do if… What had Margery's word been? Defend. What if he defended himself against Lord Warstone? No…he made the choice and knew the consequences when he did so.

What would she think of the choices he had made?

For her there was beauty, and she could freely demand he admire the colours in the valley. For him, nothing was free. Simply this…merely walking to an orchard beside a woman he wanted…wrenched him from the maw of his duties.

Even if he deserved them there were no colours for him. There never would be, despite how much she pointed them out. He didn't see the world like others—

he knew that. What would happen when she discovered his flaw?

Deeper and deeper into the orchard they walked. Most of the people ignored them, but just as many stared. He was grateful she didn't stop to greet them all but kept walking further through the trees, where there were fewer people, but also fewer quince to pick.

Margery seemed to have come to that conclusion too, because she was now frowning accusingly at the trees as if it were their fault all the easier fruit on the bottom branches was already plucked, and it was only those on the top available.

Oh, she was fierce. Entranced by the sight of her hands on her hips, the bucket angled outward from her arm, he sensed the trap too late.

'I'll need your help to pick these.' She pointed.

She'd needed loads of help—and he was envisaging all of it...

Spanning her tiny waist with his hands, hoisting her above his head, catching sight of the curve of her ankle or placing her in such a way that her rear would be directly in his line of vision.

For days now, he had stolen awkward glances, but their height difference, and the fact they often walked close, something he'd purposely done, had precluded him from truly appreciating those rounded curves.

There was a good chance she wouldn't mind him lifting her. She'd asked for help and she kept touching him.

She wasn't afraid of him, and she also didn't approach him as if he was some oddity or a conquest to boast to her friends about. She just ordered him about, which should be insulting. It *was* insulting. But he also like it. He imagined ordering her about and he liked that better.

'Are there ladders or stools nearby?' she said.

She was already forging ahead before he could answer. To help, and to hide his smile, he turned in the opposite direction.

Margery was a force unto herself, and apparently beautiful in ways that others could tell. How had she fallen prey to men like Roul?

Roul... Just the thought of that man anywhere near her curled his hands into fists. And Ian? To Ian it was the game his parents had begun for wealth and power that was sacrosanct. It required messages in the night and information exchanged. It required absolute secrecy.

Why had he held his hand and not killed her? Both of them had killed for far less reasons. The fact Ian deviated from this and allowed Margery, an outsider, to know anything, was odd. As was Ian's behaviour lately. He'd used to never to leave him behind—now he did it almost constantly.

There was the reason he kept bringing new men who needed to be trained. Ian had argued he only trusted Evrart with them, and Evrart had left it at that, but it was a poor excuse.

There were times when he wondered if Ian was good, and trying to be as his parents wanted, or truly evil and playing at kindness.

He would have sworn Ian had loved his wife and children, but he'd taken them away. Evrart had feared he had them killed, but then those rumours had begun that they'd run, and Ian searched for them.

Why rid himself of his family, only to search for them?

Then there were the rages...the slashing of cushions. The fact his brother Reynold had played against Ian and befriended the men who'd killed their second-eldest brother, Guy.

No one had mourned Guy's death—not even Ian's parents. But to befriend the men who killed him... To openly scheme with them against his own family...

The Warstones were usually more united than that.

Ian's mind seemed to be unravelling, but so was the Warstone loyalty and power.

Where did that leave him or Margery? He didn't know, and he didn't know why he thought of her name along with his. It wasn't as if—

'Never mind! Here's one!' she called out.

What had she found? Oh, yes, a ladder.

Never once in all his years had he a bit of fortune. Those brave enough spoke of their envy for his size, but he had to fight constant challenges, women eschewed him, and those men not brave enough to fight him disdained him. Ian, Lord of Warstone, used him as a prop. He was no more than a sword in a sheath.

Finding no opportunity to stride away from this woman and gain a reprieve was simply another in a line of grievances. Not because he wanted to be away from her, but because he *should*. There was more here than the risk of his family, there was more risk to hers the longer she stayed.

Striding over, he grabbed the ladder she was righting and secured it under some laden branches.

'Can you hold the basket, so I don't bruise the fruit?' she asked.

The trees were hardly tall. The fact this woman needed a ladder was testament to how tiny she was. Even so, the distance between the ground and the top of the tree wasn't significant enough to harm the fruit. He should argue these facts, since none of the other pickers were holding up baskets.

He picked up a basket.

She beamed at him, and he quickly looked up through the tree branches into the sky beyond. Trying to think of anything other than how her smile affected him, he felt the drop of fruit into the basket he held. Each one represented a personal chastisement.

One, two, three…

Last year, he'd chopped two fingers off one of Ian's hired mercenaries who had already lost one finger to frostbite. Ian had ordered the other two to be cut off because he had been a fool not to wear coverings.

Four, five six…

What would he lose when Ian discovered he stood under a tree like some fool? What finger? What limb? He never took risks. There were reasons he didn't—

'Do you think it's forbidden fruit?'

He shouldn't have looked, but he did. She'd asked a question and he was standing right next to her. So he did look, and was rewarded by the play of light through the curls haloing her head, the inquisitive expression in eyes framed by thick lashes, and her mouth pursed in amusement because he hadn't answered her.

'Do I what?' he asked.

Margery held a quince. 'They say that in the Garden of Eden a quince was the fruit from the Tree of Knowledge.'

He'd never thought about what the fruit was. Over the years he'd seen paintings and tapestries, but he'd never paid attention. Art didn't attack or swing a sword. Thread and paint wouldn't save his family or fulfil his debt and his duty to Lord Warstone.

She dropped the quince into the basket. It felt more substantial than the rest.

'I don't mind if it is,' she said. 'It's terribly tart raw,

but sweet and succulent when cooked. If I was a fruit that was forbidden, that's what I'd be.'

His view shifted, and it wasn't because he'd stopped looking at the tree and at her. He held the basket up for another of the fruits, but it felt almost as if he was the one on offer. As if he was holding himself up and doing a poor job of it.

His arms...*shook*.

It wasn't anything to do with the weight as she tossed more quince in, and everything to do with her words of 'forbidden', and 'fruit', and 'succulent' and 'sweet'. It was the fact she kept touching him and asking him questions that didn't have to do with killing and protecting and guarding and the loss of digits for a good man.

This woman was forbidden, and he wanted her.

If they were to talk of temptation whilst he held the basket, he wouldn't last for a day, a heartbeat, a held breath.

On a growl, he placed her basket on the ground, grabbed an empty one, and strode away.

If she wanted quince, he'd get her quince—and it wouldn't take him long because the damn trees weren't much taller than him.

'Good suggestion!' she said.

As if he'd made one...

Even her encouraging words were affecting him now—making him feel something that wasn't cold, desolate, alone. Something that wasn't what he had been since he left his childhood home.

He wondered how much farther he could be from her and protect her; how much further to not see her, hear her, and somehow not still feel her.

Chapter Nine

Margery carefully dropped another quince into the basket. She'd preferred it when Evrart had held up the basket, so she didn't darken the fruit. She attempted again to make conversation with him, but it seemed his unflappable patience had finally abandoned him.

All day she'd wondered why these trees were far from the fortress and not as cultivated as the other fruit trees, which had been pruned for ease of picking. Perhaps this orchard was older, but it was large, the sun shone bright, and the scent from the broken fruit beneath their feet was intoxicating.

But none of this fecund beauty was as vibrant as the warrior who thrashed and huffed, mumbled and growled, and acted completely differently from the man she'd become acquainted with these many days.

This warrior—this man—was magnificent. She watched the arc of his shoulder as he reached overhead and dropped another fruit, before stretching both arms in the air and pacing quickly away, only to roll his shoulders, bow his head and return to the basket. Actions, he repeated many times—until he looked towards her and caught her staring at him.

Then the look he wore tugged at her in a way she'd never felt. It was something dark, surprising—like catching Hades in the daylight…like being tempted by Hades in the daylight.

What was this? Any feelings towards him were dangerous at most, foolish at least. He'd said he must be loyal to Ian—Ian, whom she knew should have killed her.

Ian… When he returned, would he make her his mistress in truth? If not, then what? He wanted something from her, but even in all her experience with men she couldn't guess. He was so distant and cold.

There was nothing cold about Evrart, and the more time she spent in his company, the more she thought she could know his thoughts. Not by his words, but by his body.

He was striding towards her now, carrying his filled basket, and there was nothing icy about his movements. He was gruff and a little awkward, as if knowing she watched him.

This man didn't want to pick quince. In truth, she'd say he hated it from the way he bashed at the trees and snatched any and all of the fruit within his reach. He indicated he didn't want to be here, told her he'd rather train, and in truth trees made for feeble adversaries.

When she looked in his basket, it was clear the fruits had been poor sparring companions as well.

'Why did you pick these?' she said.

His brows drew in. 'They're quince.'

'They're not ripe yet; they're green.' She fumbled through the basket. 'These are yellow. Did you just randomly pick quince?'

'Two baskets. Two people. It was faster.'

She hadn't thought to offer him advice on only choosing the ripe fruit. He knew how to pick the ripe, didn't he?

'You've eaten them before?' When he shrugged, she added, 'And you can see my basket?'

He didn't bother to look. 'They're all the same—small round things.'

She wanted to dismiss this as manly disdain. He hadn't been happy picking quince, had wanted to train... But the two things didn't match. He wasn't acting as if it was beneath him, and over the past few days he hadn't complained when she'd wanted to see inside the cordwainers' building or the ale house. Nothing had been denied her. So his picking unripe fruit was something else.

Curious, she held up one and then another to his nose. 'Here—smell these.'

'They smell different.'

'But they look the same to you?' she said.

'They look almost the same,' he answered, but there was something in his eyes now. Watchfulness? Amusement?

'Let me try something else.'

She grabbed his hand and unfurled his thick callused fingers to place a ripe quince in one palm and an unripe one in the other.

'Can you feel one is softer than the other?'

Keeping his eyes on her, he rolled the fruit in his palms. His hands were the hands of a warrior—one who had wielded a sword every day since becoming a man. If the difference was between a new quince and a ripe one, he would probably be able to tell the difference, but given it was autumn, and these were ripe or almost ripe, it would be an impossible task beneath his thick fingers.

Still, he looked to her, and then to the fruit, which

were tiny in his large hands. One after the other he brushed his thumbs over the knobby fruit.

When she looked up, his expression of bemusement was gone, replaced by something more intense. Something she had a difficulty blinking away. Something she didn't want to ignore now his gaze was on her lips.

He swallowed hard. 'They are the same to me.'

'What do you mean the same?' she said, her voice a little breathy. 'This is green…this is yellow.'

'If you say so.' He raised his slumberous lids.

She shook her head. Half to break her gaze, half to break his. 'Evrart, stop. What colour is this?'

'You tell me it's yellow.'

Did the corner of his mouth curl? 'And this one?'

'You told me green.'

Was this about the quince or something else?

She lifted a curl of her hair. 'And this?'

His head tilted. 'Light…almost white.'

'My eyes?'

His gaze swept to hers and locked. Stayed. But his stare wasn't blank…it was searching, searching, searching—until she looked away.

Then he did something startling. He clasped her elbow very gently until she looked at him again.

'I can't see colours,' he said, his voice low, rumbling. 'Not like you can.'

'I don't understand…' He hadn't let go of her elbow, and the heat from his palm was rapidly radiating from that insignificant spot.

'I can tell these are different because they are shades of almost the same colour, but there is no yellow or red, like you see, nor green. My brothers teased me on it when I was a child.'

She'd never heard of such an ailment. 'Can't you see a healer?'

Again there was that light in his eyes, as if he was amused at her concern. 'No—and my soul isn't the devil's.'

She remembered how she'd thought he was like Hades in the orchard. 'I know that.'

'I'm not in Purgatory, nor one of God's chosen, either.'

His words were so earnest, she couldn't help but smile. 'I never would have suggested it.'

'Don't tell.'

His expression was troubled. Because he thought it a weakness, or an oddity? Had someone harmed him because of it or thought him cursed? She wanted to harm *them* if so.

'Why?' She shook her head. No, that wasn't what she wanted to know. She pinched her skirt and lifted it. 'What about this?'

'I can't tell the colours. I don't know what they are, so I can't explain what I see. I can smell or touch the difference, but I can't *see* the difference. Not the way my brothers told me or the way you showed me just now.'

'How did I show you?'

'With smell and with touch.'

'You knew what I was conveying when I asked what you were picking?'

He gave a curt nod.

'So why did you...?'

He glanced away, cleared his throat.

Nothing of his words gave away his thoughts, but his body did. It showed in the pained expression he wore. She'd thought she bothered him, but when she touched him...

Whatever it was she felt for him, he felt it too. He

was bothered *by* her. What would it feel like to be caressed, undressed, by someone who wanted her...someone she wanted?

That way lay death.

Ian was gone now, but he would return. Yet she was loath to end things between her and Evrart. He wanted to train, but in light of what he'd told her... Not to see colours... Not to know that the warm sun above them was yellow or that late frost looked white on cowslip... Except... Were colours only experienced by sight? Maybe—

Standing, she grabbed his hand. 'I know what to do.'

Margery was tugging his hand, but it was her joyous smile that Evrart followed. Grabbing the two baskets in one hand, and letting her clasp his other, he was led by the petite woman out of the secluded orchard. It wasn't appropriate, and it wasn't allowed. Even if they'd been married, it would have been an oddity on Warstone grounds, and still he allowed it.

Once they emerged from the trees, he had to let go. So he did. Never stopping in her hurried pace, she looked at his free hand, and then at him. He must have shown something, because her open, happy expression dimmed and a tenseness settled on her shoulders. When she began to look to the side and behind her, like someone who had been attacked in the past, he had a mad urge to grab her hand again.

They'd risked much already in doing what they had. To willingly hold her hand as they walked into the kitchens wasn't safe for them or his family. Still the impulse was there...

He didn't have impulses.

He did since he had known her.

Like now.

He watched her grab things and put them in an empty bucket. Every few steps or so she'd glance at him, then ask a kitchen servant for something else. When she'd got what she wanted, she ran past him.

'Hurry, hurry, hurry. Follow me.'

She was beyond his reach and sight as he swept his gaze around the kitchens and scowled. Too many people were interested in what Lord Warstone's mistress was doing…too interested in his presence beside her.

All these years, he'd kept to himself. It was better to protect Ian, but also himself. Now he almost didn't care to protect himself. Not if letting go of her hand meant she'd wear that wary expression again. And in that was probably his demise—for he knew, for reasons he didn't understand, that as long as she kept grabbing his hand and telling him to follow, he would.

It would all end soon enough. Any day now Ian would return and whatever this was would be gone.

'There you are!' she said when he opened Warstone's private door. 'I told you to hurry.'

'Margery, now wait—' The door closed behind him and the latch fell. It was audible, and he swore he felt it. It was significant. 'We can't have the door closed.'

'We'll open it again later.' She pulled him forward by the arm. 'Hurry, because it'll melt and you won't understand.'

He didn't understand now.

He'd been guarding her with the door open whilst he stood in the corridor. He shouldn't be in these rooms; the door shouldn't be closed. It shouldn't be possible that a woman who barely came up to his chest could drag him over to the bed where she now sat.

'I should get Jeanne.'

'Not Jeanne or anyone. This is for you.'

'What are we doing?' he said.

'You'll see!'

That wasn't good enough. 'I shouldn't be here.'

'You won't want anyone watching what I'm about to show you.' She patted the bed.

He looked down to the bed and back to her, swallowed hard. Which wasn't the only hard thing. His entire body was reacting to the way she looked at him.

'Margery...'

'I'm showing you what is in this bucket, and I can't do that unless you're right next to me. Come—your reluctance is taking longer than the trial.'

Her eyes were large and in earnest. He didn't know the colour of them, but they were compelling. So he sat on the edge of the bed, as she was, with the bucket between them.

She moved the bucket to her side. He eyed the empty space between them as if it was a field between enemies. She grabbed his hand and placed it between them, palm up.

'We'll start with blue first, because it's disappearing.' She stuck her hand into the bucket. 'Close your eyes.'

He was with her in Lord Warstone's chambers, with the door closed, and she wanted him to close his eyes.

Like butterfly's wings, she brushed her hand over his eyes. He closed them as her soft palm whispered over his face, but opened them when he sensed it was gone. Then she poked him. In the eye.

He grunted.

She laughed and winced. 'Sorry, but please keep your eyes closed.'

He would—because it was dangerous otherwise. Hand on the bed...eyes closed... He felt strangely vulnerable. He hadn't felt like this since...he'd *never* felt like this. She was looking at him, and he was allowing it. What did she see?

There was the brush of those soft fingers against his inner wrist, across his palm to the tip of his fingers. His entire body tightened, and he only just hid his shiver. He heard another dig into the bucket. It wasn't only his body that was tightening. It was his thoughts as something cold and wet was centred in his palm. His fingers flinched.

She laughed low and he wanted to toss the ice to the side. No, place it on her skin and—

'That's blue like I see it,' she said.

'What?'

'No, don't open your eyes.'

He closed them again. 'When you're told something is blue, this is what it looks like to me.'

'It's cold. I thought the sky was blue?'

'It is blue, but it's warm today because of the sun. But when the morning is cold, just think of that as blue.'

'What else is blue?' He opened his eyes again.

'Snow in the morning, or water.'

He looked at her, his gaze speculative. 'Ice is like water?'

She flashed a grin and snatched the ice. 'That was a terrible example.'

'No...'

She laughed again. 'Close your eyes. Now I'll show you yellow and red.'

He laid his hand on the quilt and felt her leave the bed and come back. But she didn't sit. Instead she stood, and he felt the weight of her skirts against his leg before she put something heavy in his hand.

Cursing, he jumped up, and dropped the hot metal.

'Sorry!' She grabbed his hand.

He stilled immediately when the cool air from her pursed lips brushed across his palm. Truly stilled. And he wasn't sure he could draw a breath when she did it again.

He swallowed hard. 'I believe you should have shown me blue *after* yellow and red.'

Letting go of his hand, she sat down hard. 'Will it blister?'

He opened and closed his stinging palm. 'No, it is merely...red.'

'Oh!' she said. 'That's terrible.'

'Pain is not red?' He couldn't help grinning.

'Actually, it is. Your palm that is...it's red. And... blood when spilled is red.'

He looked at his hand. 'Pain is red? Blood is red? The sun is red?'

'The sun is yellow.' She grabbed the tiny scrap of ice, placed it in his pained palm, and curled his fingers around it. 'This is a poor test. Your hand hurts, and blue is impossible to show you.'

Keeping his hand in hers, he sat on the bed, rummaged through the bucket and pulled out a weed. 'What's this?'

She snatched it from his hand. 'It's lavender. Dried. There's nothing fresh, but you can still smell it. In the spring we can go out and you can feel how soft it is and... But this is foolish.'

'What is it supposed to be?' he said.

She huffed. 'My eyes.'

He snatched the dried herb out of her hand and tossed it aside. 'That smell isn't your eyes.'

She blinked and looked away. 'Well, no...it's dried and doesn't have quite the scent. But the colour is.'

She wasn't understanding, and how could she? He

barely used words, let alone the right ones. 'Your eyes are *you*. Your softness, your scent. I can't see colours, but it doesn't mean I can't see you.'

Her gaze swung back to him. Her eyes were wide and searching. His instinct was to move away, to look elsewhere, but there was a delicate wonder there and he stayed still for it. For her.

'I want to give them to you,' she said.

Had anyone given him anything? His mother, certainly, and his sister had bundled some weeds with sticks when she'd been very young. For what purpose he didn't know, but she'd been three, and he'd taken them when she'd handed them to him. But other than family, no.

'Why? I have given you nothing.'

She looked down at her hands in her lap, and then up. 'I wouldn't say nothing. I have a whole bucket of quince I can't use.'

Chapter Ten

Evrart grinned. The kind of joyous happy smile that crinkled the corners of his eyes and creased his cheeks.

He was breathtaking.

On impulse, Margery laid her hand on his cheek to capture it.

He froze; she swallowed hard.

'How is your hand?' Not truly wanting to know about his hand, she didn't look away.

Not looking anywhere but at her, he opened his hand, wiped the pool of water there on the quilt. 'It is fine.'

The intensity of his eyes drew her in. What more would he allow? Keeping her touch light, she trailed her fingers along the angle of his jaw.

His lips parted as he took in a shaky breath. His skin was warm, alive…the feel of his beard was rough but the skin underneath soft, as was his startled expression.

'Is this acceptable?' she asked, further exploring the areas he'd allowed, behind his ear and along the shell of it.

'What?'

'My hand here?' She gently pinched his earlobe before going over his temple, then his brow.

He closed his eyes briefly as her palm skimmed to explore the other side. 'It's...different.'

It was as if his bones were mountains, his skin the earth. She wanted to explore him. 'How?' she asked.

'You touch me all the time. On my shoulder, on my arm, on my hand...' he said.

He held so still she wasn't certain that he breathed or that his heart beat.

She shifted closer.

His eyes widened. Was he alarmed?

She felt the fluttering of apprehension in herself, but also the wonder of this moment. All her life she'd kept her family close, but fled from others. From the tug and pull of them. Their demands and orders. She'd gone with Josse as willingly as she could under the circumstances, and with Roul reluctantly, but it hadn't been about her... it had been about them and their needs.

This man... She wanted him.

Reason told her she should keep boundaries as large as the fortress. That she should play the game of false smiles and false words and then hide. Not be alone with him...not want to kiss him. But hadn't she already realised he was different? That despite their differences in size and gender they shared similarities? They were alike because he needed to defend himself, too.

Keeping her eyes with his, she continued what she'd started, what she seemed unable to stop. He fascinated her... She moved down the thick cords of his neck and under the softest part, just under his chin. She darted forward to kiss it.

He started back.

Pulling away, she placed her hands in her lap. 'Sorry.'

'What are you doing, Margery?'

She shook her head and lied. 'I don't know.'

If his gazes were touches, they couldn't be more potent.

'No woman in many years has touched me.'

'Nor tried to blister your palm.'

His brow drew in. 'No, I mean…the women who've tried I could never trust,' he said.

What was he saying? That he'd had no women in… *years*?

'You are the most singular woman I know.'

She'd been imprisoned in a room, but over the last days had been allowed to wander, and had seen women here. 'I can't be so unusual.'

His lifted his hand, as if he meant to caress her in return, then lowered it. She eyed that hand, and his wary expression. She added what his body was telling her to his words…

'You're afraid of me.'

He huffed. 'Any man would be.'

'Because of Ian?'

'I haven't thought of Lord Warstone all day. I do not when I'm with you.' He looked away, as if he'd revealed too much.

She grabbed his hand, which was gripping the quilt. He looked at their joined hands as if they were something wondrous.

He was beautiful to her. Maybe he wasn't like Josse or Roul or even Ian. Still… 'Why no women?'

'This is what makes you singular.'

People avoided him. Did they purposely not talk to him either? 'Because I ask you questions?'

'Because I am not a man to others. I am Ian's guard— a Warstone acquisition. I am a way to get what they want. I learnt that early on.'

He talked as if it hadn't been early enough. Had they hurt him?

He released the quilt and rested his hand on hers. 'You never talk of my size.'

She didn't. 'Am I supposed to?'

He looked flummoxed at that.

'I don't believe I've ever mentioned someone's height before,' she said. 'You never mention mine.'

'I'm large.'

'Almost everyone is bigger than me,' she said. 'I like it that I can spot you easily.'

'Women talk of my size.'

'Well, of course they do,' she teased, but then she saw his expression… 'Are they scared of you?'

A quick nod.

What an odd concept. 'Not *all* of them can be scared of you.'

'There are women at the Warstone fortress,' he said. 'I have met them here, and at many other holdings as well. If it is not me…it is my relationship with Lord Warstone that precludes any of them getting close. And if I am with him elsewhere I am guarding him.'

Ian needed guarding…but she was still missing something. Evrart talked, but his body…his expression… He was still so reserved.

Carefully, she turned her hand in his, so their palms faced each other. Then, while she watched him, she curled and fanned her fingers around his.

He shivered.

'When I do this…do you not like it?'

'No.'

'No? You don't like it, or you do?' She trailed her fingers over his wrists.

His eyes lit up, but he kept silent.

'Other women must have tried?' she pressed.

The light in his eyes fell. 'It was wrong.'

Evrart was at the beck and call of one of the most powerful men in the country—it shouldn't matter if he was ugly or frightening. If she'd learnt anything under Roul's house it was that women wanted power. So it couldn't be that women didn't try.

'Wrong because you would not compromise Lord Warstone in your duty to guard him?' she said.

He gave a half-jerk of his head. 'That is the reason I gave.'

'But not the reason you felt?'

'It felt wrong.'

She pulled back her hand and laid it in her lap. He gazed at her hand as if he wondered why she'd moved it. Wasn't it obvious? He'd just told her he didn't like it.

'I'm sorry.' She looked around, pulled her entire body away from him. When had she become so coarse, so disrespectful? She knew what it was not to want touch... to simply endure it.

'What are you doing?' he asked.

'I know what it's like.' She waved her hand in front of her. 'And I want to say how sorry I am for—'

His brows drew in. 'I want to understand—especially since even I can tell something is changing the colour of your skin—but I don't.'

Would he make her say it? 'I am sorry for flinging myself at you. I know what it's like to hold still when all you want to do is run away or clobber someone on the head with your comb.'

'You believe I don't like your touch?'

'You just told me of those women touching you and it feeling wrong.'

He looked around the room once, then again before he shook his head and looked at her. 'It was wrong because of why they touched me. But you... You don't touch me for conquest or to boast. You don't say words to me that break me from my duty.'

Oh, how was it possible? But it was, and it was true. Evrart had been *used*. Used by Lord Warstone because of his size, and used by women who wanted to boast.

'If there is anyone to apologise it's me,' he said.

She thought back; he'd never once touched her. 'For what?'

'I hold still. And I do more than that when our height or proximity won't suffice.'

What was he telling her? 'You allow my touches?'

'I do. A shoulder, an arm… You hold my hand. A warrior doesn't allow his hands to be filled unless he wishes to die. If we found enemies and I could not get to my sword quick enough, you would die.'

'But I hold your hand all the time.' At his knowing look, she added, 'Because you allow it.'

The corner of his mouth curved, and his eyes softened.

In her head she had often compared him to a great oak, but that wasn't right. He was a flesh-and-blood man who could move. All those times she'd brushed her hands and fingers against him. Laid her head on his shoulder or bumped her hip into his side… He'd allowed it.

The odder part of it all was—now that she reflected on it—she'd realised just how much she did touch him.

'Are you thinking of how much you've touched me?' he said.

She put her hand to her mouth, utterly embarrassed. 'I'm horrified.'

'Horrified? It shocked me because you don't touch other men.'

'Of course I do. I'm Ian's mistress.'

He shook his head. 'You're not. He told me. But even

so, he touches you. You don't do it back. You clasp your hands in your lap and go still, like a deer who hears a branch crack.'

That was an apt description for exactly how she felt. How she'd always felt since Josse had first touched her. And Evrart had observed this.

Which didn't adequately explain why she touched him. At all. Was it familiarity? How much of her feelings had she revealed to this man?

'You're my guard. You're always around. You're just *there.*'

'You don't walk stiffly in front of me like you do with Ian. You walk by my side.'

How often did her shoulder brush his arm? Or her skirts get caught around his legs when she passed him in a doorway? On the narrow stairway, how often did he stop so she ran into his back?

Every day.

'You truly allow me to touch? You've been given me opportunities to touch? To test?'

'To know.'

'To know what? Whether it felt right?'

'To know whether you would. Because from the first moment you touched me it was right.'

Margery's insides flipped—and it wasn't because of embarrassment, but because of something lighter… happier. All this time Evrart had been purposely putting himself in places where she would touch him. For what purpose? That was a question that didn't need to be asked. She felt the pull of it now.

She wanted to.

In fact she felt this need to climb onto his lap and give him a thousand kisses all over.

'You've been…courting me,' she said.

He jerked. 'What?'

That wasn't right...there were better words than that. 'Trying to woo me?'

At his expression—half-desire, half-longing—she broke. This man had seduced her beyond all reasoning or comprehension.

'I believe you need to move towards me now,' she said.

He looked at the distance between them, straightened, and rubbed his palm down his thigh as if bracing himself to move. Something inside her recognised him. All her life she'd avoided people, tried to protect herself from them, from men. But with Evrart, she brushed against him.

Hopping over, she straddled his body and laid her hands on his shoulders. He froze, his mammoth hands hovering somewhere along her back, her hip.

He pulled back, his brows raised almost to his hairline.

He was startled—which was good, because she was startling herself. 'Is this acceptable?' she asked.

'*Yes.*'

Chapter Eleven

Nothing of this was true. It couldn't be. Not this room…
not this woman. Nor the facts of her kindness—no, more
than that…her caring. She cared for him.

At any time he could have told her he couldn't see
colours, like her, but saw her eyes were lit by something
he'd only seen from the stars at night. But he'd kept his
mouth closed, and everything else about him open to
her. To the light touches of her fingertips as she'd placed
objects in his palm. To the light way she breathed. To
the tiny gasps she'd made as she picked something up
and then the other little hitch as she'd placed them in
his palm.

In the silence of the room everything became about
her.

Everything was about her now.

She straddled his lap, her slight weight significant
against him. Her eyes were sparkling, with a light of
mischief in their depths that was darkening more the
longer she gazed at him. He saw the curve of her lips in
her delight that she surprised him.

And he *was* surprised.

'You're supposed to touch me now,' she said.

She shifted her hips, brushing against his breeches, brushing against him. Touch her? If he did... Caressed, kissed, suckled her small breasts, dug his fingers into the curves of her ample hips? Would he see if he was right that the span of his hand could wrap around the tiny waist?

She gave him a knowing look before dropping her eyes down between them. He hadn't even laid his hands on the small of her back. He hadn't even kissed her. And he couldn't be harder...couldn't want her more.

Pressing on his shoulders, she curled her weight against him. 'Oh!'

'Margery...' he growled.

'This will do.' She tilted her hips again.

His hands dropped to her waist. The warmth of her skin beneath the mountain of clothing undid him. Wrenching it up, he wanted it off, off, *off.*

'Wait!'

He stilled.

'I have to untie it here.'

'I want to rip it from you.'

She jerked. 'Oh, well...' Laughter. 'I want that, too.'

He meant it. Watching her fingers daintily tug this way and that, it felt as if she tugged at his own braies. He grabbed her hand, shoved it out of the way, fisted the silk and jerked it free. There was a slight ripping sound as her body flattened against him. Clenching the wrecked fabric, he pulled it over her head, tossed it away, and was left with a fine chemise and Margery, who was grinning at him.

'Better?' she quipped.

He couldn't answer. His mouth was dry, his chest constricted. His cock was flexing against her.

Her eyes widened and then her lids lowered. 'Oh, that is better...'

'Is it?'

He felt as if he'd soon tear off the rest of her clothing and devour her. Bury himself—his entire body—right underneath her skin and wallow in the very essence of her. Wrench her soul right out of her heart, hold on to it and defy the very heavens because it was his.

He felt *alive*.

His hands skated up the small of her back, feeling the slight furrows of her ribs, the hills of her spine, until he cupped her shoulders and pressed her undulations down harder on his body, feeling the spike of lust. Releasing her shoulders, he kneaded the small of her back, the roll of her hips.

She gave a low moan and lowered her head to his shoulder. 'Oh, I don't know why that feels so good... but don't stop.'

Spanning his fingers against the generous globes that had fascinated him since she arrived, he flexed her against him.

She shifted her head, breathed words and sounds into his neck. 'Yes, Evrart... Yes.'

He did it again and again. Her scent, her noises, were driving him mad and he buried his nose in her neck. She smelled of that flower he had been told was white. The one that grew in the chapel gardens and the kitchen gardens, like the rosemary from the shrubs that dried their clothes. Like *her*.

Did she taste as sweet?

He licked. She gasped. He licked again, from her collar to her ear. She giggled. He rubbed his face, kissed, nipped, licked, until she was laved by his kisses, his touch. Every sound, gasp, laugh and purr encouraged him.

And all the while the pressure of his hands never stopped. Palms spread over curves, thumbs forked into her hips as he moved them both. Until the hitches of her breath against his neck stopped and stuttered. Until he pulsed with the need to release, but just held back.

Until she said, 'Evrart... Evrart.'

Her fingers dug into his arm, her body shuddered and thrashed, and he slammed her down hard against him, feeling the fluttering heat of her core press against him. He raised his head to the ceiling and clenched his body, holding until her shivering stopped. On a low growl he ripped off her chemise, rolled her underneath him and latched his mouth on the plump rosebud nipples that had teased him since the day she'd slid into his life.

The more Evrart touched her, the more Margery's body starved for more. Something in her might have begun this, but everything between them was so much *more* because Evrart touched her and kissed her as if he hungered, too.

It was the feel of his hot hands rubbing her back. The piercing draw of his mouth as he encompassed her entire breast with his mouth and pulled until he had the very tip, which he lightly bit. He went to the other breast to do the same. Then back to the other. And when she expected a nip, he swirled his tongue.

She clutched his head, tugged his hair. She had released in pleasure from a man for the first time before he unleashed his mouth upon her breasts and now her body wept for more.

'What are you doing to me?' she asked.

'Tasting you...'

He ran his kisses up to her collarbone, down the valley between her breasts, squeezing her breasts together so he could lave them with his tongue.

She wanted to laugh...wanted to moan. It felt so good. She wanted to do the same to him as he descended to her navel. It was as if he was marking her, claiming her—and he was still fully dressed.

She plucked at his tunic. 'Please...'

He lifted his head, and a brown lock of hair fell across his shoulder and slid against her stomach. 'You want me to stop?'

'I want this off.'

He hesitated, his eyes on hers, as if determining something. She didn't know what words he wanted to hear, but she kept her eyes on him, letting everything she felt in this moment be seen.

Lowering his head, he began to explore again.

She pulled on his hair. 'Evrart,' she said. 'Please.'

He huffed and eased back. Her legs were stretched wide to accommodate his bulk, to make room for him. Something she hadn't even been aware of. Giving freely wasn't something she'd thought possible, but she did because of him. Her reluctant giant.

He reached behind him and she was temporarily mesmerised by the flex of the muscles in his arms, before he pulled the tunic up over his head and flung it towards her gown.

Then he held still, and she held still with him.

She'd seen men in her life...had touched two of them. Never utterly freely, but she had known the softness of Josse, a man twenty years her senior, and had hidden from Roul, with his whip-like body, as much as possible. But this man she chose over them—chose for herself.

Warm skin over tissue and strength. But a strength that didn't seem humanly possible. How often had she compared him to the fortress? The breadth was there, but the fortress was cold and he was heated. Alive.

Corded muscles crossed shoulders, the defined ridges of his stomach narrowing to his breeches, only to flare out for his thick legs. Down to what no amount of clothing could rein in. The fact he was a man who wanted a woman. Who wanted her very much.

With layers of clothing between them, he'd used his need and she had taken her pleasure. Yet now her core clenched with greed all over again.

Gathering her thoughts, she judged the width of his torso against hers, noted the difference in where her feet ended and how much farther his legs spanned beyond the bed they lay on. She splayed her hands against his arms, realising it would take four of her hands to wrap around one of his arms.

Feeling his gaze, she glanced up at his face. Amusement was there, as well as desire and heat.

'I'm comparing, aren't I? Like those other women.'

'So am I.'

He smiled, and her worries faded.

'I thought you were a warrior?' she said.

His lips twitched. 'Is there something about me that looks as if I'm not?'

She'd seen him in the lists. None of the men held back as they swung their swords. She'd seen men limping from the lists, holding an arm, a stomach. She'd seen the trickles of blood. But Evrart...

She grabbed his arm, felt his resistance before he lightened it for her. She stared at the expanse of his hips. Craned her neck to see more of his back.

His expression was changing from one of confusion to amusement and back again. 'What are you doing?' he said.

'You don't have any scars on you.' She lowered her arm and felt along his back with her fingertips. His heated skin was smooth and unhindered.

He looked down to her hand, which was clenched on the wrist of the arm that held his weight. She was trying to move it, and he wasn't helping her this time. So she tugged harder.

'Why are you smiling?' she said.

'You're flinging my arms about and touching me again.'

She wasn't flinging anything about. 'You were allowing it,' she huffed, and gave up.

'I was.' He swallowed. 'You're not afraid?'

'You're always asking that question.'

His eyes dimmed.

'Are you waiting for it to happen?' she asked.

His eyes told her the answer.

She was afraid—afraid that this connection would be just for now, just this one time. That beyond this she wouldn't see or feel him again.

She laid her hand on his stomach and the muscles rippled. 'My hands are cold?'

He pursed his lips. 'No. Never.'

She flattened her palms, revelling in the bumps against her palm, the light smattering of hair between her splayed fingers. She touched until she, too, wanted to taste.

Dragging herself up to his shoulders, she kissed the jut of his collarbone and across the mounds of his chest. She moved down the bed and against him to flat brown nipples, where she nipped as he had done to her. When he jerked, she laughed. When he growled and pushed himself up and away, she laughed some more.

And then all of him hovered, as he bracketed his arms

at her sides. She stopped her exploration to gaze at the length of them. She could see her feet, but not his.

Her fingers hooked in his breeches at his waist. 'These too.'

His breath heaved through him. 'Margery…'

It sounded like a warning. *This man…*

'You knew you couldn't see colours the way I do but you let me try to show you. Why?' She laid her hand against his mouth. She didn't need his words. She knew the answer. 'You wanted me to touch you…that's why. Now I want these off.'

'You're so small, and I'm…not.'

There should be something that frightened her now. Not because of him though—not because it was Evrart—but because he was a man. None of her experiences before had gone well. None.

'I'm not afraid, Evrart. You'll have to wait forever for me to be afraid, and even then I won't be.'

He clenched his eyes tight at those words, then breathed out slowly before piercing her with his gaze. 'We're going slow on this—you understand?'

Why was this only making her want more? Moments ago he'd fulfilled her more than any man before, but now…now she felt as if there'd been nothing at all. Nodding eagerly, she hooked her fingers into his breeches again.

'Put your hands above your head,' he said.

'What?'

'I need your hands above your head.'

Her entire body sank into the thick blankets and the mattress at his command. She hated being told what to do. But this…?

Awkwardly, unevenly, trying to get her arms to work properly, she arched her hands above her head. When his eyes watched hungrily, she linked a few of her fingers and was rewarded with a heavy-lidded, lust-darkened gaze as he swung his eyes back to her.

'Stay there.' He pushed himself off the bed.

She would if she was to be rewarded like this. With this man standing before her, his heated gaze never leaving her. Moving from her eyes to her hands, to the curve of her waist and down her legs. And all the while he undid the belt of his breeches, unwound the fine linen of his braies. Held it there.

It made her restless, eager.

'Still your legs,' he said.

She did, and she kept her knees together and off to one side, feeling vulnerable, feeling too much. Every order he made was unexpected.

'Why are you like this?' He looked down to the curl of her toes. 'Do you know how finely you're made? How utterly beautiful you are to me?'

She waited for the moment of disappointment. Other men had complimented her, other men had noted her beauty, but her happiness at being with this man did not dim. Because she knew he said it not because of her hair or her eyes. Evrart saw *her*.

'You shouldn't be anywhere near someone like me… someone who does the things I do. But there you went… touching me, talking to me. Offering me your food.'

She didn't want to hear those words. He was perfect. Didn't he realise she saw *him*, too?

'I thought I just bothered you.'

His brows drew in. 'You do. Constantly. Even late at night, when you're sleeping on the other side of my door.' He looked away and huffed. 'Especially then.'

He thought of her when they were apart. Yet he kept them separated now! 'Please, Evrart.'

He still held the braies to his waist, the excess linen fluttering to the ground. Under that frustrating fabric was a shaft that no amount of fabric could disguise. She wanted to feel him, to taste what his skin would be like.

'I don't want to hurt you,' he said.

There was the man she knew. The one whose hand she had clasped to gather quince. The hand that had twitched when she'd placed the shard of ice in it.

Here was a man who looked as if he was in pain. The flush around his neck, that pulse beating hard in the cords of his neck…

'You can't hurt me,' she said, and realised how true it was. No matter what he did, Evrart couldn't hurt her. Everything in him already balked at merely touching her. She was more concerned about that.

'I ache already,' she said.

His hand gripped hard around himself, as if stopping himself from spilling like that fabric. That wouldn't do. That was not what she wanted—what they both wanted.

Pushing up, she grabbed a corner of his braies.

'Margery…' he said.

'Evrart,' she said back.

She tugged a bit. He held, giving her a warning look, so she tugged harder and he released his hand, but kept it at his side as he rolled his shoulders.

She'd never seen him restless before. He was always aware of his body, so he probably knew those little movements would seem overt in someone like him. Was he nervous? She glanced at his face. His expression had turned resigned. No, this wasn't modesty. This was something altogether.

'Still waiting for me to run away?' she said.

'You should.'

He was simply…in proportion. That was all. He was

large, his bones thick. It was reasonable for any man like him—

There were no men like him.

She looked at his shaft, the veins thick, the head a rich plum colour. He didn't look as if he was in pain— he *was* in pain.

Lying down again, she raised her knees and parted her legs.

His eyes, which had darkened until there was no more blue, lowered to see what she freely offered. Her sex plump with need, wet with desire. That she needed him as much as he needed her.

Because that was what she saw when she gazed at him.

Need.

And if he was simply going to stand there...

Rising to her knees, she laid one hand along his hip-bone, thumbed the vulnerable soft skin there, where sunshine and men who fought in the lists never saw. Her other hand hovered just underneath him.

He looked anguished. 'We won't fit.'

They would. In the most blissful way they would fit. Didn't he know that they already did in all the ways that truly mattered? She had known him for so little time, but the time they'd had...it counted. In her heart, and in her soul, it counted. She wouldn't be here with him otherwise.

Grabbing his hand, she tugged and shuffled back on the bed. His eyes glanced from their joined hands to the hand still at his hip. It was urging him forward until he placed one knee on the bed, and then the other. She felt her heart soar.

'Lie back,' he said.

'Why?'

'I want to control this a little longer. And besides…' His eyes were knowing, and he bowed his head.

She liked it. His kisses and caresses were different this time…meaningful. Before he explored he seemed intent on torturing her, pleasuring her, and he did. Until her hands grappled against his back and her legs clung and slid along his sides. Until she reached up and kissed him as much as she could and he didn't tell her not to. Until he hovered above her again, his hair a tangled mess from her fingers, his lips swollen from her kisses.

Until she tilted her hips and arched towards him so he'd know her want.

And in this he did not hesitate, but took his hand and notched himself to her core, slid forward until he breached. Then he paused, and she wanted to clamour for him to continue.

How could she feel this way? Only anticipation… only need…

She clutched and tugged and writhed.

He pushed forward again and bowed his head.

She felt the hot exhalation of his breath against her chest, her belly. Felt the slight burn and stretch to her core. Felt the need for more.

'No more control,' she begged. 'No more holding back—please, Evrart.'

'It's too much,' he said.

It was…it was. Her body was throbbing at the intrusion and vibrating for more. His own massive body was flushed with colour, with a sheen of sweat as he fought for control. As if, he too, had been slammed with only instinct.

'No more gentle,' she said.

She dug her heels into his thighs and pounded them against him, but he didn't move. She wasn't a virgin; she knew the ways of men. The first time she had been taken hadn't been brutal or cruel. She'd had that moment for comparison all the time since then. But she didn't know this man, and it had never been like this.

He huffed out a laugh, part in humour part in anguish laced with surprise, and she saw some sort of spark to his eyes that felt like a revelation.

'Margery, are you touching me and pushing me around again?'

'I want you.'

'I can see that; I can feel that.'

His eyes shut, and a shiver rippled up his spine that she scrambled to follow with her hands.

'I can feel...*you*,' he said.

This man! Her core was clenching...everything in her was begging for faster, harder, *now*. This man! When he talked, when he said those words...

Laying a hand against his cheek, she kissed him softly, tenderly, letting him know that what he was saying, how he was being...she felt it too, not just in her body but in her soul.

In her heart.

Wrapping her arms and legs around him, clutching him as close as she could, she moaned when he lowered himself as he answered her request to give her everything.

He held still. Time stilled. And then that building restlessness, that need, consumed them both. There was more here than the joining of their bodies. There was something more that was tangible. Felt.

It was tearing her up inside and building anew. Ripping her at the seams. Her body shivered. There were small trembles in her hands and along her legs. He was undoing her.

'Evrart...?' His name was a question, a demand, a plea.

A muscle popped in his jaw as he jerked a nod in response. And then he moved. There was no hesitation, no control. Words were said like prayers of intent. He whispered in that low, gravelly tone she adored how sweet she was, while all she could repeat was how much she wanted, wanted, *wanted*. And his hands lifted her up as she pulled him down. And—

'Evrart, I'm going to—'

Her entire body sang her release and her joy. A hard thrust, then another, jolted her higher, until she felt his own heated pleasure, until it was only them somewhere else, not on this bed, not in this room, not subjects trapped by duties and locked doors.

It was only them.

Evrart collapsed at the side of the diminutive woman who had felled him, his body lax, his breath evening out.

His heart, however, trembled and shuddered. All the more when she turned towards him, her breasts pressed to his side, her leg sliding along his, one palm gliding across his damp stomach until she was curled against him.

He kissed her forehead, scenting once again that delicate white-petalled flower—the one he still couldn't recall the name of. All he knew was that if someone told him the true name it wouldn't matter. The scent was Margery's. The flower couldn't compare.

'Evrart...your legs,' she said.

Ah... He thought she'd noticed his scars before, had been gladdened when she didn't react. Although if she had noticed perhaps she would have seen him as she should have. As ugly on the inside as he was on the outside.

Her delicate hands traced along one long slash, then another. Cuts that were flat and thin. Made by many swords. His torso was unmarked, but his legs looked as if he'd slashed a year of months into them.

'Lord Warstone tells them to go for my legs.'

'Your legs? They'd have to…' Her eyes roamed around him to see that no sword had touched him elsewhere. They should never have touched him anywhere. His training and his sword reach should have precluded such weakness.

'Why didn't you move?' she asked.

He stayed silent. She was clever enough to come to the right answer. He never wanted to repeat it. The act of standing still to appease an irate lord was not an act easily given.

Her palm lay flat against a particularly bad one, her expression turning dark, threatening. He wanted to laugh, to squeeze her in gratefulness that she felt anger at Warstone and not pity towards him. He wanted to—

There—there was that sound.

'What is it?' she whispered.

Pushing himself up, he heard it again. Something that made ice fly through his veins. The sound that the gates made when they were being closed and the portcullis was being lowered. The sound made only after someone had entered the courtyard.

He shoved himself off the bed, grabbed his tunic. 'Get dressed.'

She sat up. 'What do you hear?'

'Ian's returned.'

Eyes wide with fear, she crawled to the end of the bed. There was another sound from inside the great hall. Already that close?

She pulled on her chemise as he tightened his braies and grabbed his breeches.

He looked around the room. 'There's no time.'

The mattress of wool was a lump, gone askew—something only his large body could have done with great force and movement. It would have to be shaken, the wool redistributed.

No time!

'Get under the covers. Pretend to be rising if you can't feign sleeping.'

He grabbed everything else and flew to his private door, held the latch, feeling a spike of fear up the back of his neck as he heard another sound. A door. Was someone coming in, or leaving?

No time for anything!

There would be guards outside Lord Warstone's door in the corridor even now.

He rushed into his room, his heart only slowing when he realised it was empty. Although... He looked more closely at his belongings. Nothing was disturbed, but that sound still clanged in his head, and he swore there was a scent in the room, as if someone had entered and left.

Quickly dressing in new clothes, he bound his hair and stormed out.

'Ah, there you are,' said Ian of Warstone.

Evrart froze. Ian was leaning against the opposite wall, directly between his rooms and Evrart's. As if he was...*waiting for him*. He kept his gaze away from Ian's door. Had Ian already opened that door and seen Margery in the bed he'd left her in?

'An odd time of day to be sleeping,' Lord Warstone said.

'Not sleeping.' Evrart shoved open his door so Ian could see his undisturbed bed. 'Changing clothes.'

'Ah…' Ian nodded slowly. 'You may need to pack some more. You're leaving.'

'Leaving? You have just returned. Where do we go?'

'*We* do not go anywhere. You do.'

Ian pulled a scroll out of his tunic and handed it over.

Evrart knew what the scroll was. A message to be sent via messenger. The messenger to meet another at a designated spot and if no one arrived within three days to travel to the next and the next. Five in total. If no one arrived after that, the messenger was to return to the fortress via a circuitous route.

He knew this because there were other men here whom Ian had ordered to do such things. Other men. Evrart had never been ordered to do it himself. He was here to protect Ian, to train new men.

'I'll inform the men of my departure and be gone on the morrow,' he said.

'Now,' Ian said succinctly. 'Go into your room and pack. You will do nothing else. Take the provisions I have returned with and leave immediately.'

His first instinct was to fight. Like this, he could kill Ian—but there was no certainty in what the rest of the guards would do, and there were too many between here and the outer gates to risk it.

Ian's grin slashed across his face. 'Do you think I'm displeased with you because you disobeyed my exacting orders to keep that woman in her room? Rest assured that I'm well aware this is your first offense against me.'

Evrart's body turned to ice. He'd risked his family and Margery. 'My lord?'

'Come my friend, I wanted you to have—' Ian's eyes grew distant before he blinked, and he returned his pale gaze to Evrart again. 'You're the only one to do this. If the…item is obtained the game will continue, if not, it will go on as I know it must. But there's matters afoot, and you will be gone.'

Ian wanted him gone. For what purpose, and to get what? He feared it was about the game and legends and the lost dagger. About families at war with countries. And he couldn't ask because he wasn't supposed to know anything of it.

He simply feared. But if Ian wanted his family dead, it would have been done.

What plans did Ian want to make that he couldn't be a part of? Because that must be what he was doing. Ian wanted him, his personal guard, gone from Warstone fortress... So he could harm Margery?

If Evrart brought Ian's attention to her and it wasn't his intention, it could be worse. He wanted to call out to Margery. To warn her. To hold her once more and kiss her sweetly on the lips because he feared it would be for the last time.

But whatever it would take, whatever Ian forced him to do, he'd come back to her.

Trapped, heart thundering, he risked another question. 'What is it you want me to do?'

'The same.' Smiling almost gently, Ian pushed off the wall and went to his chamber door. His hand on the latch, about to enter the room, he continued, 'Serve me as you always have done. As you just were.'

Chapter Twelve

Another day of pacing the length of Ian's rooms. Margery was half out of her mind with fear, with worry.

Ian's private chambers were a large enough space to house four families if they were back in her village. Each room was decorated differently for comfort, but if Ian was out, she took advantage of the chamber with the reading table and chests, because the different windows allowed her some access to outside. At least she could see the activity in the surrounding courtyard, and look beyond the wall to the village, the orchards, the far forest.

Despite her daily fear, she was uninterested in everything around her. Not even searching Ian's belongings again held any interest. And all because— No, she wouldn't think his name.

Ian had returned for over a fortnight now, but was little company during the day, despite the fact he stayed in the chambers almost as much as she.

But he got to leave the rooms whilst she was trapped.

There were guards outside Ian's chambers. They allowed her to go to the garderobe, but she didn't dare look outside through the archways or lean against the wall to see the chapel's garden.

Jeanne came every day, but when she greeted her or Ian she spoke with that same timidity she'd had when Margery first arrived. Her friend was afraid, and Margery wouldn't do anything to risk her life—not even give a smile or a greeting.

To make everything worse, the fare was different, which meant she didn't get her favourite foods. Did it also mean that Cook was better? There was no one to ask.

And Ian...

When he was there, she stayed in the other rooms. All the time aware he was there at this table with men coming and going. Always a threat. His quiet was disquieting.

Margery couldn't help it. She cried.

It was Ian's knowing gleam as he watched her—the fact he ignored her presence while mumbling to himself. The messages written at his table were more frequent, and he was hiding his activities less the longer he stayed. But when he left the room she had no access to what he'd done, for he cleared it thoroughly each day.

When she might be free, he wouldn't say. From the smirk on his face, it seemed he enjoyed it when she asked. He'd captured her because he had caught her spying on him delivering one of his messages. One paltry message. Now he'd allowed her to witness so many more. Every one of them felt like an accusation.

And all the while she worried about her family. She agonised over whether her message had ever made it to her sister, Biedeluue. She hoped it had. She hoped she stayed away.

What of Mabile and the baby? Their last message had told of how ill her other sister had been. Was she better or worse? And when were their taxes due? How were her family faring without the coin she used to send home when she'd lived with Josse, and with Roul, and hadn't sent since Ian had captured her?

And her brothers! She should never have sent the message telling them she was in danger. At the time, she'd wanted her family to know, perhaps to try to help her. She'd falsely believed Ian was like Roul and would have days of forgetting her or trips away when she wouldn't be watched. Thus they'd have an opportunity of helping her escape.

She needed to get out of here!

At least Ian wasn't in the room now and she could pace in peace.

Peace!

There was no peace for her. It had been weeks and she'd had no word, nor any sight of Evrart. She tried not to think of him and failed. In the days after he'd left, her body had still felt an ache in the places he'd touched, where they'd joined. There had been surprising bruises because he'd kissed and touched her so fiercely. Those pains had grounded her. He was gone, but they were proof he existed and would come back. Would somehow keep her safe.

But those early days were fading like the imprints of his fingertips at her hips.

Now she was left with only memories and dreams and thoughts of the sun's warmth in the quince orchard, of the way he'd closed his eyes as she had placed the ice in his hand. His weight and his kisses. Her boldness. The sheer wonder of wanting him. Of still wanting him, of knowing the joy in being held, being cared for.

Had he cared for her? He hadn't said so, but she swore she had felt it in his touch, in the way his eyes had darkened and softened when he'd looked at her, in the fierce way he'd clenched her skin and then tried to soothe it. He hadn't wanted to hurt her, and it was the pain of him that had made it all the more precious.

Despite her past—despite what she knew of men—she'd been different with him. Now that he was gone she feared she should have protected herself, but she hadn't. Not her heart, not her body.

He had to be different from the others.

He'd looked at her differently…he'd touched her as if he wanted to give, not take. But where was he?

She missed him.

All those moments shared had been ripped away by the cold terror of Ian's return.

Evrart had rushed out of the room whilst she had burrowed under the quilt, kept her back to the door, and willed her heart to stop pounding.

She'd heard men's voices in the corridor, but they'd been muffled, the door's latch had rattled as if to be opened, but then stilled. No one had burst through the door. No guard had come in to slice her throat or make threats.

Hours later and Jeanne had entered. Without looking at Margery, she'd stripped the bed and made it new. From Jeanne's averted gaze, Margery had been certain Ian had guessed what had occurred in his bed, but Ian hadn't entered the room until the next morning.

When he had, he'd acted as if nothing was amiss. As if he hadn't been gone for weeks…as if Evrart hadn't disappeared.

Evrart.

After what they'd shared, she hadn't dared ask Ian what had happened to her guard, and her fear hadn't been eased when Ian had announced she was to have a change of guard.

Her pacing sped up but she willed her feet to slow. If this was all the space she was to be left with, she needed to savour it. Make it last.

Was this her life now? All that it would be for years and decades? Would her family forget her or go to Josse? To Roul? Did Roul even live?

Oh, my... What if Mabile wrote another letter to Roul's home to tell her of her health and their mother's? Who would open it? And if he was alive, would Roul have it delivered here, or read it himself?

What if Biedeluue travelled to Roul's, only to discover she wasn't there? Why was she only thinking of this now? Biedeluue, who travelled for work, had often gone to Josse's, and once she had gone to Roul's. That hadn't gone well, but still it was a possibility...

At least her protective sister didn't know to look at the Warstone fortress. She wouldn't want her to come here, no matter what. And maybe there was time for her to escape before her family looked for her. Perhaps—

There was a stamping of feet outside, the slam of a door nearby. Servants cleaning? Or maybe a tryst in the corridor or the storage room?

But the next sound was closer. Much closer.

A click, and Margery gazed at Evrart's private door, which had swung open. Two steps backwards and she saw a figure standing in the doorway. Stunned, it took her moment to understand who it was.

'Evrart!' Margery stumbled closer.

She'd forgotten how large he was. Not only in stature, but in the way he filled her heart, her head. Her thoughts never strayed far from the moments they shared, his taciturn words and those he'd whispered with his body shuddering above hers. How was she to forget those tender moments?

But it seemed it had been easy for him to forget her.

Weeks with nary a sight of him. He hadn't even slipped Jeanne a piece of paper. Any message at all. With Ian in residence she hadn't expected them to have the freedom they'd enjoyed for the last weeks, but nothing…?

And now he stood here, staring at her as if he belonged. She'd have a few words to say about that.

Margery was here, right where Evrart had last seen her, held her. For weeks—night after day after night—Evart had kept seeing her everywhere. In the shadows of a tree ahead of him, at the end of long corridors, underneath him. He would have sworn he could still taste her and hear her cries as she came. The images of which he'd repeat in his mind until he'd practically mauled the bed he lay in. All beds, any beds. Because they hadn't been her.

Now she stood before him, serene. Gone was the abandon of their last time together. Every lace of her shiny light dress was tied, but there were echoes of those moments when he'd held her: in the unbound hair tumbling over her shoulders, the slight parting of her lips. They were there in the tightening of his own body as he tracked her appearance now and recounted her passion as he'd driven into her until he had come undone.

Like he was doing now.

Her eyes were wide, surprised. Was she pleased he was here? 'You look tired,' he said.

'I look…?' She trailed off.

'There are dark circles under your eyes.'

Her eyes narrowed. 'You look filthy.'

He hadn't changed from his travelling attire. His only thought since returning three hours ago to the Warstone Fortress had been getting to her. If he'd taken a bath, and that had been the moment when Ian left his private rooms, he'd never have forgiven himself. His torture had gone on for too long. He was a man obsessed.

Wishing to bathe, but not wanting to waste the time, he'd washed his hands and face in the courtyard when the stable boy had lifted the bucket of water for the horse, gone to his chambers, and waited. Listened until the heavy latch of the door had clanged shut. And then he'd burst through the private door that led into Ian's room.

If it had been Ian, he'd have the excuse of protecting him—but it wasn't. It was her, her, *her.*

'How long will he be gone?' he said, his words barely audible.

She shook her head. 'I don't know. He mentioned something about the watch guards and the porter.'

That meant Ian would be gone at least enough for him to…to what? He was barely controlling his baser instincts and he merely stood in the same room as her. She wasn't his. She belonged to the man he had vowed before his family and God to protect.

'What are you doing here?' she asked.

Where else would he be? Mere heartbeats after entering under the portcullis, he'd wanted to be here.

She, however, had her arms crossed and her foot looked ready to tap. Was she unhappy he was here? He had risked much getting here, taking paths he would most likely be caught on to cut away the hours, to return to her sooner.

And here she was…stunning, beautiful. Everything he wished for.

Perhaps he should have had a bath in the cold lake before standing like some beast before her. This had been a terrible plan. But he had left without telling her. Not one word exchanged between them. One moment he had been crushing her beneath him, the next he had been gone for weeks. He didn't even know if she wanted him still.

'Evrart, why aren't you saying anything?'

Her words were filled with umbrage, a little wariness. Was she cross with him or concerned? Neither was what she should be feeling. She had no idea of the primal maelstrom of need he fought against. His body was pumping blood through his veins, his heart was thundering. He needed to charge into battle with a war cry—not stand before a petite female with his muscles engaged to attack.

'I have a few words to say to you.' She frowned, placed her hands on her hips, then dropped them again. 'No, just one. Why? Why did you go? Why did you leave me?'

Why was too much. There was no *why* to his travelling during darkness, or freezing in the night because he couldn't light a fire. Constantly checking over his shoulder as he stood behind trees with his hood raised. No cloak could hide him if someone wanted him dead.

There was never anyone there—no messenger to pass the scroll to, no item to retrieve. They had all been killed or had never arrived. Or it had been a fool's errand to get him away from here.

There was no 'why' to anything the Warstone did. No reason Evrart cared about. There was only her.

Her lips parted, as if she too found breathing hard, and her eyes darkened as they moved from his to the tightness in his shoulders, then down to where he was trying to release his curled fingers. It was a tell-tale sign that he wanted to rip the gown off her.

'Do you know? Can you guess?' he said. Not telling her what she asked, but how he felt.

'Do I know what? What are you telling me?'

Margery took two steps towards him and his body reacted.

'This.'

Pinning her arms against her sides, he spun and pressed her up against the wall. She gasped, but didn't try to writhe out of his hardened grip. He almost wanted her to fight against him, so he could fight back. Release some of his strength elsewhere and not against her plump lips or between her narrow hips.

But her eyes darkened, her arms broke his hold and she buried her hands in his hair. He dropped his own hold, supported her weight with his knee thrust between her legs and his hand on her hips. His other hand trembled as it hovered around her wild tumbling tresses, where her hands cradled his face as if she wanted to make certain he wasn't going anywhere.

As if he could be anywhere else.

'Evrart...' she said, half in wonder, half in desire.

'Ian sent me on an errand. I had to go right then. I don't know why, and it's not safe to tell you where.' His breath bellowed through his lungs. 'Should I stop?'

Her brows rose; her lips parted. Her eyes were studying him as if she wanted an answer, as if she needed to ask a question.

'Margery, do you want me to stop?' It was all he had.

Her eyes lit, her breath brushed against his, and she whispered, 'You haven't started yet.'

Hands gripping her hips, he pressed his mouth to hers and he eased her lips open to sweep his tongue inside. To taste her once again was heady, intoxicating, and he wrapped his arms around her, arched her breasts against his chest, and exposed her neck to his feasting mouth.

'I missed you,' he said. 'I longed for you.'

Every word was punctuated by his lips, his teeth, the

suction of his mouth. She answered him in the dig of her fingers into his shoulders, the clasping of her legs around his hips. In the breathless whimpers escaping from her lips and moving across his cheeks as she peppered him with her own kisses.

'I wanted you every single night. Tell me it was the same for you. Tell me—'

He couldn't get enough. Tighter he squeezed her. He was starving to roll his hips against hers, to feel her forehead slam against his shoulder as she met his thrusts. They were nothing but panting breaths, ferocious need. He wanted their clothes off, all barriers gone. He wanted her to be his.

Not his.

On a low groan of pain, he released his strangling hold to rest his hands against her thighs, to pull his nipping teeth away from the succulent tender flesh of her neck.

Pinned against the wall and resting on his knee, she was weightless in his arms—but she felt like everything.

Slowly raising her head, pressing her hands against his shoulders to pull herself up, she eyed him. 'You stopped.'

He almost hadn't. When at any moment Ian or the extra guards at the door could have stormed in, he had been half a heartbeat from ripping away any restraint.

She laid her hand on his cheek, the concern and desire in her expression undoing him all over again. He was never like this. Always a brute of a man, he was a beast with her.

'Did I hurt you?' he asked.

She brushed her thumb across his cheek. 'Not enough.'

He tilted her head to the side and cursed as he eyed her neck.

'Can you see them?' she said.

Her eyes were wide, excited. His own must be horrified. 'You're marked. I've put you in danger.'

'Do it again,' she said. 'Then we'll argue on why you were gone and how you should have told me where.'

Slumberous large eyes, swollen lips... Too swollen. Had he hurt her there, too? He had just wanted... And she...she wasn't concerned at all. As if—

'Did I do this before?' he said.

Her hand fluttered to her neck. 'For days I covered them. He didn't see them. They were *good*. You don't understand... I know it doesn't make any sense or reason—and not to me either—but they reminded me of you. I liked it that you—'

'I can't do this. He's here.'

His blood was ice and fire. His body was forged steel; his thoughts were scrambling like tumbling dry leaves. He needed to step away completely, not to be in this room. But he couldn't stay away—couldn't release his fingers from the folds of her gown. He was physically incapable of it. Words. He needed to say them—to tell her what he should have before.

'There's more at risk. I have... I have a family,' he said.

She jerked in his arms. 'You *what*?'

He held her tightly, until he realised she truly was fighting him, and then he slid her down to the ground.

'You have a family?' she said.

Of course he had a family. Everyone had a—

What a fool. It had never dawned on him to form that sentence any differently because the thought of himself with a wife and children was so beyond his reach as to be not even a dream.

'No, not like that. My mother and sister are alive, and Ian knows where they are.'

'You're not making sense...'

He brushed a hand against her neck. 'You're bruised.'

She put her hand against his, held it to her, and he took some heart from that.

'What do your family have to do with Ian?'

'He was travelling through my village when he saw me. My brothers... It was just me, my sister and my mother that day. He offered coin. You were right—he did threaten them.'

'Are they well?' She gripped his hand.

'As long as I do what he wants.'

A look of disbelief raced over her expressive face, and she suddenly looked to the left. He took a few steps back.

'Where have you been?' she said. 'What did he make you do?'

Nothing of his past—all about his present. Not an odd question, but not the one he'd expected.

'I truly can't tell you. This is not something I can defend myself against.'

'You must. Or perhaps... Maybe...'

'What is it?'

She swallowed. 'Maybe what he's making you do is what he wants from me?'

Never. If Ian sent her on a task...if Ian had her play some part in his games...he'd find some way to escape with her—some means to get to his sister and mother in time or warn them of—

But wasn't that what Ian was doing simply by having her here? He was a fool!

'I don't know what he wants from me. Why am I here.' She opened her mouth, closed it. 'I tried to lie with him. In the beginning, when he took me from Roul. But he walked away.'

The thought of Ian combing his fingers through her

soft curls blinded him with rage, but he had to keep his temper. In Warstone games, those who kept their heads stayed alive.

'He calls you his mistress, but he's never taken one before. I think it's for appearances—for something that I don't know of yet. I know he's been sending correspondence to his parents.'

'That woman at Roul's…was she to deliver a message?'

She was part of it. Even though she'd only accidentally stumbled across Ian's game of legends and treasures. 'It's not safe for you to know this!' he said.

'You believe he would usually have killed me?'

He nodded.

'Something isn't right. Ian wants to dine in the Great Hall tonight and he has been acting…*gleefully*, for him. He's frightening. And now you're telling me you have a family you're trying to protect…' She waved at him. 'And you're acting…unhinged.'

He couldn't think! Some of it had to do with Ian, but mostly it was to do with her. To hold her, kiss her, lie with her had been everything. To give her up immediately afterwards…his body, his heart, had rebelled.

Torn in two—that was what he was. Torn between his duty to his mother and sister and the vows he'd made to Lord Warstone. Not that they were worth as much as other vows, but he intended to uphold them.

Compare that with Margery, who needed…wanted him. He'd made a vow to her as well. He'd make a vow of his very soul if he was allowed to have one anymore. If he had a soul, it was hers.

But then that vow went both ways, didn't it? If he was going to be good to her, in body and soul, he needed to say goodbye. To keep her safe, he couldn't have her.

'We can't do this,' he said.

'He doesn't want you to guard me?'

'No, I'll still guard him.' And her. He'd watch over her somehow.

'What will he have you do? Are you going away again?'

'I'll be here. I'm not one of Ian's typical guards or hired mercenaries. I'm paid far more than them. But I was…bought.'

'Bought?'

'I have told you I have a mother, a sister. I also have two brothers. My family are all large. My brothers are gone from home. Their size got them noticed, and they've made their own way. I was the last one living at home when Ian of Warstone noticed me, offered to train me and take me under his employ. I said no.'

'Because he's a Warstone?'

'Because I was helping my mother. Unlike my brothers, I never wanted to leave my childhood village. I liked it there, very much. The fields, the fact everyone knows who you are…'

'So he threatened your sister and mother.'

'He knows I don't want to be here. Coin alone wouldn't purchase me. He didn't threaten to harm them or ruin them.'

'He threatened to kill them?'

'At first I declined. I was all my mother had, and she needed me for farming. He offered coin…and then a threat. He took me because I had no choice. It was their lives or mine.'

He gave her time to understand, and when she nodded he thought she did. Her eyes were no longer warm, or concerned, they were…they were still *her*.

'You send your coin back to help them?'

'I do—but my life is not my own. Please believe me, if it was—'

She held up her hand. 'I believe you more than you can know.'

It was she who took steps away from him, holding her arms around her waist. And this time she shook her head as if the conversation she was having with herself was one she didn't want to hear.

'You kissed me,' she said.

'I've… I've never broken from him until you. You need to know what I've done. What needs to be done now—'

'And then you kissed me again. You burst into this chamber after not saying goodbye…for *this*?'

'I had to.'

'You *had* to? For your own selfish reasons, you are here now. You could have told me this before. You risked him seeing us like this, you kissed me so that I have to lie to the Warstone, risking my life to do so, to tell me that we…we can't be together?'

What could he say? Words that might make it sound less harsh…but she spoke the truth.

'Margery, please—'

'No. This was… You guarded me before, as well as any of these cold stone walls, but no more. I won't have it. It should be different now that we have shared…now that I have waited. I hoped we were different. I hoped *you* were different. I wouldn't have—' She pulled herself up. 'I would have protected myself from you. Get out. Go. You tell me there's no future? Then there's none.'

He took a step towards her, saw the shadows on her neck from a kiss that would permanently mark his heart. Keep her safe, when he had harmed her?

'Christ, I've hurt you.'

'Your kiss didn't hurt me—your words just now did.'

He had hurt her—he saw it, and there was no comfort for that pain. None whatsoever. He was a fool, and for once—for just this one time—he needed to do the right thing.

So he left.

Chapter Thirteen

'You look beautiful, my dear,' Ian said smoothly as he scratched a quill across the parchment on his desk. 'I do wish you'd tell me how you injured yourself.'

She waved her hands and fingers around her neck. 'I bruise so easily. If I stopped to remember how I got them, I wouldn't get anything done. I've even got one on my leg. I wonder if I bumped into something...'

He looked at her leg, but then bent his head and continued to scribble. Did he guess she had hit herself in different spots, to mask the bruises Evrart had put on her neck? She'd been able to think of no alternative. She didn't want any harm to come to him, though it didn't mean Ian wouldn't harm *her*.

Evrart had left the room, and she'd barely righted herself before Ian strode back. He'd taken no notice of her and, since she preferred this room to the others, she'd curled herself up on a bench to stare out of the window while Ian had gone about changing his clothes and sitting at his writing table.

How long had it been since Evrart had held her only to say goodbye? It had felt like forever in that kiss—as if he'd missed her and wanted her. As if she was worth the risk. Instead, he'd told her of his family and said they had no future.

She did understand—fully, completely—about protecting a family. She protected her own. She also understood about protecting herself. That she'd been doing all her life. Her decisions over Josse and Roul had put her soul at risk, but she had gone against her own self-preservation instincts for her family.

It seemed Evrart had done the same. He worked for Ian—a man he despised, who threatened him—and he didn't defend himself because he protected his family against the Warstone.

But she had gone further than Evrart. With Evrart, she hadn't defended or protected herself. She had pulled him towards her, held him. She had kissed him and hadn't hidden. She had been alone with him in this room and had felt no fear, only need and want. She had felt…love. She had thought Evrart felt the same.

A future with him would be difficult, given their loyalty to their families and the threats against them, but she had included him. Had thrown away her instinct to protect herself to be with him. Something she hadn't thought she was capable of except with her family.

She'd thought he saw her. Evrart couldn't see the colour of her eyes or her hair, like everyone else. What did he see, then, when he looked at her? Did it matter when she could feel the cavern of her own heart cracking wider?

He didn't want her—wasn't willing to risk being with her.

Right now, she was fiercely grateful for the prick of pain under her jawline—a reminder to her this man had held her fiercely. *Held her.* Maybe she could pretend a while longer that he meant to keep her.

'Your lip is swollen,' Ian said.

She jumped.

'Everything is well?' he asked.

Not with the lumps of fear rolling through her stomach, Evrart's crushing kiss… 'When I harmed my leg, my hand flew up and hit my face.'

'Clumsy.' Ian blew across the parchment and set it aside.

'I have always been clumsy.'

And even more so now, with these words. Who hit themselves in the face? Did he believe her? It was difficult to tell, since he wasn't raising his head. There wouldn't be a chance she'd believe it.

He looked busy with his task. 'Are you hungry?' Ian pulled another parchment in front of him.

She welcomed the change of subject. 'I am looking forward to dining in the hall.'

He raised a brow. 'You do not like living in my quarters?'

A mistake! 'Everyone would love to live in your quarters.'

What to say next? That she had overstayed her welcome? That she'd soon go mad if she looked at the same cracks in the stone? It was lavish confinement. If she complained, she had no doubt her comfort would be taken away.

As if Ian knew her thoughts, he smirked. 'You are clever. Too bad you weren't clever enough to avoid me in that corridor.'

'I avoided you when I ran the other way and hid in the kitchens…when I told no one. And I've told no one since.'

He tapped the quill and began to write again. 'Didn't you tell me you knew nothing to tell?'

What was wrong with her? She'd blame this on Evrart too. Her heart hurt! Her words were being skewed. It wouldn't matter if Evrart had put a stop to any life they might have with each other. Ian could end her life now.

'What happened to that woman in the corridor?' she asked.

'What woman?'

Why had she asked? If she said too much she'd reveal what she knew. 'The one you were with in the corridor when you spotted me.'

'Oh, she is dead.'

She was going to be sick! But why it surprised her she didn't know, since she'd already guessed.

'Once you had spotted her, I couldn't use her to deliver my message because she might have talked of you.'

He said everything so coldly. Easily. And he had killed that woman because *she* had gone down to the kitchens to eat. The thought...

She didn't want to think.

Had her brothers received her note saying that she was in danger? She hoped they hadn't. She now truly understood that they couldn't help her, but she consoled herself that at least they'd know where she was, that she was thinking of them...

'You're wondering when I'll let you go?' He blew on the new ink and then took both parchments to lock them inside the small chest on the table.

'I'm always wondering what you'll do to me.'

He stood, inspected his hands, and straightened his tunic. 'I know, with certainty, that you're not always thinking of me.'

She hoped he meant when she was sleeping. He couldn't mean when she was with Evrart. He couldn't know of that.

'What will you do with me?'

'You keep asking me that question. For now, I can let you know you're doing as I hoped.'

'Questioning you?'

He smiled. 'Are you getting comfortable with me that you should use such a tone? Interesting...'

What was happening to her? As a child, she had defended herself—as an adult she sought the protection of her family. Because she loved him, she'd included Evrart under that protection.

Now she wasn't even trying to protect herself. With her casual words, she had willingly handed Ian of Warstone the blade to slice her throat.

Bracing herself for a verbal or physical attack, she watched Ian stride towards her. But he held up his hand for her to rest her own upon. Like royalty. It was a farce!

'For now,' he said with utter calm, 'I am escorting you to dinner.'

She couldn't.

'Come, now. I have such few opportunities to do a kindness and not have any consequences. This is one of them.'

Ian eyed her hand and the arm he held out. She laid her hand on his arm, and he patted it as if he was some source of comfort, when he was the cause of pain.

'You're here because I want to see if I can't do some good for someone who has given me loyalty. I have to admit I thought you might be useful in other ways, but I'm running out of time and there's still so much to do. Most of it is ready...yes, most... But...'

Ian had to suspect something, but his step was steady, his hand still and his breath even. Margery was loath to accept his support, but she did. Out to the corridor and towards the stairs, down one after the other… All she needed to do was not trip and fall—

'You've gone quiet.'

Because she only had more questions, and she wasn't certain she wanted answers—not from a man who spoke in incomplete riddles. Because this man frightened her, and she couldn't get the hand on his arm to stop trembling.

She was all too certain now that he suspected Evrart, and yet…was he talking of Evrart and her? He had talked of her tone, but his voice…he almost seemed happy.

The hall was full, noisy…no more or less so than she'd seen over the years at different houses and on different occasions. She was a mistress, not a wife. She had been constantly subjected to sights not meant for any true maiden's eyes.

There were some men piled in the corner with a few women between them. Margery glanced at them once and then glanced away. She'd seen it all before and didn't need to see it again—didn't need to think about the fact she was, at this moment, exactly like them. She was mistress to a married man. The fact he hadn't actually lain with her was of no consequence. She had made her choice when she made the decision to leave with Josse of Tavel.

Another sweep with her eyes, and she found herself taken aback by the opulence of the Great Hall. It had been too long since she'd dined here. When she'd had her freedom with Evrart she had simply wanted to be outside, in the gardens and beyond that. She knew of Ian's wealth—the food and bedroom linens were testament to that—but the hall was overtly ostentatious. Kings should dine here—not small peasant villagers like herself. Still,

Ian sat her on the dais, which made her terrified. It wasn't her place—it wasn't.

It was, however, Lord Warstone's personal guard's position.

Evrart stood a few steps behind Ian's right shoulder. She couldn't see him, but she felt his presence there. Felt his gaze on her head, on every movement she made. She wasn't certain she could get food down though she was hungry.

'I have an amusing story to tell you, my lord,' Evrart said into the tense quiet.

Ian's brows rose. Margery's veins froze. She couldn't see Evrart and warn him he was making a mistake. Why would he want to talk?

Her heart hurt, and he wanted to tell an amusing story? Their time together meant something to her. Meant…

Ian whispered to another guard, who quickly strode towards the kitchens. 'Come, Evrart—entertain us.'

She could neither hear nor feel his heavy steps—not over the roaring in her ears and the thundering of her heart. She did, however, feel his gaze as he glanced at her, and then at Ian, and launched into the tale of the pigs escaping during training, which had Ian laughing.

Pained, Margery didn't dare look at Evrart. Instead, she watched as a beautiful man walked unevenly towards the dais. Ian waved Evrart to the side as the man came closer. When he glanced at her, Margery swore his eyes widened in a way that was startled…and troubled. Why would this handsome man need to be worried?

She glanced at Ian, who had a predatory shine in his eyes which was frightening and completely confusing, given the content of his introductions.

Apparently, this man was the usher, and he and Ian

talked of a new cook. As they bantered, the usher's frown deepened, and Ian leaned forward in his chair. Nothing of what they said was alarming, but when she glanced behind them towards the kitchens she understood.

Because walking up the middle aisle, between all the tables and the sitting mercenaries, strode her sister Biedeluue. Her sister, who must have received her message and come to her rescue. Not her brothers…not even a neighbour with a hammer. Her sister—who was now most certainly as trapped as herself.

'I don't remember seeing you before,' Ian said, easing back in his chair.

'Is there anything of the meal that has displeased my lord?' asked Biedeluue, but her eyes stayed on Margery.

Why wouldn't she look away? She needed to look away. Ian noticed everything!

Margery picked up her goblet and took a drink. It was ale, and somewhat bitter. She tasted it again, set it down, and looked to see if anyone was pouring wine.

'The food was adequate,' Ian said. 'In—'

'The drink, perhaps,' Bied interrupted.

What was she doing here? Her sister hated cooking, so why was she pretending to be a cook? She couldn't possibly think she could rescue her… There was nothing her elder sister could do.

Margery felt ill…sick. The repercussions of this were beyond anything she could imagine.

'The drink,' Ian pronounced slowly, carefully, 'was passable. Barely, and only because I allowed it.'

'Any improvements, my lord, for the ale?' Bied asked.

Why was Bied talking of ale? Margery felt Ian's displeasure roll over her like some evil portent. His eyes were narrowed, his hand twitching. Was he reaching for his dining knife? She needed to take his attention away from her sister! But how?

'You're new.' Ian leaned forward, his voice promising retribution. 'And you're asking many questions—which is something I do not, ever, tolerate. Who—?'

Margery grabbed his knife, pricked her finger, and cried out. All eyes went to her, and not to her sister. She felt pain in her finger, but relief in her heart, and was capable of taking her first true breath since Bied had entered the hall.

'A cut, my dear?' Ian asked.

His voice was all concern as he patted her hand, but his eyes... She knew those eyes well. Those were the pale eyes she had seen the day he had trapped her. This wasn't the man who up in his rooms had spoken of rewarding loyalties. Whatever he was about to do wouldn't be good, but as long as it was to her, and not to her sister, she'd take it.

Keeping her finger in her mouth and her eyes wide and innocent, she nodded.

'Here, let me help ease your mind of that.'

Ian grabbed the fallen knife, grasped her wrist, and before Margery could react, he sliced across her palm. The sting made her ignore her sister's outrage, but not Evrart's heavy footsteps—as if he had forgotten himself, forgotten he'd said goodbye.

'See? Now one cut is worse than the other. Isn't that better?' Ian carefully wrapped a linen around the hand he'd damaged.

She nodded, unable to take her eyes off this predator with pale eyes. This man who terrified her.

Out of the corner of her eye she saw the usher order Bied away and she was able to take another breath. All would be well—

Ian called to her sister, who turned.

'I expect to be fed better on the morrow,' Ian said.

Margery tried to take her hand back so she could leap to her sister's defence if needed, but Ian cradled it to his face. Outwardly, it looked as if he was soothing it, but she knew better. It was a warning he'd cut her again—or worse.

When he finally let go, she sat still, waiting for him to strike. Waiting through a conversation about food that wasn't about food. Some undercurrent seethed between all the parties that she couldn't comprehend. It wasn't only between Bied and Ian, but with the new usher, now at their side as keys were exchanged.

Then her sister's eyes went to hers again, and Margery's stomach plummeted. Her sister was up to something—but what? Schemes? Games? She looked worried.

All the while she was aware of Ian at her side, Evrart just behind him…

Him she felt most of all. She wanted to know if his stepping forward when her hand had been slashed meant anything.

But all she could do, when the meal was finally over, was avoid looking his way.

Chapter Fourteen

The morning's early mist settled heavily on Evrart and soaked through his tunic. It was a fitting discomfort for the relentless hell he was being forced into.

Seemingly, he was standing in the courtyard of the Warstone Fortress, conducting his duties in directing his guards and guarding Ian of Warstone, who stood to his left. In his thoughts and his heart, however, he was grabbing Margery, who was locked in the private chambers, and escaping.

What he wanted to do was grab Ian of Warstone's hand and slice across it with a dull knife, then take the other hand and slice it as well. And if he got that opportunity, he wasn't sure he'd stop there with his blade.

That bastard hadn't touched Margery in all the weeks he'd had her. Not once—not in any overt way, not in any way. Then last night he'd dined in the Great Hall instead of in his chambers, and he had walked beside her as if presenting her.

For what—or whom?

Evrart wished he could curse, could rail and roar. Instead, he shifted, and even that seemingly innocuous movement had caught Ian's attention, for he looked him over with one brow raised.

Damn. Lord Warstone had played a Warstone game last night, and it could have been for no one except for some new usher named Louve and a new cook named Biedeluue.

Two people hired by the steward after Evrart had left. Two people who had inexplicably held the interest of Ian.

No one who held his interest was safe.

Which meant they'd either crossed him in their duties as his servants, or they weren't his servants at all. They were something else. But who were they? And what game did they play?

He knew they were suspicious. He'd been in Ian of Warstone's employ long enough to know that things weren't always as they appeared. So he had watched, he had been careful, and he'd noticed that neither of them had retired to their rooms last night.

His need to protect Margery had forced him to extend his search beyond what was safe for him. After all, a search of the grounds would take him far away from protecting Ian of Warstone—a duty he hadn't failed in a decade.

But they hadn't been in the fortress, nor in the courtyard, which meant they must have been in one of the buildings surrounding them.

Now he heard a familiar herald which chilled his blood. The herald announced that Lord Warstone's unstable and scheming parents had arrived at Warstone Fortress for an unexpected visit.

He wanted to storm across the courtyard, to fight, to train. Not stand here for one more—

'You seem restless this morning,' Ian of Warstone said. 'Perhaps your personal guard has grown tired of guarding you, my son, and desires to finally be where he belongs. By *my* side,' Lady Warstone said, in that serene gentle voice.

Neither of them actually addressed him, and he knew better than to answer, despite the fact the Lady of Warstone stood in front of him, her hands clasped in front of her, was staring at him expectantly.

'If he wished to be part of your guard, he would have already made the request—or more expediently earned my displeasure to be set free,' Ian said.

If he'd earned Ian's displeasure, being reprimanded wouldn't have been a worry…losing a hand would have been more likely.

'I am surprised Balthus has not asked for him.'

Balthus was Ian's youngest brother, and had entered the gates with Ian's parents. It was odd because the brothers, raised as enemies since birth, rarely kept each other's company. And yet here they all were.

Another matter that made Evrart seethe for a way to free Margery.

'Balthus wouldn't dare ask for anything of mine,' Ian said.

Lady Warstone huffed. '*I* would. Simply standing there, all silent and menacing, he's magnificent… Think of what he'd be like at court. You don't take him often enough; those soft nobles would fall all over themselves if you used him as he was truly meant to be used.'

Ian shrugged. 'He's got brothers—find them.'

'They're too far away to be convenient.' She pouted.

Evrart was thrilled that Guiot and Yter had thwarted her schemes, but at the same time concerned to know that Lady Warstone not only knew of them, but had made enquiries. Which meant Lady Warstone or one of her mercenaries had visited his home.

'Now you've made him nervous!' Ian laughed. 'Don't concern yourself, my good warrior, your family is safe. My mother wouldn't be so short-sighted as to lose your good measure.'

His opinion of the Warstones had been low the moment he had known they existed and couldn't be any lower. He was already in hell.

His eyes searched the courtyard, looking for any overt manipulations as Ian and his mother slipped into conversation. He should listen, but couldn't keep his mind on them.

Near the gates, the elder Lord Warstone must be telling quite a story to Ian's guards and his own men. His gestures were large and the men were leaning forward, the younger ones with their mouths agape.

That, too, was most likely a tale he needed to hear. Information was essential for survival here. But he couldn't stay at present, and he'd already met the guards of both homes. In good time, he'd direct them again in their duties. For now, his thoughts were with Margery's precarious position.

In addition to the senior Warstones presence, there was already danger here. He needed to address the deeds of one suspicious usher, Louve, and a terrible cook named Biedeluue—because although he hadn't caught them in any act, he had, when the Warstone gates had opened for Ian's parents, seen them slink away from the ale house.

The ale house wasn't built for a tryst—not with its cobwebs and dank dirt. No, the only reason they would have been there was to converse, to spy...to poison the ale?

He needed to discover their intentions. Soon. But he couldn't while he stood dutifully by as Ian conversed with his mother, his father caused the guards to laugh, and Balthus was out of his sight.

None of these people were trustworthy. All of them were threats to Margery.

She'd hinted that she came from nothing, that before she'd met Ian, she hadn't lived in a home that was safe. She had told him she knew what danger was, but he hadn't listened. It didn't matter. Her home might have been terrible, but nothing was like Warstone Fortress.

Here, they smiled and clucked about 'convenience' whilst they played with people's lives. But at least Margery had him, and he meant to keep her safe.

Safe!

He needed to tell her to be careful, and never to go near Ian's parents. To run away if the new usher, Louve, or the cook, Biedeluue, approached her.

But he couldn't. Because he had a duty to stand quietly and look menacing. If he played his hand—if he hinted he was concerned about anyone other than Ian—Margery wouldn't be safe.

'No, no, I don't want to go inside yet.' Lady Warstone told Ian, gazing at her husband, who was still talking with the guards. 'Let's go to the garden, where we can sit privately. I have missed you much.'

'I thought you only missed Balthus,' Ian said.

'That is one matter we need to discuss…where is he?' she said.

'I don't know,' Ian muttered. 'The other…brother was last reported to be in France.'

'He's no longer your brother, but I do want to know where he is.' She glanced at Evrart, licked her lips before her eyes returned to her son. 'Do you have it?'

Ian paused so long, Evrart wondered if this was the time he needed to guard. If this was the end. Because the only way to defend one Warstone against another was with his life. He braced.

'No,' Ian said with finality. 'Nothing is here that you want. Nothing.'

'How…disappointing.' She waved her hand towards Evrart. 'You're dismissed.'

'Mother…' Ian warned.

'Oh, please,' she scoffed. 'What does it matter where he gets direction, as long as he follows it?'

Evrart stayed still. His life, his family, and now Margery depended on his obedience to Ian and Ian alone. Or at least the appearance of it.

Ian smiled. 'Very, very good, Evrart. Proving again why I rewarded you. You're free.'

Rewarded? He had received no reward. But he did know what he'd do with his freedom.

'Thank you, my lord.' He strode away before they could change their minds. He needed to get to Margery.

All was not well with Ian of Warstone, nor was it secure in the fortress. He knew Ian had as little trust of his parents as Evrart, and would never have normally dismissed him.

Evrart stormed across the courtyard.

And Margery… Margery!

He had not been able to see her last night. Had been barred from talking to her early this morning. How was her hand?

He swore his own hand pained him because he hadn't done anything in the Great Hall. He had ceased reasoning he couldn't have stopped it, that he couldn't have known. However, he'd spent years with Ian of Warstone, and he knew what that man was capable of. He noted Ian's hold on his knife changed, but had thought he'd throw it at that usher or the cook.

Ian had kept Margery a prisoner, but he'd never harmed her.

Were the usher and cook there to harm her?

He'd been gone for weeks, sent away by Ian, and he didn't know these two. By all reports it was the steward who had employed them. The steward had been with the family long before Evrart had been hired, and his obsequious behaviour grated so he avoided the man as much as possible. But the steward wouldn't have hired either of them without Ian's approval.

A fact he could have asked the steward. However, while he had been away the steward had been sent away too, on a personal task to collect goblets—which was ridiculous and beneath the steward in every way. Almost more so than Ian sending his personal guard as he would a messenger.

All these changes were alarming.

Ian didn't make changes because it wasn't safe to do so. Anyone new was observed by Lord Warstone himself, and then scrutinised by his personal guard for months after that.

Were these two the true reason Ian had sent him away? Were these two being hired by the steward the reason that weasel had been banished as well?

Evrart didn't know. He'd have to watch them—and not because he was guarding Ian. No, if these two were dangerous, it was his duty to protect Margery. As he should have done last night.

He'd felt that cut across his own palm! He'd barely held himself in check when it had occurred, and even less so when Ian had held her hand up to his cheek... like a lover who cared.

The sheer possessiveness he'd felt at that moment had unbalanced him. He'd wanted to roar, to lay waste to everything around her until she was in his arms again. And all the more because they had argued before she'd gone into that corridor with Ian, and she purposely avoided him. Why had he said such words to her about his mother and Peronelle when he'd had no time to tell her more?

She'd guessed he was here to protect his family, but from her reaction he hadn't explained enough. He should have told her he was here for her, too, to keep her safe. But then, what did he know about her being here?

Why hadn't he asked more questions of her? What had happened at Roul's to make Ian take her prisoner? Was she part of a scheme or completely at the whims of a madman? Why had they talked of colours he could never see and wanted to so badly because of her? He knew hardly anything of her—and she was everything to him.

Standing behind her and Ian, watching the Lord of Warstone dote on a woman whom he kissed, touched, laughed with, had been agony. Wretchedness. And it had released in him a possessive rage he could barely contain.

For now, he didn't have to. Ian was occupied, as were his parents. He didn't know where Balthus, Louve or that woman Biedeluue were, but he didn't care.

He wrestled with his unfamiliar emotions, knowing he needed to get them under control before he saw her, but he couldn't.

His instinct was to get to Margery and hope she could soothe the beast that he'd suddenly become.

Chapter Fifteen

'Are you going to stand in there and not come to see me?'

Margery didn't know what Evrart was doing, but she'd watched out of the window and seen him stride across the courtyard as if the Great Hall was on fire. When she had heard his heavy steps, and his door opening and closing, she'd waited.

After all, he knew she was in here—and why else would he have come to his rooms in the middle of the day if not to see her? Now, when he didn't open the connecting door, she'd had enough. He might not want anything to do with her, but there was so much to tell him. To warn him of!

He seemed…overwrought. His hands were clenching at his sides and his chest was heaving as if he'd run uphill. She didn't know what she'd expected to see when she released the latch, but Evrart just standing on the other side of the door wasn't it.

'Are you harmed?' There was no one behind him, and yet… 'Is there danger?'

He stormed over, grabbed the door and her elbow. When he began to push her back, she dug her heels in.

'What are you doing?' she said.

'You can't be in here.'

His voice was rough, low, and brooked no dispute.

'So we stand here, in between, then,' she said, her voice cracking. This was so hard! She should have protected herself better. Then she wouldn't feel this hurt. 'There's something I need to tell you. To ask of you.'

He released her. 'Your hand...'

'It's wrapped.' She raised it before them. It was only the shock of it that caused her to cry out.

'He cut you. Hurt. You.'

Evrart was always so controlled, so careful of his movements, of his words. She'd never seen this fierceness in him before, and the longer she stayed quiet, the more Evrart seemed as if he was to reach for his sword and storm the battlefield.

'I cut myself first, remember? People have cuts.' The cut she'd made to distract Ian's attention from Biedeluue had been deep, and still caused her pain. Ian's had been shallow. More like a scratch. 'They'll be healed soon enough.'

His nostrils flared. 'Why did you open the door?'

What had happened to him while he was away? What was happening to him now? His words were cutting, harsh, and clipped at the ends. She felt his emotions crashing against her. He was the one who had told her they couldn't be together. This anger had to be at something else.

'I saw you walking here...heard you open your door.'

'But I didn't open the connecting door. Did you not think, for one moment, that there may be a reason I didn't?' he said.

She hadn't. Because she had known he was there and, despite the fact he wanted no future with her, she needed to tell him of her sister, to ask him if he could help her. Since she was locked in here, she had no choice but to beg Evrart. And she needed to know if the new arrivals were friends or enemies. Nobody came to the fortress that she knew of, and now her sister had appeared last night, and new people had arrived in the early morning.

'You were there and I needed to talk to you,' she said, fully aware that she was repeating herself. But he looked so shocked, she wasn't certain he was understanding what she was saying.

'You didn't know if it was safe,' he said.

That hardly mattered. She'd been locked inside when she was used to independence. If she had access to the outside, she'd be there now. The fact she had access to different rooms was hardly any compensation, but while she did, and he was near, she'd always open the door.

'You have to stay safe!'

He grabbed her arms, held her still. His grip was almost gentle, almost fierce. The tension in his palms vibrated up her arms. Why was he so concerned? There was no future between them.

Right now, she just wanted her sister out of this fortress and to know why more people had arrived. So, though it hurt just looking at him, though she felt tears prick at her eyes and anger at his callousness stab at her heart, she needed to stand here and talk—for her family. Then, afterwards, when he'd left, when he'd either said he'd help or he wouldn't, she would curl herself up on the sill again.

'This isn't about me.' She raised her chin, pleased her voice didn't betray her. 'Who are those people? They entered early this morning. I saw you standing with them.'

He looked at her hands lying on his forearms, his brow raised, his eyes wide. She'd shocked him. But when he looked at her again she saw beneath the swirling brown and blue a banked heat.

He swallowed. 'Ian didn't say?'

'I didn't see him. He was in the other chamber and quickly left.'

It was how it had been since he'd returned. Some days he ignored her—other days he muttered of matters she wasn't certain she wanted to know about. Like brothers' betrayals and how proud he was of them. Like poison and fools. A smattering of words that made no sense and frightened her all the same.

Evrart pulled back slowly until their hands were released and air cooled her skin. 'They are his parents.'

She blinked, relieved. She couldn't imagine Ian having a family, but if they'd come then perhaps Ian's attention would be on them instead of her sister.

'That's good, then, isn't it?'

He looked aghast. 'Haven't you heard any rumours at *all*?'

She had. Roul had talked of Ian when he had arrived there, and she'd asked some of the servants, but nothing before that.

'They're dangerous. So is Ian. So was my life before.'

His hands were outstretched, as if to grab her again, but he pulled them back, looked at them as if he didn't know what they were doing.

'No, this is nothing like before. Ian's not well.'

'What does this have to do with his parents?'

'Everything to do with them since they're the cause of it.' Evrart shook his head. 'I've been with him for a long time. His reason is slipping. I don't know how much is truth from him. He's more dangerous than before.'

She hadn't known him before, but at night Ian tossed and turned in his sleep. He said words about his wife. He was distressed, and his cries made it seem possible that he cared for his wife. Then he'd wake again, and she'd know better than to let her guard down. It was like caring for a wild animal that at any moment could kill you.

'Do you trust me?' asked Evrart. 'I was gone for weeks. I left you here whilst Ian was in residence. I—'

He wanted trust from her battered heart? All her life she'd protected herself and defended her family. With Evrart she had been prepared to defend him, too— except he told her he didn't want her.

Yet, did her emotions have anything to do with trusting him? Because she still had them. Foolishly, probably, when they had no future. And yet...

'Were you recounting that story of the hogs to Ian to cheer me?' she asked.

'Did it?'

Her quiet warrior had embellished a humorous story. Had that been him asking for forgiveness? Did it matter when it came to her own feelings? 'I trust you, Evrart. I do.'

He exhaled roughly, adjusted his neck, but a look that was almost uncomfortable flitted across his eyes.

'Do you...not trust me?' she said.

His eyes locked with hers, but the man who rarely talked had returned.

She pointed behind her. 'We lay in that bed. Together.'

'And it was true.'

It had felt that way to her. Was he sincere?

'You told me we had no future.'

'We talked of my not seeing colours. We talked of quince and forbidden fruit. We talked of the chapel garden. But I have to know everything. To protect you if I must. To protect my family if not.'

He looked away then, as if he realised he'd said too much. He had. He didn't trust her. She'd lain with him. Given herself freely for the first time. And yet there was a belief inside him that thought she wasn't to be trusted.

'I know you were Roul's mistress,' he said.

He might as well have struck her. This was worse than being told they had no future. Now he was telling her she was unworthy of him. She just stood there, taking his words, unable to protect herself.

'And I know there was a man before who was a fool and lost you in a game,' he said.

She barely heard him through the roaring in her ears—but she didn't need to hear him because she was already backing away to close the door.

He reached out. 'No, don't. I'm saying everything poorly.'

'You are, but even if you decorate your words, your meaning is still clear.'

He looked down at the ground, before looking back at her. 'I don't want to talk of those men. I want to know of you.'

He didn't deserve to know.

His brows drew in. 'Let me ask, please. His parents are here, and I can't leave anything to chance. What does Ian want with you? Everything in me says that your reason for being here is Ian's alone, and yet he's not behaving with you as he should if you were innocent.'

She'd told him she trusted him. Now she felt like some sort of fool to have done so. She just wanted him gone. It hurt to look at him. He didn't deserve to know her past, but he wasn't leaving. Maybe when he knew some of it, he would.

'I had nothing to do with Ian before that one fateful

night,' she said. 'I chose Josse because of his age and his manners. Because he was wealthy enough to take care of my family and he did so. With Roul, I avoided him as much as he'd allow me. I ate by myself. That night I was starving. It was dark, and I walked to the kitchens where Ian held a dagger to a woman's throat. I ran, but he caught me. I didn't hear words exchanged, or if I did, I've forgotten them. He kept me, and I don't know why. He told me he killed her, but I'm still here,' she said.

He frowned. 'If you happened upon one of his games he should have killed you. It's another game of his. It's not you.'

Wasn't it? She had been the mistress of Josse and of Roul. If she hadn't put herself in that house she wouldn't have been in Ian's games. She felt Evrart's eyes search hers, felt as if her own were doing the same.

She found it odd, now she'd talked of Josse and Roul, that he talked of Ian and not the men she'd lain with. Twice now he had let that part of her past go. Maybe he didn't want to know of the men, or perhaps it didn't affect him as she thought. A part of her wanted to pursue it with him, to let him know how terrible a person she had been before Josse had ridden through town and she'd made the decision to remedy it all. But what would be the point?

She needed to get her sister free, and then she'd be gone. This man, for whom she had let all her defences down, was here for just this part of her life. He wanted no future with her. And yet she worried for him, because he was implying...

'When you left that day...that last day when you and I—'

'He was waiting for me outside this door,' he said. 'He knew I was in here. When he left, he said his time was to be interesting. I thought he meant his next journey, but now I wonder if it was…here.'

What would be interesting here? Nothing.

'Margery, we need to say so much more, but the timing… Ian's parents are here and that changes everything. Whatever rumours you've heard, that isn't the same as living with them. They are badgers with smiles on their faces.'

Ah. Back to the guests and her sister. 'I can hardly avoid them if Ian decides to—'

'He won't introduce you, but they will still know you're here.'

'Why wouldn't he introduce me?'

'He's never had a mistress before, and you aren't even his mistress. It would cause too many questions.'

'But there's all these people…and they're likely to be in this area of the castle because they're his family.'

'True, but…'

Evrart looked to the side before he looked at her again. She saw something in his eyes—something she wanted to know very badly. Something that had nothing to do with Ian and his parents.

'They have an odd way of pretending,' he continued, though his voice was a bit raspier than before. 'If nothing is said, and if it is of no import, then it's beneath them.'

She felt the heat in her cheeks. It was true. As a mistress without powerful connections, she was beneath Ian, and she knew in her heart she was beneath Evrart. Evrart—who kept looking at her as he'd devour her, or stuff her away in some burrow where no one could find her.

'You'll stay away from them,' Evrart said.

It sounded as if he cared…he looked as if he wanted her safe. And, as foolish as it might be, she wanted it to be true. Because, even if she was a fool to do so, a part of her trusted him, a part of her loved him. All of her worried for him.

'I'll stay safe as long as you will,' she said.

Evrart gaped at the woman who now stood in the doorway connecting his room to hers. She was right there. Fearless wide clear eyes, full lips, that defiant tilt to her head that made him want to bury his hands in her curls, tilt her chin up and kiss her.

'I'm always safe,' he answered.

'No, I don't believe you've been safe for a very long time. If I'm to stay safe, then you are, too.'

Had anybody ever said such words to him? Had he ever had such a reaction? He'd left Ian and his mother in the courtyard, strode as fast as he could to come here. But when he'd arrived it had been as if all the fear and rage over the last days had escalated inside him. He'd merely wanted a moment to gather himself. To not be a madman when he faced her.

And all she'd done was open the door...

A breath, some words, and reason had returned. But how could he hold on to it if she said such words as this to add to the words that said she cared for him?

Those words whipped heat around him. Her voice was telling him she wanted him safe, calling to him to take, to protect.

Possession. Protection. Those words had lashed at him since last night, when he hadn't been able to hold her, when he'd pressed his ear to the connecting door in case she came to harm.

Her hand was wrapped. Not a drop of blood had bled through. It had to have been a shallow cut, but he hated it. Hated their separation. So, though Ian had dismissed him, and he'd hurried to reach her, once he could, he'd tried to rein himself him.

He'd stood by the door just to breathe and settle his heart, and then she had pertly opened it and harangued him.

Ian's room was empty for now, and so was his. Margery was here. Another step and she'd be in his room, near his bed. All he had to do was shut the connecting door to Ian's chambers...

'Evrart, you're quiet again.' She shook her head, her curls brushing against her shoulders, releasing that fragrance he swore he'd scented in his bed last night. How she had plagued him even then!

No, there was danger. She couldn't be here.

The corner of her lip was healed, the bruises around her neck faded. He was glad. He was grateful. He wanted to mark her all over again. Simply the thought of Ian having access to her when he could not was driving him mad.

'You're here.'

She was here in front of him, and they had talked of what they needed to. Now he just *wanted*. But they had no time!

'And so are you,' she said. Simply. Easily. As if it didn't mean everything to him.

He'd gone a lifetime without her, then weeks more after he'd kissed her, held her. But these hours of being close to her without knowing her like that again were unbearable. He couldn't do it again. Not in this lifetime.

'I should have told you of my family and Ian's threats against them,' he said.

She tilted her head, her expression one of guilt, concern. 'Perhaps. And I should have told you of mine,' she said.

He didn't understand. 'Yours?'

She nodded. 'My family. Because one of them is here.'

He stepped away. Looked through Ian's rooms and then his own before he dared take another glance at the woman who unbalanced him.

'We should sit,' she said.

He'd thought her past held the danger. How much time had he already been here? How much time before Ian was to be here, or the rest of the household?

'Tell me,' he demanded.

'I sent a message, asking to be rescued.'

'What?'

'I learnt to read and write from Josse and I taught my siblings.'

'Margery...'

She closed eyes briefly. 'I sent a message to my sister, to make her keep away, and another to my brothers, asking for their help because I was in danger.'

Evrart cursed. Cursed again. 'The usher?'

'Biedeluue. She is my sister.'

'The cook—?'

There were voices outside.

Margery's eyes widened.

He held his finger to his mouth.

'You don't understand,' she whispered. 'She's here for me. I know there's no future between us, but I need you to—'

'Margery, there's no time.' He wanted that time!

'Can you...will you protect her?'

She didn't have to ask. 'I'll find some way. When Ian leaves again I'll create a distraction, if necessary.'

'His guards are here. There are more guards, too. There are too many.'

And all their swords would be pointed to her.

'There are only the ones at your door.'

'Then another will get to your family. You risk them if you do.'

How quickly she knew the risks! 'There's some distance between here and there. They have a chance if I can get to them. Your sister has none if we don't do something fast. Who's the usher?'

'I don't know. But I believe my sister knows him.'

He agreed. It had been the way the man stood, as if protecting Biedeluue—a fact that if he'd noticed, so had Lord Warstone. Something he needed to tell Margery.

'Ian knows she's your sister,' he said.

'He can't.

'Warstones always know—or they guess and all too often are right.'

'How would he guess?'

'You could have given him a clue.' He remembered. 'You cut yourself on that dagger purposely to get his attention away from her.'

'What have I done…?'

Nothing but be good, loyal and brave.

He took her bandaged hand. 'Don't do that again. Please, Margery, stay safe. Stay here until I come again. Can you do that?'

'My sister… I'm surprised she hasn't already come to these rooms.'

'Stay. Here. Even if she comes, stay here.' He looked to the window. 'I've got to go. I can't be caught here again.'

He stepped back, his eyes never leaving her.

Would this be it?

'I'll stay, Evrart,' she said. 'I'll stay if you answer this.'

He gave a curt nod.

'Why were you standing on the other side of the door?'

His dear sweet Margery. 'Don't you know? I was trying to keep you safe from me.'

Chapter Sixteen

Margery resumed her pacing and hated every step she took. She'd been at the whim of her family and her village until she'd made her own fateful decision to accept Josse. Since then she'd lived as much as she could by her own volition. She'd wanted to learn to read and write… to do sums and learn languages. She had demanded it.

Now to be confined, when she truly wanted to grab her sister and run to another country, and not to be able to…

What did Evrart mean by keeping her safe from him? She'd kept on thinking of his words and deeds all morning. Him not opening the door…him repeating the word 'safe'. She'd thought he meant safe from Ian, but then he'd said from *him*.

He said there was no future for them. She accepted that. Even if they got out of here alive, with her sister safe, his family safe, there was still the fact of her past. She'd chosen Josse—a difficult decision. But the reasons behind her choosing him hadn't just been about her poverty. They'd been about how hard it was for her family to care for her. She'd been a burden on them since her birth. She wasn't worthy of them.

And now Evrart said he wanted her safe from him. Was that why he'd pushed her aside? Not because of his family or because he had no space in his heart for her, but because he thought himself dangerous?

She loved him. She shouldn't. She should still protect herself. But there was so much about him—how could she not have let her defences down? All this time he had been worthy, not her.

Sitting down on the bench by the window, she still couldn't see Evrart or any of the new arrivals. The sounds in the castle were many, however.

At any moment she expected Ian to storm through. She expected her sister as well—but that was only because Biedeluue rushed ahead before she thought matters through. Or maybe she had come and was being delayed by the guards? Anything could happen to her! And who was the usher Louve? Why had Ian seemed so pleased with that conversation about food?

She didn't need to be safe from Evrart. She needed him. He was worried for her...for her hand. He was concerned over Ian and his madness. Was Ian slipping out of reason? What did that mean? He'd never harmed her before—hardly touched her. That slice on her palm had been almost as if he was proving a point—but what? Had he been showing off because of Bied? Impossible.

The ominous quiet weighed heavily. There was nothing to break the circle of her thoughts, and she was starving. Would Jeanne come and stay long enough for her to ask a few questions?

Standing again, she paced the entirety of the rooms which were open to her because Ian had made them so. One antechamber led to another, then another. All were furnished with chairs and tables and whatever a person in captivity might need. They were sumptuous, but by now she could count every floor stone.

Another turn about the room and she could hear the guards conversing outside the door. They never talked of anything worth hearing. It was as if they knew not to mention Ian, or the kitchens, or anything that would help her escape. Then there were other voices. A man's and…her sister's! Bied was on the other side!

Margery pressed her ear to the door. It was Bied! A click of the latch, and Margery scrambled back—to see the usual guards, and then the new usher!

'What are you—?'

Behind him came a familiar figure, ambling in sideways, as soon as the guards would let her. Her sister! The door slammed shut, but she didn't care, she was hugging and squeezing her with all her might.

'Biedeluue! How did you get here?' She pulled back, noticing the usher move swiftly to one of the windows to look down below.

'I have brought a tray of food,' Bied said. 'Jeanne's slicing vegetables in the kitchens today.'

She truly was pretending to be the cook, but… Margery glanced again at the man, who had moved to another one of the windows.

'Who is *he*?' Margery indicated with her chin.

'This is Louve,' she said. 'He's usher here.'

If he was usher, she truly was a mistress and Bied a cook.

Margery crossed her arms and tapped her fingers along her elbows. When Bied looked a bit sheepish, she arched her brows for good measure. Her sister would eventually tell the truth.

'He's here because…because…' Bied set down the tray she carried and seemed to gather her thoughts.

The sudden quiet was broken by Louve, who was rifling through the contents of a table where there were papers and a quill, opening up a large flat box and then another.

'Which one is his chest?' Louve said.

Ah. Ian's mysterious messages. Constantly he was at his writing table, and men would wait to be handed a sealed scroll. When Margery was especially bored she'd rifle through the desk, much as this usher now did.

He wasn't an usher. He carried himself like nobility, with an undercurrent of vanity. And wasn't his gait that bit more assured? She would have sworn in the hall he had limped. What was his relationship with her sister?

She looked at Bied, but she only gaped at the man, as if not expecting his question. Interesting...

Waving around the contents, Margery said, 'They're all his chests. Except for the two gowns, everything here is his.'

'Where does he keep his papers?' Louve said. 'Messages?'

Margery pointed. 'He writes everything there.'

Louve shook his head. 'When he receives messages, where do they go?'

Enough questions. Her sister now looked perturbed. Was it possible these two were working together? But this man was beautiful and her sister... Her sister did not trust men—any of them. Especially men who looked like him and held themselves like him.

'You're not an usher,' she said.

He slammed a lid closed. Opened another box. 'Tell me.'

This man might not have been truthful to her sister. Except her sister looked at Louve as if she did trust him.

When Bied nodded at Margery, she continued. 'The

messenger makes an odd knock on that door,' Margery said. 'A guard opens it. I have to turn my back and face that window until Ian tells me I can turn again.'

'Except you've watched,' he said.

Of course she had. He was holding her life to ransom. For no purpose. She had no coin to pay him, no connections for him to use. 'A bit…when I didn't turn fast enough. He doesn't like that.'

'Where else can I look for a piece of parchment about this size, with drawings? Something beautiful and colourful,' asked Louve.

Margery shook her head. 'There's nothing like that here. Trust me, I've searched. He doesn't leave the messages here, I don't know what he writes, and as for anything else I've upturned this place every day, looking for anything to get me out.'

'Does Lord Warstone talk in his sleep?'

All the time. Though he never slept with her, she could hear him talk of his wife, his children… The vulnerability in his voice was disconcerting when it came from the same man who had sliced against her palm with a knife and threatened her life every day.

'Not about papers,' she said carefully.

Louve's expression darkened. 'What, then? And be quick about it.'

'It's none of your concern.'

'Nothing about papers…nothing about gems?' Louve asked.

He hadn't answered any of *her* questions. Why should she be harangued like this? Her sister was watching both of them and staying silent, which wasn't like her at all. Had this man threatened her life to keep her silence?

'Nothing that should concern an usher, only a wife,' she said.

With one last measured gaze at Margery, Louve strode back to the window, peered one way and then the other, cursed, and then gave out a huff of amusement.

Margery kept her gaze on her sister. 'Why are you here?'

'Won't you ask him what he wants with those questions?' Bied said.

'I've been in this room for far too long and I am certain it's safer not to ask.'

'I brought her here—I'll keep you both safe,' Louve announced.

Margery doubted that. He was conceited... Arrogant. This Louve acted like every man she'd ever met, with the exception of Evrart. What was her sister doing with him?

Turning her back on Louve who was looking out of the window again, she whispered, 'Why are you in the fortress?'

'You sent me a message,' Bied said. 'You said you were in danger.'

It was just as she'd feared! 'That message was for our brothers—not for you.'

Bied swallowed. 'Who has always helped you in the past?'

Margery shook her head. She had written to her sister to keep her away. She'd even said how pleased she was to have captivated Ian's attention. All for nothing—because she was here. They weren't children anymore, and this wasn't just a few bruises from a game of throwing hammers!

'With my bumps and bruises,' she said. 'How can you be so reckless as to come here?'

The usher snorted behind them. Margery ignored it.

'Me reckless?' Bied said. 'I warned you of Lord Warstone. Nothing you said in your message eased any of my concerns. All you talked about was how handsome he was…how charming.'

Margery gasped. Bied had warned her? Had she replied to the message she'd sent? If she had, Roul might have it. She couldn't think of that. It didn't matter as long as Ian hadn't intercepted it.

'Is that why you're here? I only said all that for your sake.'

Bied looked aghast. 'What?'

How to talk about this when they'd never had a true conversation about the other men? About the fact she'd left their tiny village because she had known her sister protected her, because she hadn't wanted to be a burden?

That was her fault. But it was Louve's fault she couldn't truly talk now. She didn't dare have such a painful conversation in front of him. She'd have to tell only some of the truth.

'If I had told you I was involved with a man for the coin, for his connections—which all exist, mind you— would you have let me go?'

Eyes narrowing, Bied tilted her head. 'So…you're not broken-hearted?'

No, she was terrified. 'Absolutely not.'

'You put yourself in this danger for nothing?'

Margery glanced at Louve, who'd gone back to the first window to look out. She didn't want to talk of this now, but maybe now was all they had.

'*You* aren't nothing,' she said. 'Our family isn't nothing. You work and give coin to Mother and to the others. Yet you save nothing for yourself. And what Lord Warstone promised me…well…'

'You did this for me?'

She would do anything for her family including stretching the facts to protect them.

'I knew he was different from the others,' she said. 'I heard rumours he was dangerous, but his offer was enough to truly make a difference. Especially for Mabile, who wrote to me and—'

'Mabile!' Bied said. 'Why didn't anyone tell me?'

There. More facts, more stories. More matters to straighten and understand. But what had Bied been doing while she had been locked up in a fortress? They would need to talk soon.

However, telling her sister anything now, with Louve listening, didn't sit well. She didn't know him, and he wasn't Evrart. Maybe when it was finally safe, when they were far away from Ian, she'd let her sister know she didn't need her protection, that Ian was mad, and that she was sorry the family had had to sacrifice so much for her. That because of her birth her father had left, her mother had broken. All those words and more—but later. Not now. She didn't trust prying eyes or ears.

'I don't know why she told me instead of you, but in truth we never know where you go until you write to us. And I've been here for so long.' Margery eyed the door and sighed. It seemed forever since she'd received that letter from Mabile.

'What is happening to Mabile?' asked Bied.

With a glance to Louve, Margery said, 'She's pregnant again and she did so poorly before. She won't be able—'

'You have only moments,' Louve interrupted.

Louve might look as if he was occupied by events outside, but she knew he listened. She was wise not to trust him—wise not to tell everything. Just enough to shield her sister. To get her out of this room and back to safety. Away from Ian.

Away from Louve.

Except he not only looked out of the windows, he also

looked back at her sister. He looked angry, determined, but also concerned. She was right not to trust him, but it was clear her sister did.

'Louve truly is protecting us,' she whispered. 'I'm curious now—who is he?'

'I don't know,' Bied said. 'He's lying.'

Louve cleared his throat, and this time Margery gave him her full attention. Though he might not deserve it. Bied had said Louve was lying, but her words had held no bite. If she had to guess at their relationship, she'd say they were close. She prayed he was good to Bied.

'Are you poisoning the ale?' he said.

Not what she'd expected. 'What?'

'She wouldn't do that.'

Bied immediately stood in front of her, her hands on her hips. Margery could hardly see the man trying to stare her down.

'There are casks that are poisoned. Are you,' Louve asked, 'or is someone you know, putting poison in the ale?'

Margery placed her hand on her sister's arm. Bied lowered her hands and stepped to the side. She truly adored her sister, but right now this was her battle. Although it was one she didn't understand. What ale had she had lately...? Oh, the ale last night had tasted off.

'Is that what's wrong with it?'

Bied turned to her. 'You didn't drink any of it, did you?'

Margery shook her head. 'It was vile. I've been drinking wine ever since.'

'And how is your hand?' Bied asked.

How many of her cuts and bruises had her sister repaired? Many.

Smiling, Margery raised it. 'Wrapped. It was only a shallow cut.'

Bied gave her a quick hug...which hurt. Margery flinched.

Bied flung herself away. 'You are hurt! Let's get you out of here. You need to rest, to heal.'

No, there was no fixing this—and Margery was all too aware that Louve kept on watching them. This wasn't a conversation she wanted to have in front of him, because she knew why she hurt.

'It's not what you think,' she said.

'You wrote that letter,' Bied said. 'You have a swollen lip, and goodness knows what else, and you tell me it's not what I think?'

It was from being held by Evrart. Did he care for her? Love her? Was he truly keeping them apart because he wanted her safe? Foolish man! They, too, needed to talk.

'It is just that.'

Bied tapped her foot. 'I came here to rescue you.'

'I can see that,' she said. 'Though you were supposed to send someone else.'

'When it comes to the family, I've always come to your aid.'

Now they were back to this—but better to discuss her sister's overprotection and not Evrart and the fierce way he held her.

'Except this time I need someone who can use a weapon against trained men. You can't fight any of these warriors.'

'If you needed a sword, you should have said,' Bied said. 'I would have found one—or some weapon. Or...'

How long would this man Louve tolerate a conversation between two stubborn sisters?

'I thought that the words "truly dangerous" would

be enough. I found that tiny scrap of paper and I had to take the chance. Ian's wealthy, but he doesn't leave blank parchment around.'

'I can see them in the woods,' Louve announced. 'The party could be on a chase, or on its way back.'

This was dangerous. Louve was no usher, and her sister no cook. She was no mistress. And the man who could kill them all was returning.

'He's no usher,' Margery said, eyeing Louve.

'He can organise a household,' Bied replied.

Again there was no bite to her sister's voice. This man wasn't what he appeared, but he meant something to her sister. Over her sister's shoulder she caught Louve's look before he turned away. Ah. There was concern, but something more… Respect. Want. This man desired her sister. Did her sister want him?

'That's good for you, then, since you're so terrible.' Margery winked.

Her sister huffed, and Margery couldn't help but laugh.

'You need to pack,' Louve said.

What? She looked to Bied, then to Louve. Then to the door, where it was suspiciously quiet. Had the guards disappeared? Why would she need to pack?

'I'm not going anywhere.'

Louve tore his eyes away from the window to look at her. 'Say that again.'

'I'm not going anywhere without Evrart.' Or at least not without truly talking to him first.

'Evrart!' Bied exclaimed. 'Lord Warstone is the one who has kept you trapped.'

'He had—he is!' Margery said, hating that she must say what needed to be said. Her sister deserved more than lies! 'He was terribly charming at first, but in the time we've been here he's become distracted. And he's never asked me... Which I'm grateful for. But it has all been very frightening. I had to send that note.'

'They are returning,' Louve said. 'Balthus is alive.'

Balthus...wasn't he Ian's youngest brother? Evrart hadn't mentioned he arrived along with his parents this morning, and why would Louve sound relieved?

'Alive?' Bied was concentrating completely on the usher, who looked suddenly irritated.

'I meant Balthus is riding with them,' Louve said, striding to the door. 'The first of the guards have cleared the woods and there's someone travelling with them I don't recognise. Lord Warstone can't be far behind now. We have to go. There's no time to pack.'

Ah. Balthus rode with Ian. Did it matter? No. What mattered was that her sister and this man needed to leave this room.

'I'm not leaving.'

Bied looked to Louve. 'Help me.'

Margery wanted to say the same. She knew her sister didn't understand, but there was no time to explain.

Louve looked to her. 'I don't think your sister is understanding.'

'And you are?' Bied said. 'What is this?'

'Your sister wants to be away from Ian, but not from this man...' Louve said.

'Evrart,' Margery supplied.

Had Louve guessed what Evrart meant to her? His lashes half hid a gleam that made her want to look away. Had he guessed why she had bruises?

'Where's Evrart now?' Bied asked.

'With Ian,' Margery said.

'Why does he matter?' Bied said.

'He doesn't,' said Louve. 'We've got to go.'

'No!' Bied said. 'None of this makes sense.'

Margery stepped back. No, Louve couldn't know what Evrart meant—which was a relief, because that meant there was a chance that Ian also didn't know. But he had guessed, and quite accurately, that there was a relationship between them.

He had also searched Ian's chests and befriended her sister, who had reported Louve was lying. If Margery had been brought here because of Ian and his games, it was entirely possible Louve was here for the same reason. She didn't know how that tied in with her sister, who wanted to rescue her. But she wouldn't know unless she asked.

'What deal did Ian make with you, usher? He negotiates like the devil.'

Louve grinned, but it didn't reach his eyes. 'He said I could have you if you left the rooms. Since I had Bied, since she'd had that message from you, and since I knew you loved your sister, it seemed as though I couldn't lose.'

Margery hugged her arms around herself and looked to the ground. Nothing was truly clear, but she could make some guesses of her own. Louve and Ian liked to play games, and she and her sister were here because of them.

'Who is Evrart?' Bied said.

'He's Ian's personal guard,' Louve announced.

'That brute?' Bied gasped.

'Don't!' Margery lashed out with her arm, but quickly pulled it back. She hated it that Evrart was being talked of this way, but it wasn't her sister's fault. 'Don't say anything bad about him. He's a good man and he has had a trying time with his appearance.'

Louve went back to the window. 'They're coming through the gates now, but it looks as though they want to attend to their horses. Odd…but we'll take it. Explain, Margery—and fast. Your sister won't leave this room otherwise.'

'I beg to differ!' Bied said. 'I'll leave within half a heartbeat if she explains herself!'

Margery kept her eyes on Louve. He cared. He cared for her sister, who obviously didn't hate him. Margery hoped he cared enough to keep her safe from Ian. Like… like Evrart wanted to do with her.

Evrart. She missed that man, and though she didn't know his feelings, she was certain of hers.

'I'm in love.'

Bied opened her mouth to speak. Closed it. Tried again. 'Are you jesting?'

Foolish choice of words. In the past, to make her choices more palatable for Bied, Margery had written and told her that she was with Josse and then Roul because of love. Now…now she had to tell the truth.

So little time!

'Truly, this time,' Margery said. 'We tried to fight it. Ian wouldn't approve, and there is danger to us both! Then it seemed Ian turned a blind eye and it…happened.'

'Ian didn't turn a blind eye,' Louve said.

Ice slid down Margery's spine. 'What do you mean?'

Louve glanced to Bied, shook his head once. When he looked back at her, she saw his expression… Gone was the arrogance and self-assurance. Instead he looked as if he was about to tell her the worst of news.

'He likes to watch.'

Margery shivered. He couldn't mean what she thought… 'You don't mean that.'

With a look of apology, Louve dipped his chin and looked away.

She would be sick—or worse. They'd only been together once, in the bedroom. But Ian had been there? Evrart had voiced his concern because the man had returned early, but Margery had thought it too far-fetched that he would have caught them and not said something.

And Evrart. That proud, gentle giant. That moment they'd shared had been special. Now it was tainted. Regardless of whether he wanted her again, the fact they had been watched when her mercenary was at his most vulnerable...

'Oh, Evrart can't ever know... I think I'm going to be sick.'

'Your sister said that to me once.' Louve glanced to Bied.

'This is not the time for jests,' Bied uttered. 'Where are you getting this humour—and would you please choose a disposition?' Bied pulled Margery's hand into hers. 'Margery, we have to go. Your lip is cut and you flinched at dinner. Lord Warstone is hurting you.'

She wanted to ask questions of Bied, but she recognised her sister's expression. She wouldn't leave unless she understood. 'It's not Lord Warstone. Evrart...his personal guard...he's big...and I don't exactly... Do I have to explain this in front of him?'

'No, you don't,' Louve said. 'I understand.'

'Yes, she does,' Bied said. 'Because I see her with a swollen lip. I see that my youngest sister has been hurt by some guard of Lord Warstone!'

Too many emotions clogged her throat. Too much worry. But she had to make her sister understand. Ian could be here at any moment.

'Bied, it's not what you're thinking. He's large. I jumped and we crashed. Please know that Evrart feels all the worst for it, but I... I don't. You saw him act like an idiot, trying to cheer me...'

Bied flushed. 'No more.'

'It seems your sister *likes* more,' Louve quipped.

At the sight of Bied taking umbrage against the man Margery giggled, then slapped a hand on her mouth. It made her lip sting, which was good. This wasn't funny. Not at all. She was slowly unravelling from all the half-truths!

Bied took in a large breath and pointed at Margery's hand. 'Lord Warstone cut you in front of everyone. If you stay, how can you guarantee he won't do it again?'

'She can't. That's the Warstone way. Has it happened often?' Louve asked.

How much to tell? Ian was a madman, threatening her life. He also mumbled late at night of his love for a wife long gone.

'I don't know him well enough, but Evrart says he's been slipping.'

Bied gasped. 'You surely can't feel for him?'

'If you heard Lord Warstone when he's sleeping—' Margery stopped. She would be as mad as him if she divulged so much.

Louve darted towards Bied and looked out through a different window. 'They've left the stables. It's time. I can't guarantee what will happen if Ian sees us here. If we get trapped on that stairway, we'll have trouble.'

'What do we do?' Bied said.

'We leave her.' Louve's voice was absolutely full of certainty.

Bied shook her head. 'We'll all go. This... Evrart will follow.'

'He can't.'

Margery eyed Louve, who had repeated the same words. Someday she'd know the history of him...

Bied pointed at Louve. 'What are you not telling me?'

'He owes Lord Warstone a debt.' Margery prayed her sister would understand. 'Ian knows where Evrart's family is.'

Bied took a step towards the door and shook her head once, then twice. 'I didn't come here for nothing.'

'You have no weaponry...no training.' Margery felt terrible at every flinch Bied gave. It was all the truth, and she needed to be brutal. 'I wanted you to bring our brothers, who at least can fight. How are you supposed to get us past the guards? I'd hoped that with a few weapons and Evrart's training, we would have a chance.'

Bied opened her mouth, closed it, then exhaled roughly. 'Bied, if—'

'You've been here for months,' Louve interrupted. 'Unless they've been trained by a demon himself, for years, nothing would give your brothers a chance.'

Margery looked away.

'You must know that,' Louve hissed.

'When I told Evrart it was my sister in the great hall, he flew into a—' Margery turned to Louve. 'Oh, if Lord Warstone watches, does he hear?'

Louve gave one nod and then locked his eyes with Bied. 'That means he knows who you are. We're leaving.'

'You truly care for him, don't you?' Bied said.

So much. And it appeared that this Louve not only cared for Bied but loved her.

'I do. Swear to me that—'

'No!' Bied cried out. Louve seized her hands. 'Stop grabbing my hands!'

He didn't let go. 'Not this time. Your sister is safe as long as Ian wants her to be. If we're here when he enters the room, we're dead. He's been listening and he knows you are sisters. That's why he wanted this game with me.'

'Game?' Bied said. 'How many games can there be?'

'Go. Go. *Go.*' Margery pushed against her sister's back. 'I'll find you. Ian can't last forever. He'll make a mistake.'

Margery kept pushing until Louve had got her safely outside the doors. The two guards there eyed them. Nothing was safe. Ian would be told. If he hadn't overheard her and Evrart talking of Bied, he'd know there was a connection now.

And all she could do in this cursed room was wring her hands and lament!

Margery eyed the writing table with its parchments and quills. Or was there something else that could be done? Another message? And maybe this time her brothers would receive it...

Chapter Seventeen

Margery heard a door closing gently behind her. Hours had gone by since Bied had delivered her tray of food. She'd been escorted once to the garderobe, and she'd dragged her steps to look through the archways. There'd been many people in the courtyard. But no signs of Evrart, Ian or her sister.

Pretending to care, she'd asked the guards where Lord Warstone had gone earlier, and for once they'd answered. A hunt. The guards seemed excited by it, but what could they possibly hunt at that time of day?

Evrart hadn't mentioned a hunt, but she'd started to guess with Louve's comments about everyone returning. She still didn't understand when or how Balthus arrived...or why him being alive would matter.

And she wouldn't know being trapped here!

She had almost broken down when the latch had locked her in again. All she could do was listen to the castle filled with noise, and the shouts of many. Some of it merry, but the rest... Exhausted, terrified, she lay in the bed under the quilts. If nothing else she could warm her cold body. For how long, she didn't know.

A distinct heavy footstep, one she could hardly hope

for; Margery turned in the bed. Evrart stood in the doorway to his private rooms. His brows were drawn, his jaw locked, and after he blinked and broke their eye contact, he rolled one shoulder and straightened, as if he was holding himself in.

When she sat up, he took one stumbling step after another until he knelt by her bed as if his legs had given out. She didn't care about anything except that Evrart was here. She didn't know how he felt, but she knew her feelings.

Shoving away the covers, she slammed between his arms and burrowed herself into him, her nose in his neck, her legs around his waist, her hands gripping, gripping, gripping, trying somehow to get closer, to be safer.

He stiffened, then he groaned and tightened his arms right back before loosening them. Hating that, she pinched his arm, and with a murmur he wrapped his strong arms around her more securely. Not as satisfying as when he'd tightened them, but better. Better because he sank a bit more of his weight against her, and that she loved.

Except he held her a bit too long, breathed her in longer than that, and whatever relief she had felt because he was here disappeared.

Pulling herself up, she brushed his hair out of his face. 'You're here. Why?'

'Margery, something's happened.'

'My sister?'

'She's well, and the usher has her.'

There had definitely been something between them. Her heart eased, but not by much. Not when Evrart kept looking at her as if the world had changed.

She kept brushing his hair, his cheek, his hand. His face was cold as if neither of them could get warm.

'Tell me. Are you hurt?'

She plucked at his clothing and craned her neck around him. Felt the broadness of his back and his laboured breaths. His breath should be sure and steady, not shuddering through him as if he'd run up a mountain.

'What happened?'

He tightened his lips. His eyes dimmed. 'Nothing that I want touching you.'

She pushed on his shoulder. 'We've talked about this. I told you to stay safe. I told you to defend yourself. I can't help you do that if you don't tell me what is going on.'

'I'm to keep *you* safe!'

She raised her chin. 'Is that why you told me there was no future between us?'

His nostrils flared. 'I'll do what it takes—whatever it takes. I'll protect you and that's all you need to know.'

'That's it?'

Didn't he realise she'd had enough of protection? Enough of being a prisoner at the whims of other people. She wanted to be right there by his side. Not watching him taking the brunt of it all.

She uncurled her legs and pushed off him. Kneeling before her, he was her height. With him staring directly at her it was hard, tapping her foot at her lover, but she'd do it if it would get her point across.

He slowly stood.

'You have to tell me something or I'm walking out through those doors,' she said.

'They're locked,' he said.

'Then I'll go through your rooms.'

Evrart crossed his arms. 'You're not going.'

She waited for an explanation, and when he merely stared back, she darted.

He stuck out his arm and she smacked her head against his forearm.

Evrart cursed.

Holding her nose with one hand, she held out her other arm, warding him off. 'Don't you dare apologise.'

'Why would you do that?' he asked, prising her hand away from her face.

She could do nothing about the tears in the corners of her eyes. And her nose stung.

'I told you what I would do,' she said. 'It's you who stuck your arm out.'

He ran his roughened fingertips across her forehead, her temple. The scratch of his calluses soothed her. As did the concern in his eyes that she adored. He *had* to feel the way she did!

'I'll make this easy on you.' She grabbed his hand. 'Do you have any feelings for me at all?'

'Any feelings?' He swallowed. 'No.'

She stepped back. What had she expected? She had told him she'd lain with men for coin, and even if he was different, he didn't know what heartache she'd caused her family before that. She wasn't worthy of him.

'Well, then…'

Faster than she could react, he cradled her face in his lethal hands, tilted her chin until she kept her eyes with his.

'I have *every* feeling when it comes to you.'

'Oh.'

'Some of those feelings you may not want.'

When he said it in that growly voice she wanted them all. She wanted everything from him. But that would take some time.

'Tell me what happened.'

He dropped his hands.

Getting this man to tell her wouldn't be easy, but if he had feelings for her he would. He now knew how much it meant.

'I'm assuming whatever has happened isn't life-threatening, otherwise you'd rush me out of here, but you're scaring me. You're hurting me by not saying anything.'

He clenched her hand. 'Ian's dead.'

Margery's entire body jerked, and she reached back to grab at something. A weapon, preferably. 'We need to get out of here. His parents will be after—'

'They left before it occurred. Ian threatened them and they left swiftly.'

'They'll be back!' She tried to wrench her hand free.

'They won't,' he said.

'Evrart, you're not making sense. Who killed him? The parents can't be far—'

'Your hands are cold.' He grabbed both her hands, searched her eyes. 'You heard the sounds?'

The arrival of the hunt, the thunder of many feet, voices, shouts and cries...

She had waited for the clang of swords, but instead she'd been left with the silence. And now she knew that was the worst thing of all.

What use was he? He had been granted this oversized, ill-fitting, body and he couldn't see the true beauty of the world. Everything was dark and grey. But he could protect. He could agree to serve a Warstone so that his mother and sister stayed alive.

He'd gained skills since then. After almost ten years in the Warstone Fortress he should have the ability to keep safe this one tiny woman who'd ridden into this courtyard. One fierce, brave, beautiful woman who wore a cloak far too big for her.

He had failed her! He'd meant to protect Margery

and still she was affected. Still the violence of his life had touched her.

Those sounds… Had she heard Balthus fall? Ian? Had she heard the steward gasp for breath after he'd drunk the poison?

What was worse? Hearing those sounds and not knowing what they were? Or guessing what they could be? Wasn't he here to protect her innocence? She didn't need to know the evil of the world or what darkened his soul.

'You give me nothing but silence? Still?' she said. 'I'm going.'

Perhaps it was worse to hear and not know? Maybe… maybe he could tell her something? Not all. Just enough so she would be informed and wouldn't want to know anything else.

'I'll tell you. If…if you let me hold you whilst I do.'

She hesitated.

He released her hands, willed himself to step back, but failed. 'I understand. You shouldn't be… I shouldn't be here, touching you. Everything's changed.'

Her clear eyes searched his, before she frowned. Fiercely. 'I don't want you to not hold me!'

Before he knew what was happening, she was in his arms.

She stiffened, then laughed. 'I just can't see what's happening in that mind of yours if I can't look into your eyes.'

'You want to look at me?'

'Evrart. You're frightening me. Remember those feelings? This is one of them: I'll always want to look at you!'

She wouldn't after he'd told her what he needed to.

He should have told her from the beginning. It wasn't as bad as what he'd done in the past.

She'd kept that bright light in her eyes because they'd taken walks in the garden, picked quince, dined on beans with extra onions and hard bread. She'd befriended servants and they'd played games with her, like letting her into his room.

Had he ever made a friend or played games?

He tucked her onto his lap and she curled into him. So trusting...and she felt so right.

'Was my sister there?' she asked.

'Yes.' He tugged at her gown so it covered her feet.

'I could ask her to tell me, if that would be—'

He shook his head, rubbing his cheek against the softness of her hair, releasing that scent that grounded him.

She patted his hand. 'Well, then...'

She was frightened. He needed to let her know some of the truth. He'd protect her from the worst.

'We left for a hunt today, along with Ian's parents. It was successful—but in more ways than one. While we were in that forest you can see from the windows Balthus, Ian's youngest brother, dropped from the trees. Do you know of the brothers? It's Ian, Guy, Reynold and Balthus.'

'Balthus.'

'You know of him.'

'I...my sister, and the usher, Louve, came to my room with food. Louve looked out the window and noted Balthus was with the party. They told me—' She looked as if she wanted to say something, then changed her mind.

Shaking her head, she continued. 'He didn't say Balthus dropped from the trees. All alone?'

He wanted to pursue her sister and Louve coming to the room, but could hear the surprise, the wariness in her voice. They, too, had been surprised and wary. Anything else could wait.

'There was no one else with him. His parents appeared delighted. Ian seemed resigned. But Balthus went up to him, clapped him on the shoulder. They didn't say anything to each other. Just looked.'

'At what?'

He didn't know. Not truly. But he could guess.

'Their parents raised the boys to be enemies to each other. Guy wasn't mourned when he died—not even by his parents. There's something going on with the two of them, though. They've been competing with each other, and Ian's mind has been breaking ever since he gathered his wife and children and sent them away. I wonder if... if Ian tried to harm,258 or to kill, Balthus.'

Margery gasped. 'But they're family.'

'Warstones are different,' he said.

'I can see that,' she said. 'Did Balthus kill Ian?'

If he talked of Ian's death, he'd avoid talking of his own part in the day. The temptation was strong, but he knew that he was being a coward. He wanted to protect her, but she needed to know his wrong deeds.

'On the road home, we saw the steward returning.'

'Did he fall from the trees as well?'

She sounded confused. He understood that completely.

'No.'

But the coincidence had been too much for Evrart. He'd walked home the rest of the way with his sword drawn. It hadn't only been Balthus, but Ian who had been amused then.

'I remember the steward from when I arrived. Did *he* kill Ian?'

He concentrated on his breath, which wouldn't come. 'He tried to—with poisoned ale.'

'Poisoned! I think… I believe I tasted that.'

'I spotted your sister and Louve, coming from the ale house.'

'Louve asked me if I had poisoned it.'

'You! You would never—'

She gripped his leg. 'Tell me. Why do you suspect the steward?'

'Because Ian knew. In front of all in the Great Hall, Ian fed the steward ale at full strength. The steward drank it and died.'

He swallowed hard. He had to tell her.

'Then Ian ordered me to carry him out. So I did.'

He waited for her gasp. For her to flinch from his hold. Or at least for her to look up at him in horror. She did none of those things. Maybe she didn't understand.

'I did it with ease. It's not the first time I've carried a dead person. Nor seen one killed.'

Still nothing. His talkative Margery was quiet, whilst he shook. When he couldn't wait any longer, he tucked a finger under her chin, marvelling again at the size difference between them. Her fierceness, her bravery, constantly made him forget.

She allowed him to raise her face to his. There was nothing but tears in her eyes, and something deeper than pity…empathy.

'I'm so sorry you had to—'

She didn't understand! He was a monster!

'It's ugly. The bodies are still warm, and because they were breathing moments before you expect them to again. At least with the Steward there was no blood. In truth, if you don't get a body moved fast enough you will be covered in more than just blood.'

There. That should give her some hint as to what—
Margery laid her hand on his cheek.

'This is the kind of man I am,' he blurted.

This was the reason he needed to protect her.

'What would have happened if you hadn't taken the steward's body out of the room?'

To have not followed the order of a Warstone, and in front of his parents?

'You would have been killed.' She slid her hand down his arm and clasped her hands in her lap. 'No more, Evrart. You need to defend yourself. Now, tell me, is my sister safe?'

Her sister. 'I left the body with the chaplain and came up the private staircase. Your door was still intact, so I went to the other staircase attached to the hall. If anyone had come after you…'

'You'd have been there.'

Always. He'd always protect her. 'I needed to see what had happened…if anyone else needed—'

'Needed your help? At the same time you were protecting me?'

He nodded, searching the clear eyes that had never changed with his story. Perhaps later she'd realise what he was, but now she was concerned for her sister, so he continued.

'Ian's parents and their guards were already mobilised to leave. I don't know why. I think they had something to do with the steward. Biedeluue and Louve stood together. Balthus was nearby, and Ian stood next to Louve, on the other side of your sister.'

She put her hand to her mouth. 'So near!'

'I was there in the shadows. No one saw me. I was there to throw a dagger if needed, Margery.'

'Thank you.'

So simply said! Here was the evidence of her goodness. To ruin it with all he knew…? Never.

'Ian threw a dagger to strike Balthus. Your sister flew from the bench and shoved him out of the way.'

Margery gasped. 'That is just like Bied.'

'Louve threw his own dagger which struck Ian. He fell.'

The dagger had been aimed at Ian's shoulder. But Ian had moved towards the blade and it had pierced his heart. To tell her that a man may have ended his life in front of all? He must protect her as much as he could for now.

'Your door was closed, but I should have seen to you. I should have—.'

'You were there for my sister. I wouldn't have wanted it any other way. I hate it that I was locked in here.'

He eased his arms around her again, revelling in the fact she let him. He pressed a bit more, to convey that he understood. If his sister had been in danger, and he had been denied the ability to protect her, he would have torn down doors. But it was safer for Margery in here, and he wouldn't have allowed her freedom anyway.

When she leaned fully into him he closed his eyes and rested his head on the top of hers. He didn't know what beauty was, but he felt it with her. They sat like that as he watched the light dim in the room and her body became heavier.

'I need to talk to my sister,' she said, her voice slow, heavy.

He'd expected that. And he expected when she did, her sister would take her away from him.

'Family's important,' he said.

'But we'll rest here now.'

He tried to lay her down.

She grabbed his hand. 'We'll rest here now.'

He could deny her nothing.

Chapter Eighteen

Despite it still being dark when Margery woke early the next morning, Evrart was gone. She didn't know when he'd left, or why she had needed to sleep. She'd been doing nothing but resting and sleeping for weeks.

It must be the fear, the worry…those shouts she had been able to do nothing to ease. The words Evrart had spoken. The fact she was locked in a room while Biedeluue simply charged forward in her life.

She hated not being able to do anything. She was useless. Had been made useless. It reminded her of all the times when, as a child, she had suddenly been swept up in someone's arms without any acknowledgement. She'd be arranging rocks, or gazing at insects, and suddenly she'd been picked up and put somewhere else.

It hadn't taken her long to realise that would be her life if she stayed in the village. And it also hadn't taken her long to know her family couldn't afford to keep her. She didn't want to be a burden, and she wanted some freedom, so she'd taken Josse's coin—for them, but at the same time doing something for herself.

Ian had been terrifying and could simply have killed her. It was as if he had known being imprisoned and forced to bend to his every whim was a worse fate. To have some independence, and then to be denied that very freedom…? That wasn't her. She—

A timid knock on the door and Jeanne was there with a tray.

'Oh!' Jeanne stopped in the doorway. 'You're awake.'

'I couldn't sleep.'

'I didn't know what else to do this morning.' Jeanne stepped in without closing the door. 'I know it's early, but I took a chance you wouldn't throw me out.'

Margery eyed the food she knew she wouldn't eat. It wasn't quite light outside. They had time. 'I'm glad you came. Set it here—stay and eat.'

Throwing herself into a chair, Jeanne grabbed a bread roll and Margery poured cold pottage into the two cups. She didn't hide her smile. Jeanne was hoping for her company as much as she wanted it herself.

'I can't believe he's gone,' Jeanne said. 'I don't know what's to become of the household now.'

Margery's heart eased at Jeanne's easy way with her. She knew she wasn't a servant—not truly—but she wasn't royalty either. Having a friendship…any friend… was a gift.

'Won't the Warstone parents or Balthus take over?'

'Did no one tell you…?' Jeanne's eyes widened. 'I'm sorry, that wasn't kind. I keep forgetting you're locked in here.'

Sequestered. Confined.

She should have checked on her sister, but Evrart had said she had Louve, and Margery had been loath to leave the comfort of Evrart's arms.

She'd imprisoned herself!

'That probably wasn't kind either,' Jeanne said.

Margery waved her hand. 'No, don't apologise. It's not… I'm free now.'

'You were fortunate to be in here,' Jeanne said. 'To have missed everything.'

Margery didn't feel fortunate—or free. She felt as if she was again being picked up and put somewhere else. Somewhere she wasn't certain she wanted to be.

'I had to serve the goblets of ale,' Jeanne said.

Evrart had said much, but not everything. She knew it wasn't reasonable to expect a man who barely made a sound to give details, but she couldn't help but wonder if he'd done it because he was protecting her. No. She had made it clear to him how important it was to her to know the truth.

Margery took a sip of pottage. 'Goblets?'

'They passed around wine for everyone, and then a tray of ale went—'

'To the steward, who died,' Margery said, not wanting to hear it again. Evrart had suffered enough.

Jeanne wiped her mouth with the back of the hand still holding the roll. 'To the usher and the new cook as well.'

Margery stood. 'My sister!'

'Your sister?' Jeanne said.

Evrart hadn't told her everything.

Margery looked at the open door. Enough was enough. 'Jeanne, forgive me…'

Down the staircase, across the great hall… Margery ran towards the kitchens. It was easy to spot her sister. The familiar hands on her hips, the hair waving with riotous indignation.

'Bied!' Margery skipped down the steps.

Biedeluue turned and enveloped her in her arms. Familiar. Wanted. Cherished. Their mother had always been fragile, and it had been Bied who had cared for her.

'Margery, are you well? Are you harmed?'

How could she be harmed when she was cut off from life, and protected all the time? Jeanne had made it sound like a benefit; it was a curse. She hadn't known her sister's life had been in jeopardy.

'What of you?' She pulled back from her sister and looked her over. She was here. Not poisoned. Breathing. 'You're here in the kitchens!'

Bied clamped her hands on Margery's shoulders—which, given their short stature and Bied's curves, didn't separate them much. 'I'm only here because I was promised some tarts with extra honey. I'm starving.'

Margery didn't want to eat. She wanted to know what had been happening in this castle. Whilst she'd been surrounded by pillows, others had been killed and had narrowly avoided drinking poisoned ale.

'Can we simply—?' Margery started, but then she spotted a woman bringing over a tray.

'Thank you, Tess,' Bied said.

'If I'd known you had company in the kitchens I'd have brought more.' Tess handed Bied the tray.

Margery didn't want any food. She wanted her sister. 'There's four tarts here,' she said.

'Hardly enough,' Tess said with a wink. 'You'll see.'

Bied linked their arms and pulled them into another room with a roof full of hanging herbs and a long table. Margery dragged two stools closer together.

'Tell me what is going on,' Bied said.

'Isn't that what I am to ask you?' she said. 'The ale that killed the steward was poisoned.'

Bied blinked.

Margery didn't know where to begin. Half of her

wanted to strangle her sister for risking her life; the other half wanted to keep hugging her.

'Jeanne said everyone got wine, but a few were served ale. You and Louve and the steward.'

Bied nodded. 'Ian ordered ours not to be poisoned.'

'You didn't know that when you were served it though, did you?'

Bied hesitated, then shook her head.

Margery pushed off her stool, wrapped her arms about herself and stepped away.

Bied shifted in her seat. 'I haven't been here long, but I've learnt if a Warstone wants you dead, then you're dead. And they like their games.'

From the tone of her voice, it seemed her sister liked them, too. Margery walked to the other side of the table and stayed there, because she was furious.

'Margery...'

She held out her hand. 'Not yet.'

Whilst she'd been swept up at the whim of some Warstone scheme she knew nothing about, Bied had come here and risked her life. But Margery needed somehow to make the people around her see that she needed to rescue herself.

'How do you know the usher?'

'I met him here,' Bied said. 'But—'

'How long have you been here?'

'Less than a month,' Bied said. 'But—'

Margery shook her head, turned her back again.

No. No. No.

'I love him.'

Margery turned around. 'The usher? You have only just met him.'

'I love *you*.'

'What do I have to do with it?'

'I thought you were probably being served the ale as well. That you would be caught out.'

Margery leaned on the table. 'You shouldn't have taken the ale.'

'What wouldn't I do?'

All the fight left her. She loved her sister just as much. What would she do for her family? Everything. She'd accepted Josse…that way of life. It hadn't been easy. Roul had been even worse, but she'd accepted that too, because she'd refused to be a burden to her siblings. She'd wished to ease her mother's mind.

'You're not dead,' Margery said.

Bied's eyes watered, as if she was taking in Margery's fear. 'Neither is Louve. Nor you.'

'Evrart told me what happened in the hall. That there were daggers thrown. That you pushed Balthus out of the way.'

'Evrart!' Bied said. 'I don't know how he did what he did.'

Hefting a body and carrying it to the chapel grounds. Explaining to the chaplain what was to be done?

'He's done worse,' Margery said.

'He told you?'

He'd told her enough. Enough to scare her away or to protect her from him? No more. From here on she'd never be forced behind a locked door again. She didn't know what she'd do to avoid it, but it would be something. Because by hiding away she had only these words now. Words from Evrart, from Bied, from Jeanne… And she knew she still didn't know all the facts that threatened those she cared for.

Already she had nudged Evrart into not treating her as if she was fragile. He wouldn't betray her like that, would he?

Instead of crying here in the kitchens, she took a bite of tart. 'Oh!'

'Good, aren't they?' Bied said around the bite in her mouth.

Margery brushed the crumbs off her fingers. 'They're delicious.'

'I'm sorry I called him a brute before, when you do truly care for him,' Bied said.

And he had feelings for her—but why did she feel unsettled? Was it her past, and the fact she knew she wasn't worthy of him? And yet if they cared for each other that shouldn't matter. She should be feeling as free as she'd ever been. Not this unease.

He'd hurt her, though, even if it had been inadvertent, and letting down her defences and not protecting herself would be harder somehow.

'What are you to do now?' Bied asked.

Return to the village where she'd grown up? Never. To Josse or Roul? To another man to earn coin for her family? Not now. Not after Evrart. Not even for Mabile, who needed the coin.

Stay here? That didn't appeal to her at all. Although Evrart was here. Ian might be gone, but Balthus would need a guard who knew the way of things. Still…

'I don't know. I think that depends on you,' she said.

Bied shook her head. 'Not me.'

Margery finished off her tart and grabbed another one. 'You've never *not* made a decision about my life.'

'Is that why you wrote me that letter?' Bied asked. 'You told me how charming Ian of Warstone was and I was just to believe you? To stay away?'

She'd hurt her sister. 'I didn't want you to worry. So I told you of Ian and asked you to be happy for me.'

'Except I got the other message.'

'It was supposed to go to Servet and Isnard.'

'The messenger told me so, and I said I'd deliver it. I even wrote a reply to you, since the messenger was still there to return it. A day later I couldn't wait, and I opened the one you intended for our brothers.'

'So you did write to warn me of Ian?'

When Bied nodded, Margery winced and took a large bite of her tart. Roul would have received that message. Had he read it and laughed? Was he even alive?

'And you came to rescue me.'

'I only wanted to help.'

Margery squeezed her sister's hand. 'You have saved me and cared for me in ways I can never repay.'

'I don't want repayment,' Bied said. 'I only want—'

'What's best for me. Do you think…?' Margery shook her head. She needed this to be said, but was half terrified if she asked the question and Bied said no, her life would never be her own. 'Do you think you could just let go? Let me be?'

Bied played with the crust of her tart. 'I think I will have to. I don't know if I have a place to live any more.'

Margery was certain if Bied and Louve talked they would find a home together. 'What of this fortress?' she asked.

'Ian's dead, and I don't know about this brother Balthus who has taken over.'

'Simply ask Balthus. You saved his life by pushing him out of the way.'

Bied's gaze slid away.

Evrart had said Bied shoved Balthus out of the way, but he hadn't said what had happened afterwards. 'Did that knife hit you?'

Bied shook her head. 'Balthus was injured before. We didn't know how badly until I pushed him away from that knife. Louve has had to cut off his hand. He isn't waking now, and is racked with fever.'

Evrart hadn't explained this to her. He hadn't wanted to tell her anything at all until she'd told him she'd leave if he didn't. Had he lied to her?

Too many uncertainties!

'What happens if Balthus dies?' she asked. 'What happens if his parents return?'

'We don't know.'

Margery cared about Evrart's fate here, and her own…maybe she couldn't leave that readily either. But this Louve—he was somebody, and he was far too self-assured not to have some power or skill. Her sister loved him, so why wasn't he here?

Her sister…her brave sister…had uncertainties too.

'You are with Louve, aren't you?'

Bied looked to the side. 'I don't know.'

Her sister loved this man. Talk of Evrart, of Balthus or any Warstone, could wait. Margery knew what sacrifices Biedeluue had made to protect her from the men of the village. Biedeluue had offered herself. Margery had been only a child then, and no part of the decision, but still she couldn't forgive herself. Not truly. It was another reason why she'd accepted Josse's offer. After what her sister had done, how could she have done anything less?

'Are you uncertain of Louve because you don't trust?' she said.

Were they both to be ruined because of their past?

'I want to trust, but…' Bied gave a small smile and shrugged. 'I've been a terrible sister and I have been blind to how strong you are. You saved me in the Great Hall, and you've been surviving in this fortress.'

Margery didn't blame her sister for changing the subject. She would too, if she had to talk of Evrart and trusting him. 'I've had Evrart.'

Bied shook her head. 'You've had your wits—which must have been honed far before you entered here. You haven't been living in leisure.'

Terror had been her constant companion. Was it all truly over?

'Louve loves you.'

'That can't be true,' Bied said.

Her sister had been hurt, just as she had been growing up in that village. Biedeluue had always seemed so strong. It pained her to know she had suffered and couldn't trust easily.

'He does love you,' she insisted. 'It is in the way he looks at you, and how he rushed you out of my room. The very fact he brought you to my room. I'm certain that took much effort.'

Bied worried at her bottom lip. 'He doesn't know me.'

Evrart knew some but not all of her past. Her sister, however, was noble and kind. Bied's deeds had been done solely to help the family, whereas her own... Her birth had been a burden...accepting Josse had been merely a means to make matters right.

'Maybe it's time you told him.'

'Louve has some duties. I think they'll keep him here with Balthus, who was his friend. But I don't know where to go next. If I stay here, will you stay too?'

Louve was friends with Balthus? A Warstone? That explained his bearing and his vanity.

'Stay here? But Louve killed Ian—how will Balthus keep him? I know that the brothers were enemies, but—'

Bied shook her head. 'Louve didn't kill Ian. Louve threw the dagger at his shoulder, but at the last moment Ian moved towards it,' Bied said. 'It pierced his heart.

Louve was beside himself. Held Ian as he died. Promised him that he'd find his wife.'

Margery didn't understand. It wasn't what Evrart had told her.

'It's confusing, I know,' Bied continued. 'But Louve is friends with two of the brothers—Reynold and Balthus. I think he was trying to save Ian when he…did what he did.'

Margery looked at her eldest sister but didn't see her at all. Weren't enemies to stay enemies? If Ian had thrown a dagger at Balthus, why would Louve care for Ian? All she had seen of Ian was his cruelty. Except at night, with his murmurings. No. That kindness was for his lost wife. No one else.

'So…what of the Warstone parents?'

'The children are against their parents.'

Margery had a mother who had been physically exhausted when she was born. Soon afterwards her father had abandoned them and she had been raised by her siblings. It had always been a struggle, but there had been love there. The fact her sister could talk of family betrayal so easily was beyond her comprehension. Nor did she have any desire to understand.

'You like their games.'

'I don't play games.'

'You're in the kitchens, ordering servants about,' Margery said. 'Cooking… You're pretending to be someone you're not, and you love a man who isn't an usher. What is he truly?'

'He's a mercenary to Reynold, and he's here for other purposes.'

Fools. All of them. Her most of all. She had been swept up in the arms of everyone and deposited somewhere. If she'd heard someone talk about her sister's deeds, she wouldn't have believed them. She was fierce, and she did charge into matters, but she never pretended to be someone else.

Margery hadn't only been locked in a room surrounded by pillows—she'd been living a lie. Did she know *any-one*?

'Louve is friends with a Warstone, who is enemies of his brother, and yet when he died, Louve comforted the enemy?'

'It was all to save Balthus!' Bied said.

'But Balthus is at death's threshold, isn't he? Louve had to chop off his hand. And it wasn't Louve who saved him from Ian's dagger. *You're* the one who shoved him out of the way. You're as culpable as them.'

Bied's expression was half-hurt, half-horrified. Margery didn't care. She'd been hiding away and hiding her feelings. Giving everyone the benefit of not telling her the truth. Evrart because he was quiet, Jeanne because she'd forgotten Margery was confined, her sister because she was so brave.

Except it hurt her to be separated from everyone. Pained her not to be told the truth.

'Everyone here is pretending!' she said. 'Is it only me who was threatened with death, kidnapped, then held captive awaiting decisions to be made that I could do nothing about?'

'I'm not pretending anything,' Bied said. 'I had to be someone else to save you!'

'Maybe I don't want to be saved anymore.'

Bied opened her mouth, shut it. 'You sent that letter.'

'And it was a mistake!'

A terrible mistake. Not because she hadn't wanted to risk her siblings' lives, but because she should have done something on her own. She'd thought she taken risks because she'd written on some scraps of parchment and hidden them from a murderer, but she'd been wrong. Being truly brave would have been not to journey with Ian of Warstone. To have fought him. Not to have begged the palfrey to run the other way.

Because that was what she had done as she'd stared at the fortress gates: begged a horse to save her!

'It was a mistake, me coming here?' Bied said. 'A mistake!'

Now that she knew more, she was certain Evrart had purposely not told her what had happened in the hall—or on any other day for that matter. Did no one believe she could be strong, equal enough to be by their side? They were so intent on protecting her—didn't they think maybe she could protect them too? No. Because they believed her to be useless. Only useful for her hair and eye colour.

'Stay out of my life, Biedeluue. Protect someone else. Go and play your games with this Louve and his Warstones.'

Chapter Nineteen

Evrart spied Margery in the chapel gardens. Unlike the last sennight, this time he strode towards her.

There had been so many changes since he'd left her bed while she'd fitfully slept. Despite all he'd told her, his heart was light. She was alive, and well. Ian was dead—as was his debt to him. For the first time in a decade his family was safe. Louve, the new usher, was actually a mercenary of Reynold's, and he cared for this woman named Biedeluue, who happened to be Margery's sister. The Warstone parents hadn't attacked, and Balthus, after many nights, had awakened.

If he hadn't believed in good fortune before, he certainly did now. His life had been one thing for almost ten years, and now it was something else. Something he thought he'd share with Margery. But after she'd spoken to her sister she'd hurled words at him he hadn't fully understood, had avoided him or ordered him away. So he'd watched her from afar.

He could wait.

His changing duties kept him occupied. He was no longer Ian's personal guard, but Louve and Balthus had brought other mercenaries here, and they didn't get along with the guards already in residence. Then there were the new ones Ian had brought that day he'd arrived with Margery.

All men who worked for coin, now he needed them to work for loyalty, for skill, for something other than the reputation of a Warstone. Because with Ian gone this fortress was defended by Louve—a person with no power, and no noble blood or connections. A man from whom mercenaries weren't pleased to be taking orders.

It was one thing to be paid in coin, but quite another to be linked to a house with power. Most of the mercenaries wanted both, and some had already left. Unfortunately, because the Warstone parents might lay siege any day, they couldn't afford to lose more. For the last week it had been a constant battle bringing the men to heel.

Thus, he had given his Margery time, but more changes had come, and he could wait no longer.

More than that, he missed her. Missed the light brushes of her hands against his arm, his cheek. Missed her voice and her demands he talk. He'd lived most of his life in silence, and now he no longer found it comforting.

'I thought I'd find you here,' he said.

Margery did not stand or turn around, but she did kneel amongst those flowers she smelled of. He might not see all the colours, but could discern she was more beautiful than those flowers, more precious to him than the land they grew on.

'I have news for you.'

She adjusted herself from kneeling to sitting, but she did not turn or give voice to whether she wanted to hear him or not. He took hope from the fact she hadn't simply stood and walked away.

'Balthus is awake. He bears no ill will for his hand,

and has agreed when he is healed, he will search for Ian's wife, Séverine, and her two boys.'

Margery laced her fingers together and laid them in her lap.

'Louve and your sister will stay to defend the fortress,' he continued. 'Balthus will send missives to the King of England, requesting the title be transferred to Louve. If that fails, he will defend it in Balthus and Reynold's absence, against his parents. They're staying, Margery; I am certain you can have a home here as well.'

'What makes you think I want a home here?'

Her voice wasn't bitter, but it didn't hold that light lilt which had teased him in his sleep. For all the days she'd ignored him, he had wished only for her attention. Now she was talking of leaving.

His thoughts scattered. Had he not made himself clear? If she left, so would he.

'You're leaving?' he said.

Margery looked over her shoulder at him. He wondered what her light eyes saw. A man too crudely made for her, too imperfect? A man who could hear of her beauty, but could not see it? At least not the way others did. He wished, again, that with her he could. Still, he loved the beauty he did see.

He held her gaze for as long as she was willing to look at him. Wished it could be more.

'Warstone Fortress works very well without me,' she said. 'Is there a reason for me to stay?'

'Your sister is here,' he said.

'But I'm ignoring her too.'

He felt that familiar tenseness and rolled one shoulder. She was sitting on the ground whilst he stood over her. He must seem enormous, frightening, to her. Carefully, he folded his legs under him and sat as she did.

The gravel path wasn't comfortable and, unlike her, he was hardly hidden. It wouldn't do for his reputation or his authority to be seen like this, but he didn't care.

'You're not ignoring me now,' he said.

'That's because you're sitting on the ground with me.'

'Does it help?'

She twisted around to face him. 'Oddly, yes. I may have not been fair these last days, ignoring you. But it wasn't only you. It was Jeanne, and my sister. It was… everyone.'

He'd watched her ignoring everyone. Seen Margery stride smartly by her sister, and seen the resignation in Biedeluue's face afterwards. He knew he looked that way too. But Bied never forced Margery's attention, so he didn't either.

'I needed to understand a few matters,' she said. 'I didn't feel like talking with any of you.'

He could believe that. 'I took hope in that.'

'In my ignoring you?'

He had simply been relieved that she's stayed when she could so easily have left. Except…

'Have I done wrong now? By coming here?'

Her eyes softened and a curve went to her lips. 'Never. You have made my apology easier.'

'What were the matters you needed to think on?'

'My life has been subject to others' desires. Ian forced me here. I know I'm not anything more than a woman who sold her virtue—'

'Don't,' he said.

He wouldn't hear it. She hadn't given up her honour by doing what she'd had to to help her family, any more than he'd given up his for his mother and sister.

Her eyes searched his, looking for answers. 'I still want the truth, though. I need it.'

She was questioning his honour? 'And I've lied to you?'

'You speak words—but do you speak enough?'

He spoke more with her than he did with anyone.

'I have talked to Jeanne and my sister. Both of them told me far more than you,' Margery said. 'I know you're quiet, but did you deny me knowing what happened in the Great Hall because of the way you are, or because of some other reason?'

If a sword was aiming for her neck, he'd block it with his own. If a blade was thrown, he'd stand in front of it. If harsh words, deeds, the ugliness of life, which he had known of for almost ten years, was directed her way, he'd block that to. What good was he, what use, if he didn't protect this woman?

'I would deny you nothing.' Including the life he wished he'd been spared. It did him no good to know of the killing of innocents or that a mother pitted against her sons.

Margery would have a life of orchards and kneeling in gardens that smelled like her. And he knew he'd answered her rightly when all the lightness of the gardens in sunshine lit her from within and she smiled at him again.

She'd overreacted. Margery had hoped she had. It was the worry over the lives of everyone she cared about. The sheer rage at her captivity. But to have judged this man as she would have the villagers who had thought they knew better than her? Evrart wasn't like that. He was simply quiet. She needed to stop having doubts—at least about trusting him. Her past, however, would have to stay in the past.

Of course, her anger didn't start and end with him. But Jeanne didn't deserve her avoidance. Did her sister?

Well, that was still possible, but Margery would have to apologise to her, too.

Standing, Margery brushed the dirt from her gown and then held out her hands. He looked at her waving fingers, then back at her face.

'I can help pull you up!' She laughed. 'Oh, you do have the best expressions.'

He stood on his own, brushed his clothes as she had. 'I have no expressions.'

Margery straightened and stretched. 'The sky is changing again.'

Evrart rolled his shoulders and exhaled roughly. Then slowly, slowly, he looked up at the sky like her.

'You don't notice the sky, do you?' she said.

'Rain, storms, snow, heat…my duties don't change for the weather other than the tasks are easier or harder. They still need to be done.'

He didn't see the sky like she did, but he still looked at it because of her. The more they found about each other, the more she realised how different he was from other men—including her brothers. They would never have sat on the ground in a garden.

And he was different from the men in her life who had dictated what she could and could not learn, what she should be and what she should do. He didn't care she had sold herself to save her family. Or at least he didn't want to talk of it. She still felt she should tell him, but then…he was different. And he didn't care what she looked like because he didn't see the world like everyone else. Maybe he was different enough.

She felt as if she was repeating hope to herself. But maybe for now she needed to do so. He might be protective, but he told her of matters when she needed to be told. When she asked. To have found a man such as him when she'd spent weeks terrified...? Her fortune was too great. Perhaps that was where her doubt lay.

'Now what do we do?' she said.

He looked down at her.

'What's to happen now?' she repeated.

This was the other matter that occupied much of her time while she was wandering around, going from the cook to the pantler, to the chapel gardens. Seeing if there was some other occupation she could have. If perhaps she could earn coin another way.

But always she came back to this man. His life was here—but had that changed since Ian's death?

She didn't think so. She'd often seen Louve and Evrart talking. She'd tracked the hours he spent with the guards and mercenaries. As much as she teased him on not being skilled, he was, and to take him away from this...

But then...where did she fit? And this man was quiet again.

'Evrart, what do you want here?'

'It has never been about my wants.'

They were so similar, and yet she longed for more and was willing to include him. His feelings aside, what more could there be for them? She had her past, and he had his future here.

'But isn't it now?'

'There is much to do here.'

She was a fool even hinting at a future together. 'I'm finished. Should we go?'

'So soon?'

'I am certain you are eager to be training instead of sitting in a garden.'

Evrart shrugged one shoulder. 'There is much training to be done, and even more loyalty to be earned before Balthus departs.'

'When Balthus returns surely he'll help with the men?'

Evrart looked to the courtyard, to the many people hurrying past them. Only a few looked their way. Margery couldn't get used to their lack of curiosity when it came to her. It was welcome, but still odd.

'When Balthus leaves we may never see him again. The loyalty between the brothers is tenuous.'

Hence why Ian had thrown a dagger at his brother, and the reason Guy's death hadn't been mourned.

'What if he leaves with someone to help him?' she said. 'Someone who would want to return here?'

His brows drew in. 'None of the guards or mercenaries would want to.'

'Not even for protection or their family?' she said. 'This is a formidable fortress.'

'If Balthus leaves, the safety of this fortress will be suspect. Especially with the Warstone parents, who will want it back. But...' Evrart exhaled roughly.

'What is it?'

'I wonder if they are pulled in too many directions.'

'What do you mean?' she said.

'They know of Ian's death and Balthus's injury. Louve sent messengers to Reynold. The first one was captured.'

'If I had a child...any child...' She couldn't understand not wanting to protect family. 'And they are still not here?'

He shook his head. 'Reynold has been working for many years to undermine his parents' influence. I wonder if it has begun.'

'Then Balthus will want to return here all the more—to claim his right.'

'He doesn't want this home. He has barely visited in all the years I've been here. No, this is one piece of rubble he'd gladly give away.'

'He should still be here to help Louve establish his authority. And for a man who is silent, you certainly have opinions.'

'I stood at Ian's side as his personal guard. I heard much.'

Somehow she'd forgotten that. What this man knew would be beneficial to Louve's defence here. He might not be able to go.

'What is it?' he said.

He was needed here. She was not. And, in truth, even if she was, she didn't want to stay. She might have met Evrart, but she'd been captive here, and spent too many hours wondering if her life would end.

Why burden him with any of that? She was supposed to be living a life of her own. Not writing letters asking for rescue or begging favours from horses. Or wondering over a future together with a man she wanted...

'So no mercenaries or guards for Balthus or else he might not have reason to return here after he recovers Ian's wife and children. What of Henry?'

'Henry? The butcher?'

She might have stayed away from everyone, but she did enquire about the man who had looked so friendly that first day.

'A Warstone wouldn't want a butcher, a mere servant, at his side.'

Ian wouldn't have, but they didn't know Balthus. She didn't like that the very fortress her sister lived in might be under attack. It would be better fortified if Balthus was here as well. 'I'll let Biedeluue know maybe she can make the suggestion.'

'Balthus won't take orders.'

'No, but if it is suggested, Balthus can think it was his own idea. And a butcher would be perfect because he'd want to return here and not go wandering about. Thus, Balthus would return as well.'

Evrart's eyes narrowed. Margery kept hers wide. It was so obviously a ridiculous plan. They held their eyes like that until they both laughed.

'Did you have a decent butcher in your village?' she blurted.

'My village?'

Why was she asking questions about his village? To see whether she'd hate it? Or to torture herself with what she couldn't have?

'We never used his services. The sparse meat we caught was cut by my mother, and all too often put in soups to stretch it.'

This was another commonality they shared—both of them had come from poor rural families. She hated her village, but Evrart's eyes shone with memories. Were his village and its people decent?

'And your mother and sister?'

'They live in the same village. I send them coin, but fields don't tend themselves, so there is always work to be done. My brothers are built like me, and others have trained them with swords and weaponry. It has been a long time since I've seen them.'

Margery rearranged the flowers in her basket. He sounded wistful. As if he missed his family and wanted to see them again. Was that true? Or was it her wishing it was true so they could ride together and live—?

A gentle finger under her chin raised her eyes to him before he quickly let her go.

'Margery, these are very curious questions you ask.'

They seemed bold and obvious to her. Hinting for him to take her to his village… The poor man!

'I don't want to stay here.'

'To avoid your sister?'

She needed to apologise to her sister. It wasn't the first argument they'd had, but it was certainly the worst. She had written that note and, as she always did, Biedeluue had come to help. That was hardly Bied's fault.

'Is it your sister?' he asked again.

How to explain when she barely understood? That she just had a feeling, but it kept getting stronger the longer she stayed. It wasn't merely because she missed the danger, intrigue and carnality of her former life. None of that ever called to her. The garden called to her. Being outside, watching and feeling the weather change called to her. But Warstone Fortress was too well run. She wasn't needed here. She had no place.

'Not her, truly. But it is Biedeluue's home now.'

He frowned. 'And it can't be your own.'

It was a ridiculous argument—what person had a home of one's own? If a family was truly wealthy or truly poor, it lived and worked together. And that was where she'd failed.

'There's not enough to do here. For me. I don't think the pantler will let me near his supplies again.'

Evrart's lips curved. 'What is it, Margery. Your eyes tell me so much.'

'You can't see the colour of them.'

'You shine out of those eyes you tell me are lavender.'

'Is that all you see?' She tried to make her tone light, but her need to know cracked her voice and she clenched her hands. Was she so desperate? 'I have no place here, but you...you don't have a place back there.'

His eyes widened. 'My village? Oh, Margery. I have never, not once, wanted to be here. I was taken from my home.'

'Taken?' She looked away. 'When Ian came through your village.'

'I didn't freely take the coin.'

She looked back to him, her eyes searching his if she pained him by bringing it up or letting him think she forgotten. When she hadn't…couldn't. 'I know; I understand. What happened?'

Exhaling, he continued, 'That is a tale I don't wish to tell now. Just know that I was given no choice but to be here.'

That didn't answer the question of whether he liked or didn't like where he currently lived. 'So you didn't want to leave your village? You liked it there?'

'It was all I knew. This…here…is all I know now.'

'And you're good at it.'

He gave a curt nod.

There was no solution to this!

He chuckled.

'This isn't humorous. For a sennight now I've been trying to find a way… But you are always occupied and needed. I don't want to deprive my sister of your skills. What if we leave and then they are attacked?'

'So serious… Margery, if you're asking to go to my village, and for me to accompany you, I would do so wholeheartedly.'

She couldn't hope!

'My village is only three days away. If the fortress is attacked, who is to say that my coming from behind would not be a benefit?'

He flexed his hands, as if he wanted to hold her. She wished he did. Instead he tilted his head, his eyes searching hers. 'You would go to my village?'

'If you would go with me.'

He leaned down, as if to kiss her. 'You've never been to my village. You might not like it.'

But she loved him—though she hadn't said it to him. Some seed of doubt or cowardliness was not letting her tell him. Or maybe she was just trying to protect herself, as she had all her life.

He had told her he had feelings for her, but what those were, she didn't know. If he loved her, he would have said that—wouldn't he? Yet feelings counted, and maybe it wasn't everything, but with her past she wasn't going to ask for more. He was a good man. His family were probably good, too.

Perhaps at his village it would be different, and she could be useful there. She wrapped her arms around his middle, felt him stiffen before he held her back.

Her heart was so full it pained her. Did she deserve such a man? No. This was too much, even for her. She pulled away. He wore that same puzzled expression that endeared her so. As if he was half confused and half de-lighted by her.

'I'll need to talk to Jeanne…let her know what we're doing.'

'Then talk to Jeanne.'

'Could she come and visit, or me visit her?'

'If it's safe,' he said.

Could it all be this simple? She didn't want to be here, so Evrart would take her somewhere else. How could it be this easy? He'd simply tell her things when she needed them, and not care about her past? She hated these doubts. Hated them and still…

She had to know.

'What happened with Cook and Thomas?' she blurted.

She'd seen Michael, the cook, wandering around the fortress. Some days he was in the kitchens; other days he was in the gardens. He wasn't an old man, but he walked like one. She could have asked Jeanne, but since she had seen him she'd held herself back. It seemed too intrusive.

'You wanted to know of the butcher and now of Cook?'

'When I arrived, he wasn't well. He's not...'

Evrart's eyes softened. 'Cook's son died. Thomas isn't much older, and he often cares for the boy. They're both grieving.'

She shouldn't have asked, and yet she was glad she had because now Evrart talked to her. She hated these doubts, but maybe in time... If he was protective, she'd be protective right back.

'Do you miss your family?' she asked.

'Every day.'

'Did you not mention it before because of your past, or because you thought I was happy here?'

'You ignored me, so that made it difficult to tell you anything.'

She slapped him hard on the arm, and he held his arm as if injured, at the same time giving her a wide smile.

'Tell me why,' she demanded.

'I thought you'd want to stay with your sister.'

Because family was important to her and he knew that. How could she doubt him anymore?

'I want to go. I do.'

He wore that expression again, as if he couldn't believe his good fortune.

Taking his arm, she picked up the basket, now filled with chamomile to be dried. Maybe she could take some with her to her new home...

Chapter Twenty

Margery bumped along in the saddle, holding on for all she was worth. The sky, which had threatened all morning, finally gave up the rain it held. All at once. She swore her bones were wet.

However, they'd were still climbing hills, and Evrart was determined to make their destination.

She wouldn't be concerned if it meant shelter, but she could see none in sight. Just a bunch of trees that steadily grew larger, until he led them under their expansive canopy while the rain pounded on the leaves and branches above.

Her ears were still ringing, and it took her some time to realise that the rain no longer drowned her.

Shoving off her hood, she marvelled. 'What is this place?'

He dismounted and helped her down. Stamping, her horse shook its head and splattered her with more rainwater.

Grinning, Evrart moved her away from the beast. 'Mulberry trees,' he said. 'They were once cultivated and trimmed, and now their leaves and branches provide cover.'

'You knew this was here?'

Nodding, he wandered underneath one. 'I can stand under them—unlike your quince trees—and if the birds leave enough behind, I can usually find a few.' He plucked some berries and held them out to her.

She picked one, and he popped the rest in his mouth.

'They're delicious.'

'The hills will ease soon as they slope to the river.' He strode to the burdened horse—the one carrying their supplies.

'I'm not so worried for the hills, but for the rain.'

'The rain will end—the hills will not. This is as good a place as any to rest.' He pulled at the bindings of one satchel.

'You know this area well?'

'We're near to the abbey.' He tossed the satchel to the side and began on another. 'Most of our travelling will be easier as they've cultivated much of the land.'

'There's an abbey?' she said, her teeth chattering despite the warmth of the day.

'You'll see it soon, and then it will always be in the distance. It may be as large as Warstone and its lands, and it's near to my home. Let me get your cloak.'

'No, I can do it.' She was no better than the three horses waiting for Evrart to take care of them. Two to ride...one to carry their things to Evrart's village.

She still couldn't believe she was going. Biedeluue hadn't been surprised when she'd told her, but even though they'd spent years apart, for some reason their parting had been difficult. Still, it had been full of promises and love.

Jeanne, on the other hand... She had her family at Warstone Fortress, and couldn't leave, so they'd both cried until Margery had gone under the portcullis.

Here she was about to cry again!

Breathing deep, she tried to remember the good. The day was warm, at least, and her hands weren't chilled. The cloak came free, but when she strode to hang it from the smallest tree, she couldn't reach it.

Evrart came up behind her and hung it on a branch. The rain had slicked back his longer locks, displaying his blunt features. His face was not refined, but brutal, the forehead wide, the jaw square. But those eyes...a bit more brown today than blue.

Their clothes were saturated, and the smell of wet linen and wool, of damp leather and soaked horse permeated the air. But still she scented the man. Her Evrart.

When he stood this clos she was more aware of his size, of how her eyes were at a level with his belly versus his chest. The expanse of both was twice or more than hers. His arms were heavy at his sides.

This close, he was larger than a horse and more steep than any hill, and yet not once did she fear him. But she wanted him. Yet, she'd treated him so horribly, by ignoring him and then begging him to take her to his village. She didn't want to beg or push him further.

They were travelling to his home, but he had never made a declaration of love and certainly never said he'd marry her. She'd been trapped and forced to live one way by poverty, by her care for her family, and then by Ian. Now she was on her own and felt a bit lost.

What did she know thus far?

That Evrart was good...protective. That he'd said he had feelings for her. She was certain he hadn't told her everything, but maybe he only needed time because he was quiet. And maybe her fears of being useless were merely present because of those last days at Warstone Fortress, when she'd found nothing to do.

Perhaps her past and this feeling of being unworthy would dissipate the farther she got from it.

Maybe she just wanted Evrart in any way she could for as long as he'd let her.

Aware of his eyes on her, she cleared her throat. 'Tell me of your family.'

Evrart blinked and stepped back. He had been certain Margery would kiss him. Or perhaps place one of her hands on his arm, indicating that she wanted to be kissed. Not talk of his family.

'My father died suddenly in the field one day. My mother, Blanche, is much like me. I have two brothers older than I and a younger sister, Peronelle, who is a handful.'

His had been a happy home. Not as happy as he wanted his own to be with Margery. *If* he was to have a home with her. He'd never pursued a woman before. It had been so natural when she'd attempted to show him colours. Easy because she'd touched him so much his body had given him no choice.

Ever since he'd been nothing but a brute with her. Grabbing her and taking her kisses, desperate to keep her safe. And then she'd ignored him for days. In the garden he had hoped all was settled—except she'd asked only to travel to his home. She hadn't said she cared for him and he didn't know how to ask her to be his wife, and that he wanted it to be at his village, and not at Warstone. Though she travelled with him, there was a distance between them he didn't know how to close.

Turning away, he tended her horse. 'It was a happy home.'

'Then how…?'

He looked over his shoulder at her. 'How did I meet Ian?' he offered.

He'd been out in the field, tilling with oxen, when a procession on the nearby road had caused many of the children and the villagers to run out to greet it. Evrart had kept ploughing. With his back to the road, he hadn't seen the lone rider gallop across the field.

But when the horse had kicked up the mud and stones, he'd noticed. When he'd turned and seen the rows he'd carefully dug were destroyed, he'd noticed.

'He came up on a nearby road, saw me, and made my family an offer we couldn't deny.'

His only attention on having to redo his work, Evrart had not immediately addressed the man on the destrier. But when a sword was pointed at his throat, he'd noticed that, too. Ian of Warstone hadn't asked for loyalty in his employ, he'd taken it.

'By threatening them.'

Evrart nodded. That had been ten years ago. Ten years of hard training, first learning to become a squire and then to gain the skills of a knight. Evrart would never obtain knighthood. That was impossible, but Ian had always gloated he had the training of one.

Years later, when they'd attended court, Evrart had realised how odd it was Ian did not have the usual guard. Years after that, he had come to know why. Ian couldn't threaten noble families as he had Evrart's. He couldn't force their loyalty. And no family with any decency or with any love of their children would allow those children to be raised by Warstones.

No, he had been bought, sold, and with his mother and sister crying, he had entered into Warstone service.

'What of your brothers? Were they not there to protect you?' she asked.

'Yter and Guiot were already gone. Else without a doubt Yter would have volunteered his services in my stead.'

'He's different from you?'

'They are both as large as me. Yter was always restless, loved adventure, and played games only to win.'

'Guiot?'

'He studies things. To me there are rocks…to Guiot there are *kinds* of rocks.'

'Are you close?'

'I have not heard from them in many years. I have never learnt what you have Margery. I do not know letters or writing.'

'I should not have learned either, but I… Well, when I did learn I taught my siblings with a stick and some earth. I could teach you. Perhaps Guiot has learnt by now.'

Was this an indication that she wanted to stay with him? 'I'd like that very much.'

Margery looked at the sky, though she could see only a bit of grey. She was chilled, but not cold, and very little rain fell through the leaves. Some quick walking under the trees would dry her well enough.

'Do you want more berries?' he asked.

'Is there more bread from this morning?'

He nodded, and she went to the pack, dug around until she found the bread and dried meat and handed him some as well.

'The rain is easing,' she said.

'We'll go when it stops. The horses won't be happy to be carrying packs in the rain.'

'Is it much farther?'

'A day—but with the rain, maybe it will take till tomorrow. You'll see many buildings before we get to the centre of the village. My family is on the other side.'

His village sounded larger than the one she'd grown up in. Perhaps in a bustling atmosphere there wouldn't not be so many prying eyes. Maybe a large village meant there were more resources to pay taxes and there wasn't the abject poverty of her village. If Evrart, who was good, came from there, then it must be good.

'If it's only days from Warstone Fortress, what protection does it have?'

He shrugged. 'Protection from the abbey—and, in truth, it's between Warstone holdings.'

'Between?' More Warstones? More intrigue and betrayal? Would she ever escape danger?

'Be at ease. At first, the Warstones didn't own the lands. Once they did, they gave Ian the fortress and kept the other land for themselves. The Warstone parents aren't often there, however.'

'Could they be near now?'

'We should not run into them on this road. I would not have risked it otherwise.'

When she'd left her village, she hadn't thought of risks. She hadn't thought of matters that could be worse than having no food and a mother who hunched while walking. Instead, after Josse, with Roul, and especially with Ian, she'd made matters worse. She'd risked her sister's life, sending that note asking for help.

With Evrart, the risks would be lessened, but only if they were together.

It might be too soon to think of them being together, but her heart couldn't help but hope. He might not have said he loved her, but he had lain with her...he was taking her home to his family.

'If they are spread too thinly, they'll head to Philip's court or Edward's, to reinforce their losses. Certainly when it becomes known that Balthus wants to deed Warstone Fortress to Louve, a no-name, no-blood hired sword, they'll be at court to contest it. Most likely they'll travel to England.'

'Why is that?'

'Because Lord Warstone is English, and they have other matters afoot there.'

Louve was English... 'Is this something to do with why Louve was searching Ian's chests?'

Evrart tensed and rolled his shoulders. 'How much do you know Margery?'

After she'd apologised, her conversation had gone well with her sister, who had been saddened, but not surprised she wanted to leave.

'Nothing—truly. Bied would tell me nothing, and I left it at that.'

Not because she hadn't wanted to know, but because Bied had said it would risk Louve. Margery hadn't asked more. Bied loved Louve, and he loved her. Whatever she could do to protect her sister's happiness, she would.

'Louve truly won't miss you?' she asked.

'I talked to him. If we stay in my village, I will need to travel at odd times and days to the fortress often. They can't trust messages.'

'Is this to do with Ian and...and that scroll in his hand?'

'Everything to do with that.'

'What is "everything", Evrart?'

He looked at her for so very long she didn't know if he'd tell her. Then, 'I may have been his guard, but I don't know everything.'

She immediately wanted to demand what he *did* know. But this was Evrart, and after her last questioning she'd

vowed to trust him more. Could she let his answer stand?
She knew this had something to do with Louve searching Ian's rooms, but she'd let her sister not tell her. She
wanted to fight it now, but was loath to lose this time
they had today. And in truth, didn't she have secrets of
her past she hadn't told him? Maybe patience was key
for them both.

'When you return to Warstone Fortress, will you give
messages to my sister?'

He gave a curt nod. 'You truly are on better ground
with her?'

'We're both stubborn, but she is my sister,' she said.
'The fortress will be odd, though, without an actual Warstone living there. Do you grieve for Ian?'

Evrart exhaled roughly. 'There were times, especially
after he married Séverine and had his two boys, when
I thought he would become a decent man. But after so
much mistrust and betrayal, reason isn't easy to hold on
to. Guy was reported to be the cruellest of all. Reynold left early. And Balthus was much protected by his
mother. I think, in the end, he let his wife and boys go
to keep them safe.'

'But she ran from him. He must have frightened her.'

'He frightened most men.'

'Ian talked in his sleep,' she said. 'He said he loved
her still, but he also wanted to...'

Evrart searched her eyes, and she let him see the answers there that she didn't want to say. To love someone and yet want to harm them... To throw daggers at
brothers and poison servants... She'd thought Josse was
controlling, Roul cruel, but the Warstones and their intrigue were something she wanted no part of.

Was she being a coward not demanding answers from
Evrart? No, not now. She liked this peace between them.

Liked it that she travelled with him and they were able to talk without the prying eyes of guardsmen or servants.

She liked the way his dark brown hair was drying, the hacked-off pieces framing cheekbones and shoulders that were better suited to some mythical giant of old. But all she could envisage was Evrart's impatience and a knife. She hoped before he cut his hair again he'd let her—

What was she thinking?

Pivoting, she strode past the horses. They were talking of Ian and his runaway wife, not of them being together. Not of how she could feel the way his hair grew, remember how it felt under her touch. How she wanted it all again.

Margery kept walking in a circle...around the trees, around the horses. Two of them didn't pay her any mind, but the gentle palfrey kept eyeing her as if she would attack. Maybe she would. She had been uneasy since Ian's death. Would that playful woman who had filled a basket with quinces return, or had he not protected her enough? Had he told her too much of what had happened in the Great Hall?

She wanted to know what Louve had searched for in Ian's room. He suspected it had to do with the legend of the Jewell of Kings. Over the years he'd caught snippets of conversation between Ian and his parents...something of treasures needed. But he had been careful not to listen. That way lay death. He had been certain Ian would kill him if he'd realised he talked aloud of such matters.

If Margery had come across Ian talking of it, it was a miracle she hadn't been killed. Maybe in time they would know. After all, it seemed her sister knew—as did this Louve. But for him, he only wanted to protect Margery, and that meant her not knowing of Warstone matters.

'The rain has ceased,' he said. 'We should leave.'

She stopped her pacing, looked at him in a way he wished he could understand. 'Could we get some more berries before we do?' she asked.

There was a tree that hadn't been plucked clean. She dug in her satchel and pulled out some fabric wrapped in a circular band.

'What's that?' He indicated it with his chin.

'It's a headdress.'

'For what?'

'We have no baskets and I need something to carry the berries.'

'Seems too fine. It'll stain.'

'My clothes are all too fine, and this I cannot wear in public. Roul—' She stopped, frowned. 'All that doesn't matter. We can't pour them into the satchels.'

He eyed the contraption. 'How many berries do you want?'

'As many as you can find.'

It was easy enough picking the berries, since he knew which of them would be ripe. It wasn't easy having Margery at his side, holding up the head covering while he dropped in each find. He swore she purposely kept moving the stiffened fabric around to see if he'd miss.

When she curved her lips, and turned quickly to the side, he determined to keep a better eye on her. Which proved complicated. For one, with the ceasing of the rain the sunlight was filtering through the leaves and casting her in different shades. The shadows played across the curve in her cheek, the fullness of her lips. The sunlight highlighted the fan of her lashes, the grace of her fingers twining around the silken fabric.

This mulberry grove had once reminded him of his

childhood, of kinder times, but he knew it would now remind him forever of how she looked up at him.

'Are there more berries?' she asked.

They would need more since she ate almost as many as he picked.

'Because you have stopped.' She plucked up another.

'Stopped?' Watching her rhythmically chew the berry in her mouth, he felt that tenseness in his shoulders thicken and move lower down his spine.

'You have stopped picking berries.' A small smile, closer to a smirk, curved her lips. 'They're delicious, but they don't have as much of a smell as quince.'

Moving lower yet, that feeling he knew was lust wrapped around his waist and pooled perilously close to where she lifted the basket. To her fingers which flitted along the silken hem. To her lips that were damp with the juice from the berries.

'What colour are they, Margery?' he asked, his voice roughened.

Delight kindled in those eyes of hers. Lavender eyes. As if a mere flower could adequately describe what he saw in their depths.

Scooping a couple of berries out of the fabric, she held them out. 'Compare them.'

His mind was on the curve of her lips, on everything except her words.

'Quiet again?' she teased.

He growled and reached for her.

Laughing, she skipped away. 'Not so quiet, then. Come, Evrart—guess.'

Her eyes darkened, showing him she felt what was between them as well, and he complied.

Grabbing her wrist, he pushed her sleeve up. The berries cradled in her palm were the shade of the skin he revealed there.

'Do you compare these berries to your skin?' He lifted her palm to his mouth and ate the fruit there.

The headdress that had still been clenched in her other hand dropped to the ground. He didn't give a damn about those berries. He cared for the ones he crushed in his mouth as he kissed and nipped her hand. He cared how she tasted as his tongue and his lips brushed against the seam at her wrist. He cared about the sound she made when he did so.

Continuing his kisses up her arm, his other hand pushed the sleeve, applying his thumb to her inner elbow. Holding her still...holding her captive.

'These berries aren't as warm as your skin, nor as sweet,' he said. 'They don't flush when I do this...and this.'

Her free hand, which had hovered, now clasped his upper arm. Pulling her closer, he kissed, licked and nipped her neck.

'These berries don't feel as your skin does. They don't make *me* feel as your skin does.'

Her eyes fluttered. The wrist he held trembled. 'How?'

He caressed her cheek. 'So soft... So soft and yet it heats my blood, my body.'

Her lips parted, and his mouth hovered above hers. 'What colour am I, Margery? What colour would you make me?'

Her eyes opened. Their depths were unfathomable now. 'Everything.'

She was everything. On a groan, he captured those sweet lips, delved with his tongue until he tasted the berries she'd eaten, until he tasted her.

Scooping her up, he held her against him, kept his eyes locked with hers, asking her only, 'Are you showing me colours, Margery?'

A question, but not. He had seen the answer, guessed it when she'd played those games as he'd dropped one berry after the other. Still, much had happened between them since that day in the orchard, and they faced other uncertainties ahead.

Laying her hand on his jaw, she caressed his lower lip with her thumb. So soft, so sweet!

'Show me,' she whispered.

Gladly.

Setting her down, he worked to loosen her gown and push it off her shoulders. He gripped her fine chemise and pulled it over her head, revealing all of her to him. Her flesh pebbled, her nipples tightened, and as he gazed at them they tightened again.

She smiled wide. 'You left my shoes on.'

Gripping his tunic, he said, 'You take care of those.'

Shoving off his breeches, his braies, his eyes never leaving her, he groaned as she bent over. He ripped his boots off and grabbed her, throwing them both off balance as he fell to the ground with her on top of him.

'Your back!'

He could feel the damp earth there, but didn't care—not with the heat of her body against his. He just wanted her. But he needed this time to be gentler.

'I'm being careful...' He brushed his fingers against her neck, where he'd kissed too hurriedly, too much.

Shaking her head, releasing that maddening scent, she said. 'Careful? No. I want you.'

'You have me.'

'No, I want...' She grabbed his arms, dug her fingers in. He felt the bite, felt her need.

'Margery—' He groaned.

'Please, Evrart. I want you as you are. All of you.'

Cupping the back of her neck, he kissed her. Her hands were going to his chest, her legs scrabbling around. He gripped her waist, held her against him. Delved with his tongue deeper, until he had to breathe, had to taste more.

'Like this?' he said.

Turning her over, he pulled at her gown and laid her over it. Spread her hair along the paleness of the sleeve, the blades of the grass. There were colours there, he knew. But they couldn't compare to her.

'I know what colour these are,' he whispered. 'Red.'

Margery murmured against Evrart's kisses. Gripped his hair, let it fan through her fingers, then rubbed her palm against the shaved bits. So many textures to explore...so she did it again.

She felt flushed with heat, with want, as he continued with kisses on her lips, against the shell of her ear, then lower. She tried to pull him to her, to kiss and taste what she could as he moved a shoulder, his chest... Then it became impossible.

'These are red, too, are they not?' His eyes were riveted on her breasts.

She'd always thought them unimaginably small, but with Evrart's gleam of pleasure she knew he did not feel so. Under his gaze they tightened until they ached, and she arched her back, rolled her shoulders against the ground, begged him to end his gaze.

'Red is heat, is it not?'

He captured her nipple in his mouth, swirled his tongue and pulled. Swirled his tongue again and peppered her breast with heated breaths, with tiny licks, before he engulfed the entirety with his mouth and suckled.

'Evrart!' She gripped his head, held him there until she felt that pinch, felt the dampness between her thighs.

He pulled back. Gave her hot, fast kisses down her belly, along her hip, until he sat between her splayed legs. She saw the wicked gleam as he took her in.

Her legs looked tiny around his hips; she tried to pull back. 'I want to touch you.'

He grabbed her ankle, held her still. 'I'm showing you colours, remember?'

'You're showing me?' She swallowed.

'Assuredly.' A victorious grin as he circled her core with one finger, then flicked her nipple with the thumb of his other hand. 'These are the same... I love it when they flush darker.'

He sank one finger into her folds. She moaned.

'I love it that this makes you moan and whimper.'

He bent and kissed one nipple, then the other. Palmed her breast as he pulled back again.

'But this is a bit more, isn't it? It gets darker, redder, wetter...' He swirled that finger and she couldn't take any more.

Grappling for his shoulders, she pulled him down. Planted her feet on the ground and pushed against the little relief he gave her.

'Evrart, stop this showing. Please...' she begged.

When he didn't stop, when he teased her that bit more and pressed his thumb against her clit, making a hard circle, she spasmed.

'What colour are you, Margery?' he asked in a low voice. One that was half a growl, half a plea.

Panting she answered, 'Everything.'

He released his finger and she opened her eyes. The curse on her lips quickly died when he grabbed her thighs and pressed them to her chest. When he made enough room for himself...for them.

No more soft touches or whispered words. He pressed himself forward, impaling her steadily, deeper, until he could move no further and she could take no more.

But she wanted more. Even as Evrart stilled to allow her body to adjust, to accept. Didn't he know she had already accepted him?

Tugging harder on his arms, she pulled him closer yet, and he buried his face in the side of her neck. She felt the hot air of his breath, the low rumble of his growl. Heard his tortured groan as he pulled his hips slowly back.

But she followed him with whatever part of herself he allowed her to use—her mouth, her teeth, her hands, her arms. Her heart. She didn't want to let him go.

His darkened eyes went wide at her sudden franticness and a shudder racked his large frame.

A shiver echoed in her own, and with a curse, Evrart clenched his eyes.

Then she didn't have to think about restraint, or showing, or anything except him.

Chapter Twenty-One

Margery was both grateful and yet not that they rode on separate horses as they entered the village. She missed the strength in Evrart's touch and in his presence against her back as she faced these curious people. She knew that if she'd been surrounded by him she could have pretended speculative gazes weren't looking her way.

And they were looking at her.

Smiling at one of the waving children, she turned to the next and tried to look kind. At least, however, by riding beside him, she might be seen as an equal to this man. Perhaps be respected.

As more greetings were shouted Evrart, in his usual way, was quiet, but there was a light to his eyes that was more joy than sorrow, more calm than wary. It was a look she'd rarely seen, if ever, at Warstone Fortress. His obvious pleasure helped ease her own emotions, which she barely contained. Happiness at being free from the Warstone Fortress was warring with her trepidation at entering the village.

She couldn't help but compare the village where she'd spent her own wreck of a childhood to this. It was larger than her old home, and seemed interconnected with others. One village after another, surrounded by miles of furrowed land. And the abbey in the near distance was beautiful.

Visually, it couldn't be any more different from the mud-laden narrow lanes she remembered. But one thing was the same as in any other place: those curious eyes.

Secluded as she had been for three days with Evrart, she'd forgotten what it was to be stared at. To hear whispers and know the subject was her.

She gave a smile to one person and a small nod to another. This time a mother holding baby. What she didn't do—what she forced herself never to do—was look at the men. Maybe later, when these people knew her better. Maybe…

She hoped with Evrart her life would be different.

The streets became busier and Evrart dismounted, leading the two horses behind him, with her coming up far behind as the crowd thickened.

There were hand gestures and slaps on his back. Many were talking animatedly with Evrart, who increasingly lost more of the tension around his shoulders. Words were leaving his mouth. There were some sounds of joy, and exclamations from little ones who pointed at his height. There were no other men as tall as her Evrart.

Her Evrart.

So many changes since Ian's death, and even more in the three days they'd travelled, when they'd shared much of their lives and even more kisses. Now she was seeing a whole other side to him. One she liked, but wasn't certain of her place with.

Again, she was happy he was back home—but she didn't know these people. They didn't know her. And the advantage of riding a horse whilst Evrart led wasn't favourable. By perception, with her clothes and the horse, with her looks, it would appear she was some fine lady being led by her servant.

Evrart wasn't her servant. He was her…lover. But that was hardly an improvement when it came to the hierarchy here. It neither boded well for Evrart nor herself. Why hadn't they talked of this?

She knew why she hadn't addressed it. Because part of her still believed she wasn't worthy of him, and… and she loved him. But if he didn't return that love, it wouldn't be right to trap him.

They hadn't married because he hadn't asked her, and she hadn't hinted. Now she wished she had—if for nothing else so she knew where she stood, knew who she was to him. Because Evrart was introducing her. There was a grin on his face, and though his gestures were careful, they were not stilted as they had been at the fortress.

She continued smiling, but all the gazes skittered away before throats were cleared and the people returned to talking with Evrart, actively avoiding looking at her. Were they displeased? How would she have felt if her brothers Isnard or Servet had brought home a woman in fine clothing who obviously hadn't worked a day in her life, or at least not recently?

She cursed the gown she had on. What would his family think of her? His family… She didn't know what his home was like, but she knew they must be close as Evrart stepped them along and two women came barrelling around the corner.

One was older, the other noticeably younger than Evrart. Both were large of bone, their hair matching Evart's. When he stepped away and opened his arms, the youngest flew into them.

Something tugged at Margery then. Both nostalgia

and missing her own family, but also trepidation at what it all meant.

She didn't have time to think on it as Evrart pulled them through the crowd and he helped her dismount, right in the centre of everyone. Three boys took the horses away, so she didn't even have them for cover as more eyes looked at her and Evrart. And then, in a voice she hardly heard above the others, he announced she was his Margery, from Warstone Fortress.

She couldn't feel any relief at his proprietorial hand at her back. Or at the way he looked at her as if she mattered. His sister, Peronelle, looked at her with narrowed curiosity. His mother, Blanche, simply said, 'She's small.'

Evrart couldn't recall when he'd felt such lightness. Most likely not since the last time he'd returned home, which had been years before. Ian had loathed letting him see his family. When he had let him go, it had been with a fellow mercenary who would report independently to Lord Warstone on what he'd done.

He had, however, been grateful to be allowed to return to his village when the rest of the guards and mercenaries had not. But although Evrart had been afforded certain liberties they had been burdens as well. Mostly because he'd yearned for the life he had been torn from, and every time he'd gone from home to the fortress, he had been reminded of the bargain he'd made. His family lived, and so he served.

But now he was free, and at his side was a woman whom he adored, whom he intended to spend the rest of his life with. He had shown her that honour by dismounting and pulling her through the village rather than simply going around to the far side, where his family lived. He'd wanted to introduce her to everyone and he had, pleased that he had refrained from marking her neck or other places they could see.

He was also pleased that the places he had kissed roughly, she'd asked him to kiss some more. She liked him—brute that he was. And though he'd vowed to be careful, she didn't want that. She wanted him.

Bringing her home—this moment—was more than he'd dreamed.

He'd smiled so much his jaw was sore, but that hadn't precluded him from smiling all the more when he'd seen his sister run around the corner of the last hut on the path, quickly followed by his mother.

And now they saw the woman he intended to call wife, and his quiet, taciturn mother, who kept her head down and ignored everyone, had actually spoken.

His life could not be happier.

'She's hungry, too—as am I,' he said.

'You're always hungry,' Peronelle said. 'I bet *she* eats nothing.'

He turned to Margery, expecting a full debate on food and her choices. Some competition such as who could eat the most bread rolls or berries. Her happy liveliness, her ability to pull him along with no fear, would be a good match for his sister's cynicism. He swore that Peronelle had been born with a suspicion of life.

But Margery's eyes were dim. Ah… It had been a long journey, and since that moment under the mulberries he hadn't stopped touching her. Stealing as many moments as he could while it was just the two of them.

'Food and perhaps some rest, first,' he said.

'If you'd sent a message ahead of time, we could have prepared,' Peronelle said.

'When have I ever sent a message ahead?'

His sister looked behind him. 'Where are the other guards?'

'No others. There is only Margery and I.'

'Is there something I can do to help?' Margery asked.

'I'm getting to it!' Huffing, Peronelle turned to him. 'Is she always so impatient?'

Frowning fiercely, his mother grabbed Peronelle's arm.

He turned to Margery. 'I must apologise for my sister. She likes it when I travel with the guards, for they know to bring her gifts.' He leaned over to whisper in her ear. 'I'll explain later.'

Margery rubbed her hands along her skirts. She wasn't certain she wanted Evrart to explain *anything* later. She wished the horses hadn't been taken away. Not that she could safely ride one, but she was terrified enough to give it a try. Her doubts on their relationship and about her own worth were quickly turning to dismay. Had she made a mistake coming here? It was as if his mother had looked at her and known she wasn't good enough for her son.

'Where are our things?' she asked.

Evrart shrugged. 'They'll bring them by soon enough.'

Who would bring them by? She'd thought he had grown up as she had. In poverty and desperation. But this village wasn't poor…these people had sturdy clothing and happy expressions.

'Do you have servants?'

He chuckled.

But what villager helped other villagers? When her mother had crumpled and fallen into herself, when their father had left, no one had helped her siblings with their land, their home or their taxes. When it had got truly bad, a neighbour had bargained with her sister. They'd be allowed to use his oxen if he was granted *favours*.

Her brothers...what they had suffered! And Mabile. She had married early, but that had provided little care, for she'd had babies so soon...when she was barely old enough. And Margery had worn torn clothing and shoes that had been handed down until they were more holes than any leather or cloth.

'Come, let me show you my home. It is not much, but there are some separate rooms. My brothers and I demanded it when Peronelle was born.' He grabbed her hand. 'You're cold.'

She was freezing.

'Margery...?'

She squeezed his hand. 'I'm well.'

'Maybe some rest.'

He tugged, and she followed.

Many of the villagers had returned to their homes; only a few lingered in the lanes. It was easy to guess Evrart's home. The thick roof was by far the tallest. Still, Evrart bent his head in the doorway and stepped a few feet in.

The square room contained a kitchen and a thick oak table with benches. At each end of the room were other openings. Blanche and Peronelle were nowhere in sight.

'You have doors,' she said.

His gaze was quizzical. 'They have rooms behind them, too.'

This wasn't the same; this wasn't the same at all.

She had grown up in one square room where they'd all slept together. If Biedeluue or Mabile had ruined dinner, their eyes had burned all night with the smoke.

Panic sweeping her, she felt the small of her back prickle with sweat. Evrart's past life hadn't been like hers, with cold winters and no blankets. He'd had family, and doors, and villagers.

Holding her hand, Evrart dragged her to the room on the right. 'This one is occupied.'

The room was large, with three massive beds and nothing else but foot boards where she imagined clothes were hung. It was plain, but far nicer than anything she'd had growing up. The wooden slats were tight, the daub and wattle thick. The room felt secure, with nary a draft.

Across two of the beds were clothes, and various lavender and rosemary branches. There also appeared to be some unwashed dishes. The third bed was unmade, with the quilt partially on the floor. It was a disaster.

But the freedom of such abundance only made her hands clammy. She had known she was different from him, but she'd counted on their past being some commonality. This wasn't the same. Now what did she share with him? She couldn't think!

'Let's see the other.'

Releasing her hand, he walked around her. Stepped through the living area to the other door. He glanced in and stepped back. 'That is still my mother's. You didn't see a large tub in the other room, did you?'

She saw everything else, but not that.

'I didn't see it leaning outside either. No matter—we'll have Peronelle move.'

As if conjured up, the front door banged open and his sister and mother entered. Margery jumped.

'The meat and potatoes are still roasting and not nearly done.' Peronelle turned her full glare on Margery. 'You'll have to wait.'

Of course she would wait. Did Evrart's sister think she would stamp her foot and demand food? Did they think her vain and spoiled!

'That is good,' she said, trying to keep her voice as friendly as she could. 'There will be time for us to talk.'

'As if I have time for that,' Peronelle said. 'Azamet killed some chickens—they'll need plucking and draining—and Mama needs to wash the clothes.'

Margery drew herself up. She could do this. It couldn't be as bad as she feared. It was simply returning to a village that had caused this frenzied tension inside her. 'If you show me where to go, I'm sure I could help. When I was a child I—'

Peronelle made a scoffing sound. 'In those clothes?'

Margery felt her loud dismissiveness as if it was a blade. His mother frowned in their direction. She was certain it was aimed at her.

'Tomorrow is a much better day for all that,' Evrart said.

Blanche turned to her. 'You rest.'

Margery didn't want to rest. If she rested she'd feel useless again.

Peronelle went to her room. 'Why is the door to my room open?'

Evrart crossed his arms. 'That's my room. And where's my tub?'

Peronelle shrugged. 'It was too big, and you were gone.'

'How am I to bathe if it's gone?'

'Like everyone else. Outside.'

Evrart looked at his mother.

'Peronelle...' Blanche said.

Peronelle flinched, but quickly rallied. 'Why does he think he's better than anyone else and gets to bathe in private? And why is she ousting me from my room?'

Margery looked to Evrart. The tub they could find or build, but didn't he understand that if he said nothing she'd have no position in this house? Her vision narrowed and she felt ill. This was like her own village, except there would be no chance of accepting Josse. No making a decision to help her family and help herself. She'd chosen Evrart, who seemed blind as to what was happening around him.

'I don't need your room,' she said. 'I'll help with the chickens, and we'll resolve where I sleep later.'

'We won't,' Evrart said. 'There's nothing to be resolved. We'll move Peronelle's things now, and then when our supplies arrive from the stalls we'll have a place to put them.'

Blanche gazed at her son as if she'd never seen him before. What was going on here?

'You can't move my things!' Peronelle said.

Evrart growled. 'We're resting *now.*'

'No!' Margery said, much louder and more desperately than she'd intended. But she *was* desperate. If she stood there much longer, she'd faint or be sick. 'I can sit in the chair, here by the fire. Or maybe I can check on the firepits outside and stir some pots.'

Peronelle eyed Margery's hands, and linked her arm with her mother's. 'We'll take care of the food, since you're obviously too hungry to wait.'

Evrart uncrossed his arms and exhaled slowly as they left and turned out of sight. 'She's grown since I last saw her.'

Was that the reason he was giving for her being rude? That she was growing? Her family had always struggled, but with three girls they'd had to work together more often than argue.

They'd left so much danger and uncertainty back at the fortress, and for three days they'd wrapped themselves up while Evrart had told her stories of his childhood here. She had been looking forward to her life in this village. But those thoughts had been dreams, which left her with this…nightmare.

'While they take care of the food, let's move her things to the other room,' he said.

'Maybe we shouldn't.' Margery was the youngest, but she remembered the arguments between Bied and Mabile. They'd always mended matters because they were sisters. Margery didn't want to cause any injury when she wasn't certain of her place here.

Evrart stopped in his tracks. 'I'm not sleeping anywhere else.'

Her heart filled, then warmed. The restlessness in her eased. He did care about her. Maybe she was simply tired…maybe her time in the fortress was skewing her perceptions. Tomorrow Evrart would be here, defending himself and her against his sister. She'd get an opportunity to talk with his mother, who had at least frowned at her daughter. Tomorrow it would be better.

They'd partly cleared the room before she realised that although Evrart had claimed the room, he hadn't truly included her.

Chapter Twenty-Two

Evrart eyed the field. 'Are there more stones than last I was here?'

Azamet, his friend since they could first tie their boots, gazed at the sky and rocked on his heels.

'You cleared your field and dumped them here,' Evrart said.

'They were to be gone before you next returned,' Azamet said. 'Didn't expect you back so soon.'

So soon…

It would be almost two years since he'd returned. Some of the village had stayed the same, but there were improvements to be noted. The biggest change was in Peronelle, whom he knew had entered some terrible time in a female's life that he didn't want to examine too closely. Never a happy child, she was now almost a woman…and she might be spoiled.

After days here, he'd expected Margery to say something to her by now. But Margery wasn't the same. He'd thought what was between them had been all set to rights when they'd shared berries, when she'd asked if he wanted to pick some.

He should have known that was unusual. His Margery would have simply demanded he pick them, not asked if he wanted to.

He had felt so joyous to be holding her again, he hadn't noticed those subtle differences. And when they'd entered the village, she'd grown so quiet, her eyes too wide. She hadn't looked that fearful...*ever*.

He'd shrugged that off as well, thinking she was tired, but days had gone by and that look hadn't left her. Could it be she didn't like it here?

He'd expected to offer marriage to her by now. He wanted at least to ask her, but now he was unsure if she wanted him in any way. At night, however, when all was dark and quiet, she curled up against him. It wasn't the same as under the mulberry canopy. He lay there but didn't hold her, and she never did anything. Just leaned into him as if she needed his support. So he gave it to her.

His mother, bless her, had given him time and the room. Quiet as she was, he could tell she was as happy as he was that he was home. When he'd told her he didn't need to return to Warstone Fortress tears had fallen and she'd patted his hand. Such affection from his reserved mother had been so overwhelming he'd almost hugged her, as Margery would have done.

Picking up another stone, he threw it to the pile he'd created. He'd propose to her soon—he'd tell her his intentions since he'd already told her his feelings. But how? And what woman would accept him, with his past, if he had nothing to offer? Building a home for them would take time, and his field was strewn with stones. The soil was good underneath, though. Crops would take a while... But he didn't want to wait. He wanted his Margery.

He remembered how, when he was young, he'd imagined working side by side with his wife in this very field. But Margery, with her tiny frame and soft hands out here, in this field with more stones than soil? *Never*. He would show his worth to her and protect her from this toil as well.

'I'll see you later tonight?' Azamet said.

Evrart bit back a growl.

'For some fine ale?' Azamet said, his voice a bit weaker.

Azamet wasn't much taller than Margery. As a boy, Azamet had shadowed Evrart, and as such he'd always been protective. Well, no longer. His duties were to another.

'We will clear this field together,' Evrart threatened. 'And if you don't want to be here as dawn breaks over tomorrow, you will acquire others to help as well.'

This day was no different from the last. Margery tried to help, was rebuffed, tried to be friendly, but was ignored, and when she tried to disappear was scorned.

Well, not verbally scorned, or rebuffed, or ignored. But Evrart's mother had a multitude of looks—none of which she could understand. Sometimes she looked almost friendly and smiled, but when Margery started a conversation, the woman would just stare at her. Which led her to believe again she'd disagreed with her son's choice for a lover.

All her life she'd protected herself from people, and here she was being battered about by Evrart's family. She had begged Evrart to travel to his village, and along the way with his childhood tales, she'd thought she knew how living here would be for them. Now it felt as if she'd been picked up and placed somewhere she wasn't meant to be.

And she'd tried to get past this feeling of doubt, because she'd sold her virtue to Josse and then Roul. But seeing Evrart in his home, with all the goodness of this village and all the love of his family, she knew he deserved better than her.

She'd tried to talk of it in the garden, but he had dismissed it. She'd let it go. Her question then had been whether he kept her in the dark to protect her, or if he was simply unused to conversing. Now she realised she shouldn't have let it go. She wondered if she had been wrong about everything when it came to this man. Maybe he didn't keep quiet to protect her but because he thought she wasn't worthy. How could a whore be worthy?

And Peronelle!

Margery was used to people gaping at her. Oddly, she was grateful she wasn't being treated as if she was something better because of her colouring. But she missed her own family. She missed being able to talk of matters like this. She wished, not for the first time, Evrart had said something of the guards bringing his sister gifts. She would have brought something from the fortress.

She'd offered Peronelle some of her ribbons, and even the headdress which hadn't stained. Peronelle had merely turned her back on them and asked what she would use them for.

She agreed with Peronelle. They were useless. And if she was to be more helpful to Evrart, if she was to stay, she'd need more serviceable clothes. Why hadn't she thought of that?

With certainty she wouldn't ask any of the women in this village to swap. They'd look at her clothes just as she did and see uselessness. Maybe there was something nearer the abbey.

'Is there a market near, where I could find some wool or linen weave?' she asked.

Peronelle stepped through the bedroom doorway, looked her over, then looked at the satchels they had brought full of clothing. 'You do not have enough clothes?'

That was not what she meant. 'I thought I could find something more...'

'More village-like?' Peronelle said.

'I used to live in a village. I still have family there.'

'But you left it, so you must not have liked it.'

Arguing with her would solve nothing. 'Please, Peronelle, where can I purchase some fabric for clothing?'

'And fill up my room with more of your things when you'll be leaving here soon enough? I hope not.'

Margery's heart plummeted. Leaving? Was Evrart wanting her gone or was it simply his sister? She'd had enough of not knowing and asking herself these questions. She needed to talk to him!

'Where is Evrart now?'

Peronelle shrugged.

Margery looked at Blanche, sitting in a padded chair in the corner. She was mending clothes. A heaped basket was beside her.

Over the last few days this was what Blanche mostly had been doing. Sitting in the corner, never saying a word, while people brought her baskets of clothes to mend.

Margery knew Evrart's mother should have been the one to answer her question. Certainly, a woman who needed thread would know where there was fabric. If she hadn't wanted to get up from her seat, she could have called out. Instead, she had allowed her daughter to enter the room and announce that her son would be sending her away.

And Evrart. Up at dawn...back when it was almost

dark. He was busy with something, but when she asked, he merely said he was taking care of the land.

He looked so pleased to be here—how could she complain about his mother and sister? She wouldn't. But they couldn't go on like this. It wasn't fair to him or to his family. Or to her.

Why didn't he merely say what he was doing? Was he deceiving her? She knew he didn't actually lie, but he had never told her everything. He'd told her amusing stories of his youth, but they'd been simple. They hadn't let her know he was from such a fine family, who with one glance had known that she was not.

And if Evrart never stood up for her, she would never be accepted. 'Where is he?'

Blanche looked up and frowned at Margery's gown. 'Fields.'

The fields—of course. Even years out of the village, she hadn't truly forgotten. It was just…well, she'd never done that…worked in the fields. Hadn't because Biedeluue had done it, and then, when Bied had left, and she'd grown old enough to be productive at harvesting, Josse had ridden by.

'You're going to go to the fields?' Peronelle said.

'You are busy with food, and your mother with mending. I'd like to help, too.'

'In those shoes?'

They were the only shoes she had. 'I suppose I'll need the cordwainer as well…'

'A cordwainer! First you want new clothing—now new shoes. Will you never be satisfied?'

Margery blinked at the tears that threatened. She looked at Blanche, whose eyes seemed to have softened, and saw that she gave a nod of encouragement. But how could she tell if she was being kind to Peronelle or to

her, when her eyes were so full of tears and everything
was blurry?

She'd been a burden to her family, and what skills had
she gained so she would not be a burden here?

She'd left the fortress because she hadn't fitted there,
and now she was even more out of place here. This—
being here and not fitting in, being a burden—was why
she should have protected herself. There she'd been, demanding Evrart protect and defend himself from Ian,
when it was her who shouldn't have included Evrart
in her heart. Because of *course* he'd have family, and
friends, and villagers who adored him. And how could
she—worthless, useless—defend herself to all of them?

Once she had attempted to explain to Evrart about
her worthlessness, but he'd brushed her off. No more.

Firming her resolve, she said. 'Point me in the direction of the fields.'

Peronelle pointed at the opposite wall. Margery didn't
dare ask for anything else.

Chapter Twenty-Three

Margery found Evrart easily enough. Following Peronelle's pointed direction, there weren't many turns until she came to an open field she hadn't explored before.

Evrart wasn't the only man in the field. Many men were rolling rocks or conversing. But he was the only one she noticed.

His back to her, he was unhinging some oxen, lifting the tackle and putting it in a cart beside him. It being a warm day, he wore only his breeches and heavy boots. His tunic was off, and his skin gleamed with sweat and dirt. He was dressed as most of the men were dressed, but Evrart stood out from all of them.

It wasn't his size; it was him.

It was the ease with which he handled the beasts and the apparatus.

As much as she'd admired him in the lists…as many hours as she'd watched him wield a sword or some other weaponry…it hadn't been *him*. She realised why now. It was the fact there had been walls around him, that there had been men who worked against, not together, with him.

He belonged out here, with the elements and the ease of camaraderie.

Which made what Ian had done to him all the worse. All those battles he'd fought, the scars on his legs... All the dead bodies he'd had to drag around and this man was still good. Useful. Kind.

She didn't belong here; she didn't belong to him.

When they'd been at the fortress, she'd known her past separated them. And though his future wasn't with the Warstones now, it was here, he should be away from her all the same.

She deserved none of this. Not the blue sky, not the friendly faces, not the man who made her mouth go dry with want and her heart hammer with so much love and need.

She deserved nothing!

And he needed to know this.

He needed to know—except the field was saturated with mud, swathes of water, and Evrart was on the other side.

No more being a coward.

A step...two.

Her foot got stuck and she pulled it out. She stumbled and her other foot stuck. Still too much space between them.

Two more steps... Enough!

'I made my sister lie with neighbours so I could have blankets thick enough for winter,' she called out. 'Me, not her—and not my sister Mabile either. No, by the time the taxes were paid and there was some food on the table there was just enough coin to purchase the wool for blankets that went to *me*.'

Evrart stopped wrapping the rope that hung from his hands and around his shoulders. Stopped midway. So did everyone else around them.

She stumbled a few more steps towards him and lost a shoe.

'I don't care if you make the argument that I was only eight,' she said. 'I did much worse before then. The first terrible thing I ever did was be born. I broke my mother and became a burden to my siblings, who could barely feed themselves.'

There was whispering off to her left, and Evrart's shoulders slumped, but he didn't let go of the rope and he didn't move towards her either. It was as she deserved.

'You know they had to stop their work to find me? I'd be stolen away by other families, and my mother's breasts would be leaking, but what did I care? Some other mother had me at her breast. I was fed, comforted. But my mother suffered. My brother Isnard told me it used to send her into laments. It only became worse, and then she lost her reason because of me. My brothers and sisters lost their father, too, because he left soon afterwards.'

She knew these things, she'd lived them, but her voice, the very breath she panted through her lungs, didn't sound or feel like hers.

Some of the men were dropping stones around her and leaving the field. Off to the side she saw others ushering their young ones away. Evrart stood still, his arms in the same position.

She stepped again and her gown dragged against the puddles. She fisted it tighter. If she'd just listened to reason and protected herself she could have avoided the villagers' stares, avoided Evrart knowing how terrible she was. But there was no hope for it; she'd do it now and be done. Tell him everything and be on her way.

She took a wider step and lost her other shoe.

'At some point even all the sacrifices my sister made to save me weren't enough. Bied had to leave the village to work elsewhere. One village after another…she never could stay in one place. But it didn't matter. She had to go farther and farther away, and we…we had to wait for the coin to borrow oxen. And the waiting…'.

The furrows in the field allowed her to walk on mounds and she was almost to him now. Close enough that she could see his expression, but she still didn't know what he thought of her screeching like this.

'I thought you were poor. I thought when Ian stole you that it was a way for you and your family to survive.' She heaved in an uneven breath. 'When I was stolen… when I agreed to earn coin for my body…it was to survive. You…you should never have left here. This place is good—like you. I don't belong. Why did you bring me here?'

Stumbling a few more steps, she righted herself. And then he was right there. Unmoving. Uncaring…?

This. This was what had been bothering his Margery. Her past. Evrart had vowed to protect her in the future, and yet he hadn't known it was her past that was affecting them now. Why had he brought her here? Because he was desperate to share his life with her.

But…

That meant sharing their lives, and he'd been quiet for far too long. All he knew was this vocal woman had gone quiet, too. And that couldn't be borne. He was a fool not to have realised it earlier.

'What else?'

Out of breath, she huffed. 'What?'

He tossed the rope which was around his shoulders into the cart. It made an awful clang and he waited until it ceased. 'Tell me the rest; all of it.'

Blinking, she swallowed hard. 'Bied was gone and our family was still struggling. My brothers worked until their fingers bled. I was harvesting one day when strangers rode through. They were always riding past the fields, and I hardly took any notice, but I was foolish and tired and I used the road to return home. It had been raining and the fields were bogs, the road was easier—but it was also easier for Josse to spot me...or rather the back of my head. I wore a head covering, but it was the end of the day and some of my hair had escaped. He slowed, and I could feel his eyes upon me, but I refused to look up. I knew what would happen if I looked up. Then he pulled his horse right in front of me, so I stopped. He asked for directions, and I gave them to him.'

He hadn't wanted directions. She knew that now. But maybe a part of her had then, too.

'You looked up,' Evrart said.

She nodded. 'I did. And then I thought I could go on my way. But he dismounted, and immediately asked for my family.'

This Josse of Tavel might have had means beyond Margery's family, but Evrart had never heard of him so he had to be of low rank and wealth.

'You went with him.'

'He went to my mother first, and when she was incoherent he went to Servet and Isnard. Josse had coin on him. A whole purse of it. They—'

'Your brothers sold you.'

'I agreed to it. He had no wife, only children grown. He was much older, and indulgent in ways that I benefited from. It wasn't...terrible. But then Josse lost me at a game of knucklebones! I was not upset. I had no feelings for the man. I didn't, however, know Roul.'

'I do.' Evrart could give her this secret...tell her this much. 'Ian visited him many times. I travelled with him on some of those occasions.'

'I never saw you,' she said. 'I hid when people came. I was hiding that night. It was long past time for bed… I thought it was safe. Why didn't he kill me?'

Evrart wanted to sweep Margery into his arms and never have the world touch her again, but he knew better.

Part of him wanted to do harm to both Josse and Roul for taking advantage of a situation they could have helped in other ways.

All of him was proud and in awe of how brave Margery had been.

'He should have killed me,' she said. 'I was no more or less than the woman in the corridor he *did* kill.'

Evrart hadn't protected her from any of this, and from the look of her hands, clenched in front of her, from her trailing shoes and dragged gown, he shouldn't have tried. They needed to share their burdens.

'I interrupted his…scheme,' she said. 'He had a dagger at her throat, and in her hand was a scroll. I don't know if I heard any words. All I saw was the knife.'

'You told him this?' he said. And at her nod, he added, 'He believed you?'

'I don't think he believed me. He just…had this interested expression. I thought he was like other men and wanted to lie with me, but he didn't. I should be dead. Not here. Not harming your family, or annoying your sister, or disappointing your mother.'

She'd used that word. *Interested*. Something unlocked inside his chest. The rest of her words could wait. This wasn't about his mother or sister. It was about them. *She* was his family, and he needed to let her know it. By talking.

'I am grateful that you stand before me.'

She shook her head. 'I'm a mistress. I've done…

seen…terrible things. I didn't even try to help that woman. I can't be with someone like you.'

He rolled his shoulders, winced. 'I could have told you that.'

On a gasp, she turned, but her gown got stuck in the mud. Good, because he didn't want her going anywhere.

'Where are you doing?' he asked.

She pulled on the hem to release it. Mud splattered her cheeks. Her hands were coated and misshapen with drying mud.

'My leaving is the best course now.' She freed one side of her gown, worked on the other.

'You think after all this time I am worthy of you?' he said.

She stopped pulling, but didn't raise her head.

'I told you I carried the steward out of the hall, glad that his death was fresh,' he said. 'Why should I care if a death was fresh?'

She didn't move, and he admired the mud in her hair, across her cheek. He anticipated the moment when he'd be able to brush those flakes away with his touch and his kisses…if she'd allow it.

'I cared because early in my training with Ian I had to kill a man. I was sick afterwards, and the Warstone wasn't pleased with my weakness.'

Margery slowly straightened. Her cheeks were whiter than usual, but her eyes stayed with him.

'We had to leave, and he had me carry that man on my back. Do you know what happens to a body an hour or two after death? His waste ran down my backside and over my legs. Ian forced me to carry him further yet.'

'Don't—' she said, blinking rapidly, her eyes sheened with emotions. 'You don't have to say any more.'

'These are my words to you. That's how I've been

with you: quiet. I thought I was protecting you, but I wasn't. You've been wanting to tell me these things and I've been denying you. Now you think I'm some person who is above you in every way, but I'm not.'

He took a breath, scanned the field, grateful that the villagers had left to give them time.

'I am certain I ended the life of innocent men, Margery. I never harmed women or children, and I tried to discern or choose my deeds, but in the end I truly couldn't. You think you have no worth. But you're standing before a man who has murdered people.'

Her eyes were wide, and the tears that had pooled slid down, but she stayed quiet.

'You're making me talk,' he said. 'You do know how difficult this is for me?'

She nodded, the tears dropping hard.

'Your tears are more difficult to take,' he said.

Giving a shaky smile, she said, 'Sorry.'

'We were both stolen from our lives, Margery. Both of us because of what we look like. You for your beauty. Me because of this great brute of body.'

'Don't… I like… You're beautiful, too,' she said.

'You're a mess,' he said.

She plucked at her skirts, waved her hand around her hair. 'I know, but so are you.'

He looked at his chest, his breeches, and wanted to laugh.

She raised her hands to her face, looked at her hands and grimaced. 'What *is* this place?'

Were they ready to talk of all his mistakes when it came to her? The villagers had given them privacy, and Margery stood in front of him still, though he had told her some of his past. So he guessed they were.

'It's my family's land.'

'This is where you've been going every day?'

He kicked the dirt. 'It's been too long dormant, and needs to be made good again.'

'Why didn't you tell me?'

'Because it's a wreck.' He inhaled. 'Because I felt worthless for not protecting you from this.'

'Protecting me from what? Working this land? But I want to. I don't want to be protected any more. Not from my own actions or from you. From anyone.'

'I understand that now. You don't do well if secrets are withheld from you.'

Her eyes narrowed. 'What secrets are being withheld from me?'

Rolling his shoulders, he jerked his neck until it cracked, watched her eyes ease from suspicion to amusement.

'A lifetime's worth,' he said. 'And they not only have to do with me and my past, but Ian's as well. They have to do with what Louve was searching for in that room. And what Ian's parents are after. I don't know it all, or how much of it can even be true, but I'll tell you.'

'Is it along the same matters that my sister knows?'

'Most likely,' he said. 'It's about legends and treasures.'

'Oh...' She laughed low. 'So nothing important, then?'

'Not to us,' he said, and realised it was true.

None of it had to affect them. Louve wanted him to return often, to ensure the fortress stayed out of Warstone hands, but other than that they were free. And he was free to tell her. To make it better between them.

'Ian...his parents...all the Warstones are looking for the Jewell of Kings.'

Her quick smile just as quickly dropped. 'Your expression! You mean this in truth?' At his nod, she added,

'But it's a legend…a story for children. No one can truly believe that whoever has the gem can make kings, can rule Scotland.'

'Not only do they believe it, they're in pursuit of it. It's an ugly green gem hidden in a dagger. Ian knows where the gem is, and for a time the Warstones had the dagger, but it was lost again. Ian believed it was switched by some thief. Someone no one can determine. This fact alone consumed Ian in the last days of his life. That's what he sent me out to get that last trip away from you. Reynold, Balthus, Ian, their parents, the King of England…all are after that dagger.'

'Who has the gem?'

'Some clan from Scotland. I think Ian, or at least his parents, had been attempting to steal it, but mostly it's the dagger. They need both. One is no good without the other.'

'You knew all this?'

'I knew bits, and in the last days Ian divulged more… accidentally.'

Because his reason had been slipping. 'His schemes and games were all for this? That scroll with a message? That woman he killed? All was so they could have an ugly gem?'

'There's more—and this part I am uncertain of, but I think your sister and Louve are involved in finding a parchment,' he said. 'Some further information that when combined with the gem and dagger would lead to treasure.'

'And the Warstones and the King of England want this treasure?'

'Very much. They have wealth, Margery, but if the rumours are true that kind of treasure could break countries.'

'And kill many people along the way,' she said. 'This is why my sister didn't want me to know. Everyone seems to be protecting someone.' She looked away, nodded to herself. 'It hardly seems as if it can be true, but it makes a certain sense now. Ian did like his messages...'

'He did.'

'I should let you know I've done some things to protect you, too,' she said.

He blinked.

'While Louve searched the rooms, I begged Biedeluue to keep an eye on you.'

'You assigned your sister to protect me?'

'She's fierce.'

He grinned. 'It appears to be a family trait.'

'I thought it prudent to protect you, given you're such a terrible swordsman.'

'Margery,' he growled, 'I'm a very good swordsman. *Very* good.'

'Doesn't mean you won't get defended by me or protected. You're worth defending, Evrart, and...' Margery thought, and then remembered. 'And I'm to keep you safe! And if this pursuit of this legend, or this gem, or treasure affects us, then I'll do whatever it takes. I'll protect you and that's all you need to know. Just no secrets.'

He shook his head. 'No secrets. And we'll share more of these words tonight in bed, when it's quiet.'

'Sounds...perfect.'

It did, and he marvelled at what fate had brought them. But maybe it wasn't fate. Ian's unusual words kept ringing in his ears.

'I think, after all this, that I know why Ian didn't kill you,' he said. 'Ian liked his games, and it's probably not the truth, but I'm going to believe it to be so.'

* * *

It was the bemusement on Evrart's face Margery couldn't let go of. After all the words they'd said to each other, all the dark memories they'd shared, his confused delight eased every dark corner of her heart.

When she'd stumbled across the field she had expected rejection. And yet he'd accepted her. He always had accepted her because of his own life. He hadn't wanted to talk of her past because he hadn't wanted to tell her about his. They still didn't know everything, but it was enough for now.

This was a good village, with kind people, but he had been stolen away from it, like her, and it had formed the way they were. Except despite their darkness Evrart was almost smiling—which was a sight she loved. He had a secret he wanted to tell her, and yet he was nervous.

'Tell me,' she said.

'He saved you for me,' he said. 'He brought you into the courtyard and said it would be "interesting". He meant you.'

Evrart looked behind her and smiled again before he returned his warm gaze to hers.

'I could never tell if Ian was good or bad. My instinct feared him, but he did odd things. Like marrying Séverine and having those boys. I thought he took them away for cruelty, but I wonder if he did it to save them. And I think he saved you for me.'

Her heart was breaking, and building, and breaking again.

She placed a hand there, just to hold it in. 'Evrart...'

What were the ways of a man who loved and hated? Who was cunning and beyond all reason? Except hadn't Ian said words to her that were almost the same—that he had other purposes for her, but he was running out of time. Could this be? Yes, if they let it.

'I think it's true,' she said. 'You are for me.'

'How could he have known it?'

'Do I look like other women you have liked?'

'How would I know?' He shook his head. 'I like it that you forget…that you don't think I'm flawed.' He frowned. 'Do you think we can let go of Warstones and their intrigues? That we can talk of it, but not be in the middle of it all. For now, whilst we can?'

For them, it wasn't about all that she had been told, it was about how much she trusted—and for once she did, and fully. She trusted Evrart with everything.

'For now,' she said. 'But if some defending has to be done…'

'We'll do it,' he answered. 'Now, turn around.'

She didn't want to. Because he kept looking behind her, and that meant there were people there. When she'd started telling him of her life, she'd thought he'd be so disgusted he'd let her leave, and she wouldn't have to face others.

'For someone who doesn't like to talk, you certainly are demanding,' she said.

'You'll want to see this.'

No, she wouldn't. But if she wanted to stay that meant facing a lot of truths.

Forcing herself, she looked over her shoulder. The field was thankfully empty, except for two people standing shoulder to shoulder, almost within touching distance.

Blanche and Peronelle. How much had they heard?

'So this is it?' Peronelle said.

'It is.' Evrart laid his hand on her shoulder.

Margery liked having his strength and presence at

her back again. She wanted to pat his hand in return, but hers were covered with mud.

'You don't even love her,' Peronelle said.

Evrart exhaled and ruffled her hair. 'Not love her? I would die for her. I almost did.'

'You didn't marry her. How come you didn't marry her if you love her?' Peronelle said.

Margery cringed. It was true—and something the village no doubt talked about.

'I haven't married her because I didn't want it to be in the Warstone chapel. Not with that chaplain...not with those funerals just done.'

He said it so simply. So easily.

She looked up at him. 'You want to marry me?'

His eyes swung to hers, and he stared at her as if she'd grown two heads.

'Peronelle, Mama, could you give us a moment?'

'Again!' Peronelle flounced away, but she was smiling as if she'd won something. 'I don't know what you intend to do with her.'

'What I intend is none of your concern. Now, go.'

'Welcome to the family, Margery,' Peronelle said with a wink. 'When you get new shoes, I want some too.'

Blanche held up the muddy ones that she must have pulled from the field, smiled, and then grabbed Peronelle's arm to propel her off the ruined field.

Now that she'd turned around, Margery could see some of the other villagers hiding behind walls and corners. Could they see how stunned she was?

Evrart turned her around. 'What is it?'

'Your mother...she smiled at me.'

'She likes you.'

'Likes me? She did pick up my shoes, but there's no

indication that she'll give them back—and how will I know when she says nothing to me?'

Evrart shook his head, as if she was woefully wrong. 'How many words do you think my mother has ever said to me? My mother smiles, pats, but hardly says a word. That's just her way. That was my way until you forced me to be a man who chatters.'

'"A man who chatters"?' Margery giggled.

'I remember being quiet with you until I realised I couldn't just give an order and you'd follow it. That being near you required *words*.'

He said it as if it had been some arduous task.

'So when she said I was small…?'

'You *are* small,' he said.

'And when we arrived and she ordered me to rest?'

'Didn't I mention you were tired?'

Perhaps. 'So your mother…?'

'Is full of joy that you're here.'

'Your sister, however… Although she winked at me.'

'Full of mischief—as are all children at fourteen years.'

Margery gaped. She had known Peronelle was young, but she towered…

Evrart just nodded, as if he knew her thoughts. 'It's because we're tall. Everyone believes we're older than we are.'

He wasn't! 'How old are you?'

His eyes crinkled. 'Old enough.'

And now he had a sense of humour… 'We have just argued. Terribly.'

He smiled. 'We have, and I was hoping for it. You haven't been yourself and I should have seen that. Can you forgive me?'

'Forgive you?'

'I shouldn't have brought you here; you probably hate villages like this.'

'Mine wasn't anything like yours. I didn't know people and neighbours could be so kind.'

'Or so curious?'

'They are trying to hide,' she said. Her neighbours would have taken advantage of the argument. Interjected and made it worse. 'There might be more arguments.'

'I have no doubt,' he said. 'We spent days together under the worst kind of strain, with Ian of Warstone, your being held captive, your sister out to rescue you, the poisoned ale... We needed to have words. And then there's you...'

Evrart's tone was still light, but was he implying...? 'Are you saying I'm the cause of our argument?'

'You're not the silent type.'

If she could put her face in her hands, she would. If she could hide for years, she would. 'I can't believe I did that!'

'Can't believe you told the entire village you love me?'

She thought back on that treacherous walk. 'That's not what I said.'

'Margery, if you had seen your face, and the fact you were so determined to get to me... Let me assure you— you told them you love me. I was so stunned I couldn't feel my legs or move them. I'm thankful my friends departed and let us get on with the declaring.'

He had been stunned. *That* was the reason he hadn't met her halfway when she had been ranting across the field.

'You told Peronelle you loved me,' she said.

'I told you as well.' His brows drew in as he took in her confusion. 'You asked me if I had feelings for you, and I told you I did.'

She blinked. 'You said—'

His brows rose and he huffed. 'When I said I felt every feeling for you, how could that not mean love?'

Evrart had declared to her back at the Warstone Fortress he loved her. All this time she had been a coward, full of doubt and worry, and all she'd had to do was ask him what he meant.

It appeared she had some lessons to learn on talking as well. Maybe they'd learn together.

'So this is it? We'll live here, where you spent your childhood, and I'll help you in the fields?'

'If you want,' he said. 'But we'll be needing a bigger, separate home.'

'Peronelle will like that.'

'*I'll* like it just to stop her asking when we're leaving.'

'Have you talked to her about leaving?'

Evrart shrugged. 'Perhaps.'

Margery wanted to laugh. She'd thought when Peronelle had said she would be leaving soon it would be only her. And his mother was simply quiet like her son. Oh, so much she didn't know!

'I like your mother,' Margery said. 'I do. If some woman dressed like me, with ties to Warstone, had come into my home to snatch my son I'd have done worse than give her smiles and quiet. I'd have been there with a hot cast iron pot at the ready.'

He frowned. 'Don't—'

'I'm not.'

She went to brush her face, looked at her hands and dropped them again. They wouldn't feel shame or remorse over their pasts, which could not be changed. Their pasts had brought them together. That she could never regret—not once, not ever.

She could only hope their children would find this kind of happiness, too.

'After dealing with your sister, I think I can just about handle anything. Maybe in a few years we can have her visit Warstone Fortress.'

Evrart threw back his head and laughed. 'To have Biedeluue straighten her out?'

She'd been thinking of something more permanent. 'Aren't there unmarried guards there…?'

Evrart's brows rose. 'A sound idea…or maybe she'll get stolen along the way.'

'Stolen?'

'As you and I were from our homes,' he said. 'It turned out well for us.'

All those years of suffering, of worry and fear, for both of them. And yet…

'It turned out very well for *me*,' she said.

'You?'

'Because of you, I'll be the one having no problem leaving this field when you carry me out.'

In flash she was in his arms. Grinning, she rubbed her mud-laden hands against his chest.

He growled and buried his nose in her neck. 'You'll pay for that.'

She could think of a few ways and hoped his mother and sister had somewhere else to go for the afternoon.

Laughing under her words, she continued, 'But you don't know the greatest reason why I have fared so well. If we ever go picking fruit, I shall never need a ladder again!'

'I'll show you a ladder…'

She arched her brow. 'Oh? You'll show me?'

Flipping her over his shoulder, Evrart ran across the field; mud splattered everywhere. He cursed.

Shrieking and sliding, Margery laughed. 'What is it?'
'There's only a pond nearby, and we can't bathe in peace!'

* * * * *

If you enjoyed this story, be sure to read
the previous books in Nicole Locke's
Lovers and Legends miniseries

The Knight's Broken Promise
Her Enemy Highlander
The Highland Laird's Bride
In Debt to the Enemy Lord
The Knight's Scarred Maiden
Her Christmas Knight
Reclaimed by the Knight
Her Dark Knight's Redemption
Captured by Her Enemy Knight
The Maiden and the Mercenary
The Knight's Runaway Maiden